Secrets

Darliss Batchelor

Word in Due Season Publishing, LLC
P.O. Box 210921
Auburn Hills, Michigan 48321-0921

Cover Design by ET Graphix

ISBN 13: 978-0-9829686-0-4

Printed in the United States of America

I dedicate this book in memory of these three special and influential women who were a tremendous blessing in my life:

My mother, Lorna Crutchfield

My grandmother, Helen Buckner

My grandmother, Annie Crutchfield

Acknowledgements

First, I thank God for the gift of writing. It is both a huge responsibility and privilege at the same time. I pray that this work is pleasing in Your sight.

Greg, thank you for always being supportive of me in all of my various endeavors. Though this was not your dream, you treated it as if it was. You've always been that way and that makes you THE man! I love and respect you for loving me through it all.

Brandon, you once reminded me that it's never too late to reach your dreams. That belief inspired me to reach one of mine. I hope this inspires you to go for every dream that's in your heart. Thank you for being you! Mom loves you very much!

Jim, I appreciate you taking the time to read my manuscript and providing your own brand of input. You are truly more family than friend.

Natayra, thanks for being a sounding board for my many book ideas and then reading my manuscript on top of it. All those many hours spent on the phone have proven invaluable to me as a person and author.

Cynthia, thank you for providing much guidance and wisdom on my path to completing this book project. All of the meetings and workshops you held have propelled me directly into my reason for being.

God has seen fit to bless me with such an awesome group of supportive and loving family and friends that it is impossible to mention everyone here. I want you to know I love and appreciate you all.

Finally, I want to acknowledge you, the reader, for reading my first novel. What you hold in your hands may be your blessing. I hope it is as much of a blessing to you as the writing of it has been for me. I would love to hear your impressions of Secrets. Email me at wids-pub@comcast.net.

Chapter 1

"Honey, how do you feel about the interview for the pastor's position at Believer's Church?" Marsha asked as she and her husband, Mitch were preparing for bed.

"Well, I'm not concerned about the interview as much as I'm wondering if this would be the right move for me. I mean, I have been assisting Pastor James for quite some time but being a pastor is a whole different ballgame."

Marsha encouraged her husband as she always did, "I believe this is God's call on your life. You have been in years of training to prepare you for such a time as this. You have been doing more work as a pastor and less assisting over time. You are well prepared to be an effective leader. You never pushed for your own church. You were very much content to submit to Pastor James for the long haul. That kind of maturity and submission to authority does not go unnoticed by the Lord. You didn't think you would be an assistant pastor for the rest of your life did you?"

"No, I hadn't really planned on staying under Pastor James forever but I really hadn't thought about becoming a senior pastor quite yet either. Pastor James always handled the touchy parts of ministry allowing me to observe him in action. Being a pastor is no joke. I mean you have no one else to pass the ball to if you have a problem." Mitch said.

" Remember you always have God. He is your Rock. Of course, you have me too. I know God is able and if He sees fit this thing can and will work out. Do you know anything about the previous pastor? "

"No, I really don't know much about him at all. I asked some of the brothers at the United Ministry Leaders group about him though. The story is Pastor Edwards left a church board meeting one day and never came back. Actually, they think he left town. Initially people thought perhaps he did something wrong and left to keep from being caught. Apparently, everything seems to be intact."

"Well what do the members say? He had to tell someone something." Marsha questioned Mitch.

"Apparently he didn't say anything to them at all. They were surprised when they received his resignation letter. There was absolutely nothing indicating why he left. I think someone knows more than they're saying." Mitch responded.

"This is a mystery. A pastor of a thriving church disappears without a trace. He doesn't take anything. There's no sign of inappropriate actions. Someone would certainly know about that and would be more than willing to communicate it if that was the case. It doesn't make sense. I don't like the way this situation feels. Something isn't right." Marsha pondered aloud.

"Marsha, Marsha! Weren't you the one who just told me God was in control of this situation? Don't lose faith now. The Word says there won't be more put on us than we can bear. Whatever is going on in that church God knows about it. If He sees fit to appoint me as pastor, I have to believe He equipped me to handle it."

Marsha got up from the bed and grabbed her husband by the hand while clearly telling Mitch with her eyes that she was behind him 100%. She gently pulled him to the edge of the bed and slowly into position to pray. While Marsha prayed for God's counsel, the couple began to feel the peace of God so strongly there was no reason to talk about the issue any further. Mitch and Marsha knew God was indeed working in this situation and there was no need to concern themselves with it anymore. They fell asleep in each other's arms in silence but still wondering what the interview would bring in the morning.

Chapter 2

Cassandra Williams was the only female member of the Board of Directors of Believer's Church. She always felt she was special because of it. She brought a woman's perspective to the discussions causing her male counterparts to be somewhat uncomfortable. The men were accustomed to being able to speak their chauvinistic comments openly. Now it was necessary to be careful about what the men let come out of their mouths. Cassandra knew the church board meetings were typically a mixture of the Spirit as well as testosterone. That much was evident when the board decided that women should have no input into the church's business. After all, if God wanted women's opinions Jesus would have recruited at least one woman when He chose "the twelve". Cassandra was not one to sit quietly when it came to things of this nature. She set out to convince the pastor that a set of ovaries does not mean God can't use them. She displayed her femininity every chance she had. Cassandra didn't act like a slut; she just made sure she appealed to the pastor's visual sense whenever she was in his presence. After a while, she knew her feminine powers were working. Pastor Edwards got to the point he was willing to let her do anything her little heart desired including infiltrating the closed-membership men's club known as the Believer's Church Board of Directors. She had switched, winked and flirted her way right into the position all the other women in the church only dreamed of being in. It was obvious to everyone she didn't always use her powers for good. They knew whatever she wanted; she had the resources to get. People often wondered what the driving force was behind her efforts. She sometimes acted like a downright bulldog when she wanted to make a point. Did she want a relationship with Pastor Edwards? In her mind, she absolutely did not want him in that way. However, based on the way she carried on around him, people thought she intended to lure him away from his wife and make him her own. It wasn't clear Pastor Edwards didn't want the same based on his reaction to her. No one knew he had entertained the thought and had actually proposed a romantic relationship to Cassandra who promptly let him know he had served his purpose...she was placed in a position of authority. That was all she wanted from him. Dejected and questioning the call of God on his life, Pastor Edwards left the church to lick his wounds. He was very much ashamed of his actions. Since no one else knew what had occurred, he felt sure he could leave the state and pastor somewhere else with very little trouble if he desired.

As Cassandra readied herself for the church board meeting, these thoughts caused her to chuckle. She enjoyed her controversial persona. When she walked in the room, everyone would stop talking as though Jesus himself had made an appearance. Because of the attention-high she got, Cassandra always made being a standout a priority. Today would be no different. It seems today they were interviewing candidates for the now vacant pastor's position. Since she was a member of the church board, she would be part of the interviewing process insuring the new pastor would be attentive to her concerns as a woman and as Cassandra. She would have to be dressed for her own unique brand of success. She chose a bright red suit, big and bold gold jewelry and matching red and gold shoes. She carefully styled her auburn hair in a very sensual but professional style that would accent her heart-shaped face. With the last hair in place, she did her makeup with the same passion and attention to detail. Everything had to be just right. After she finished dressing, she carefully inspected her appearance to insure everything was in place.

"Cassandra, you are some kind of woman," she said speaking aloud to herself. "You could convince a drowning man that he needed water," she laughed.

She grabbed her handbag shook her long full head of hair once more and headed for the door. "Wouldn't want to keep everyone waiting!" she said as she started her car and headed for Believer's Church.

Chapter 3

Believer's Church was a ten-year-old independent church. Its members came from everywhere because of their Bible study ministry. The teachings went beyond the realm of memorizing scripture to deal with the issues other ministries chose not to touch. People felt because of these teachings, they would be able to lead more victorious Christian lives. The church leadership insured that everyone felt welcome and accepted. No one felt unwanted. This provided for potential members to easily transition from Bible study group member to church member. Their music ministry was also a drawing point. People loved good foot-stomping choir singing. The well-known choir director and musicians had actually worked with other groups that had recorded. People who dreamed of recording professionally felt that singing under their direction would somehow give them an edge. For that reason, the choir provided another major pipeline for new members.

Even though the church was non-denominational, its belief system closely mimicked the beliefs of the founding pastor's former denominational affiliation. These beliefs were very traditional and conservative. Believer's Church still held very much to these views. This reflected in the way the membership related to people who didn't fit their idea of what a church member should be like. The members of Believer's Church were intolerant. From the outside, the ministry appeared to be a body on the move. What people couldn't see was the lack of relationship within the membership. People weren't connecting with one another. There seemed to be a lack of trust looming over every effort aimed at increasing the level of unity within the body. Ministries within the church weren't flourishing. People seemed tense and restless during church services. Overall, everyone knew there was something essential missing. They felt a new pastor might be the thing to jumpstart the ministry.

"Good morning, brothers" Elder Howard said as the brothers began to gather for the meeting called to organize the morning's pastoral interviews. "We have a lot of ground to cover before the first candidate shows up. We need to review our requirements and the questions we plan to ask during the interview."

"How will this process work?" Deacon Watson pondered as he poured his coffee. "We only have four candidates to interview so far and they're all coming today. Will we entertain more candidates after today or will we have to choose from today's group?"

Elder Howard referred this question to the rest of the Board. Since he was the chairman, he could make the decision but feared it would reveal his true motives. He preferred selecting one from today's group so he could stop worrying about keeping the church together. This was a big job and candidates weren't exactly knocking their door down for interviews. This caused him concern. After the pastor left, he became the interim leadership. He was responsible for insuring the church's services came off without a hitch. He also had to make decisions the pastor would normally make. Instead of seeing this as an opportunity to hone his own leadership skills, he looked at the situation as a potential liability. He didn't want to be blamed for the falling apart of the church should a pastor not be in place soon enough to take any blame. Elder Howard had a reputation to uphold and he took great care to do so. He had aspirations of becoming a pastor himself one day. He didn't want anyone else's actions or lack thereof to affect that. He had to make sure the outcome of this situation would benefit and not harm him.

Deacon Mays was the first one to speak. "I believe we have to be careful. We can't act too hastily. We have people's souls as well as the life of this fine church to consider. I think Elder Howard is doing a fine job in taking on the responsibilities in the interim. So I don't think we have to make a decision right away. If we get the wrong person in here things could quickly go downhill. May I suggest that we see what today holds?

SECRETS

There's no need to look further down the road than we have to. If there are any standouts today, we can hold a round of second interviews. If the good Lord smiles on us, we may find the man we're looking for today! How does everyone feel about that?"

Everyone present was very much in agreement. The moment Elder Howard announced their agreement Sister Cassandra Williams arrived. Her entrance to the room caused a huge groan from the other board members.

"Are you happy to see me or do you all have indigestion today? " she reacted with a chuckle. "What were you guys talking about when I walked in?"

Elder Howard responded, "We decided how we were going to handle the interviewing process. We're going to speak to the candidates scheduled for today and schedule second interviews for any we think may meet the church's needs. You were late so don't come in here starting confusion wanting to change what we've decided. You always do that and we are not going to have it today."

To everyone's surprise Sister Cassandra's face turned red and tears began to form in her eyes as she stated in a very emotional tone, "You've obviously misunderstood me. I never start confusion. I just like to make sure you hear my thoughts. I am on this board to stay and I'm tired of always having to defend my presence. Please forgive my being late."

"Thank you so kindly for stating your intentions. I am very aware that you are here to stay. However, you are going to have to understand this is a new situation for all of us and we all have to adjust. This kind of transition doesn't happen overnight. As usual, we forgive you for being late. There's coffee over there on the table if you like. We'd like to move on with the rest of the meeting if you don't mind."

Sister Cassandra wiped the tears she had successfully coaxed from her eyes and set down at the huge table where the leadership made the church's major decisions. She had once again changed the situation to make the brethren feel sorry for her. As usual, Cassandra Williams was in control.

Chapter 4

Maxine and Linda had been friends since childhood. In fact, they had been friends for so long that some wondered if they had been in cribs next to each other in the hospital when they were born. They had always attended the same school and their families even belonged to the same church, Believer's Church. In short, they were closer than most sisters were. During all their years of friendship, they had seen each other go through everything. They shared their thoughts and dreams. Things they couldn't tell anyone else they told each other. Neither of them had ever betrayed the others trust. They even knew about every encounter with the opposite sex that the other had experienced. In fact, they knew so much about the circumstances surrounding these events one would think they were both present when they occurred. Over time, they also developed a very strong loathing for men. Relationships had not been good to them.

Maxine had become engaged to Steve after six years of relationship. He had been her knight in shining armor. He had even given up his connection to Buddhism in order to continue his relationship with Maxine after she made it clear that differences in their religious beliefs were a problem. Her upbringing did not allow for unequally yoked relationships. They'd had several breakups in their relationship but each was always willing to put in the work necessary to solve their problems.

Steve's mother accepted Maxine with open arms and treated her as though she were already her daughter-in-law. The rest of his family loved her as though she had always been a member of the family.

In anticipation of their impending marriage, they opened a joint bank account in order to save the thousands of dollars they would need for the down payment on their home. Additionally, Maxine had gotten the loan for Steve's new SUV when his car finally died. Steve had encountered credit problems in the years before their relationship and could not get a loan for the automobile. The planning of the wedding had been going on for several months. Everything seemed to be going well when Steve lost his job weeks before the nuptials.

His self-esteem took a major nosedive because as a man he felt he couldn't take care of a wife and household. Though Maxine tried to convince Steve he could get a new job and that she was willing to carry him for a while if necessary, Steve wasn't receptive to the idea. She wanted him to know she loved him and would be there for him no matter what. After all, she would be his wife.

She became concerned when Steve began to disappear for days at a time without anyone knowing where he was. It seems he had begun to use drugs in an effort to soothe his wounded spirit. To make matters worse, he had traded the SUV for drugs leaving Maxine with the remaining payments and no Steve. This crushed Maxine. She immediately went to the joint account to retrieve the funds earmarked for the new house in order to pay on the car loan only to find that Steve had withdrawn everything except one cent, which was required to keep the account open. To top it off, additional bank fees were due for various transactions Steve had made. When she went to his mother's house to find him, she hadn't seen him for quite some time either.

Maxine had to face the facts. She couldn't marry Steve. She couldn't find him even if she still wanted to marry him anyway. She quietly went on with her life after canceling the wedding plans which caused additional expense. On the outside, she had forgiven Steve. It was her Christian belief that she had to be forgiving. She absolutely couldn't hold a grudge no matter what. On the inside, however, she made a silent vow. She would never be in a relationship with a man again in her life. The potential cost was more than she was willing to pay.

Linda had her share of rocky relationships as well. The last person she was in committed relationship with was Mark. She wasn't interested in getting into a relationship when she met Mark. However, she was willing to go out with him from time to time. She dated others and assumed he did also. After about two months of this, Mark insisted he wanted to commit to her and wanted the same from her.

Linda liked Mark but didn't want to limit her options so drastically. She truly believed "variety was the spice of life" and enjoyed the company of several men. One man was not enough "spice" for her.

When she turned Mark's proposal for a committed relationship down the first time, he did not give up. He almost acted desperate. He sent her flowers almost every day. On any given day she had so many flowers in her office it resembled a funeral home instead of a place of business. He showed up with beautiful jewelry for any occasion he could think of. One time Linda had a run- in with a co-worker that left her in the dumps. Mark had shown up with a pair of sapphire and diamond earrings for no special reason but to cheer her up. Eventually, Linda began to find the attention Mark was giving her exciting. He was very attentive to every one of Linda's whims. If she even thought aloud about something, Mark would make it happen. She was definitely falling for him.

The problem was that Mark didn't share Linda's desire for celibacy before marriage. In fact, Mark felt sexual intimacy was a necessary prerequisite for any consideration of marriage. He felt a relationship could be wonderful outside of the bedroom, but if it was lousy in the bedroom, the relationship didn't stand a chance of success. Linda believed that a sexual relationship before marriage was inappropriate. Not only was it biblically forbidden, it would also nix the wonderful encounter Linda hoped for on her wedding night.

She wanted to give her husband a gift that had been unopened. She thought this would be wonderful for herself as well as her husband. She understood Mark had needs he wanted her to fulfill. However, Mark didn't understand Linda's needs to remain a virgin until her wedding night. Linda found herself in a quandary. On the one hand, she adored Mark and all the benefits that came along with her relationship with him. On the other hand, Mark wasn't even considering marriage.

This became the source for many heated discussions between the couple threatening the relationship. Because Mark didn't want to risk losing Linda altogether, he decided to propose a compromise to her he knew would provide him the opportunity to get Linda to go further. He would stop pressuring Linda for sex if she would allow for physical intimacy without actual intercourse. Linda felt this option was a good compromise. After all, she felt because she was strong in her Christian faith, withstanding any possible temptation that could result would be a cinch for her. As it turned out, Linda underestimated the strength of her flesh. Mark had worked his plan with great precision and within two month's time, they were having sexual intercourse on a regular basis. Linda began to believe this was not that big of a deal. Mark and Linda became closer and closer. They were almost inseparable. That is until Linda became pregnant. Neither Linda nor Mark wanted to have a baby. However neither wanted to abort the pregnancy or put the baby up for adoption either. A solution was not clear. Mark became distant. He wouldn't slow down because of the morning sickness Linda had developed because of the pregnancy. Linda did not know if she could bear the embarrassment and ridicule of being pregnant and unwed. If she had the baby, she could never go back to church and hold her head up again. She was sure the church folks would undoubtedly have her on the altar every Sunday until the child was born. Then they would make her feel bad about being an unwed mother. She would never get past the stigma. Her family would most likely look down on her as well. Since they were staunch Christians, they might even disown her. Financially, she didn't know how she could provide for a child and herself without hardship. In her mind, there wasn't another way. She made a decision to have an abortion. Mark was in disagreement with this decision but he had no other solution to offer. Maxine had gone with her for the procedure to provide moral support. Mark never showed up. He said his alarm clock didn't go off. After the procedure, Mark decided their relationship could not continue because he was dead set against abortion and now he viewed Linda as some kind of monster. Linda had to deal with the broken relationship as well as the aftermath of the abortion. Since that time, Maxine had been the only person Linda had allowed into the inner circle of her thoughts and emotions. She decided Maxine would be the only one she would ever allow to be this close to her. As for men, they were all absolute dogs and definitely off limits.

"You know Linda, the idea you had about us living together was a good one! We're always together anyway."

"Yeah girl. We've known each other so long I don't know why we never thought of it before now," responded Linda. "We get along great. We wear the same size clothes. We share the same faith. We're almost sisters. We'll make perfect roommates."

"Since we're all settled in, what are you planning to do this evening?" Maxine asked.

"Well, I was thinking of hanging out here and maybe watching a movie. There's one coming on tonight I've really wanted to see. What are you doing tonight?"

"I guess if you don't mind sharing the couch, I'll be watching the movie with you. Scoot over".

As the movie ended, they both wiped the tears from their eyes. The movie had been a beautiful love story with a wonderful ending. Maxine was the first to rise from the sofa.

"I don't understand why Hollywood keeps making movies like this," she said.

"What do you mean?" Linda asked rising from the sofa herself.

Maxine looked at Linda as though she had said something about her mother. The frown on her face told Linda she asked a question to which she should already have known the answer.

"Linda, there is no happily ever after. What they portray in these movies is completely unrealistic. When have you ever walked off into the sunset with someone you were in love with, huh? "

Linda responded with complete silence. She knew there was no changing Maxine's mind once she had made it up. Finally, Linda opened her mouth to speak.

"Max, what is this really all about. I mean this is obviously not about the movie. What's on your mind?" she asked her friend.

"I get so frustrated with stories like that. I can't remember ever having a real strong love relationship with anyone. When I see movies like that it reminds me this kind of happiness has somehow escaped me. I don't believe it exists in real life."

"I know how you feel. I haven't been very keen on relationships with men either. Ever since that situation with Mark happened, I haven't seen men in the same light."

"That's what I'm talking about Linda. Men are not worth the time of day. I have really been questioning God about why He set this whole thing up the way He did. Why did He feel so bad about Adam being alone? Based on my experience with Adam's male offspring, they deserve to be alone. Why didn't God create dogs to provide companionship for men? They are man's best friends you know. I wonder why God didn't leave us women out of it. I think the world would be a better place if that were the case."

"Max, I hear you. But, wouldn't you be lonely if there was no one for you to relate with?" Linda asked.

"I probably would be. That much is true. However, if I never relate to another man it would be too soon!"

"Max, do you ever plan to ever get into another relationship?" Linda asked.

"Honestly I don't think that's possible. You have to be able to trust anyone you get into relationship with and I trust no one. Steve appeared to be the perfect person until his ego got in the way. I'm still paying off those bills. What about you?" Max said.

"Think about this…Mark wanted me so bad at first. Then as soon as I gave him what he wanted he abandons me. Why would I have any plans for a relationship after that whole fiasco? By the way, I thought you forgave Steve." Linda responded sarcastically.

"We're getting real personal here. You're the one who brought this whole thing up in the first place. I think you're taking it way too far considering what happened to you. I'm the one who almost went bankrupt because of Steve! You haven't gone through anything as far as I'm concerned!" responded Maxine with a tone in her voice that closely resembled the growl of the dog she considered Steve to be.

"Max, I'm sorry. I didn't mean to go there. I guess I forgot about your situation because I've been so busy licking my own wounds. We've both been through a lot. Please understand me when I say I'll always be there for you. I won't treat you the way Steve did. I'll stand by you no matter what" Linda said as she hugged her closest friend.

Chapter 5

The Believer's Church board was now ready to begin their interviews. Everyone sat quietly waiting for the first candidate. When he arrived, the receptionist showed him into the board meeting room and introduced him as Reverend Jeffrey Brown. She sat him down at the head of the table and left the room.

Elder Howard had already provided packets to the board members that contained Reverend Brown's resume and letters of reference from other church leaders.

"Hello Reverend Brown. I'm quite impressed with your leadership experience. Please tell us a little about your background in your own words" Elder Howard said.

"Well, I've been a member of my current church for about a year now. I've been faithful to every church I've ever joined. I've been a Sunday school teacher for several years as well. I believe God called me to the pastorate several years ago but now He's opened the door for me to finally step into it. I know I can do a good job for God here" Reverend Brown replied.

"I see Reverend Brown. What I'd really like to know is what vision God has given you for ministry? What would you like to do for God here in Believer's Church?" Elder Howard inquired.

"I'm glad you asked. First, I would change the name of the church to include my name. My vision, my name is what I always say. Obviously, my preaching and teaching ministry is always more important than whatever else goes on here. That's how it should be. Of course, I will need to be compensated enough to live as a pastor should. I need the parsonage to be at least 4,000 square feet and I want a luxury SUV. This would certainly glorify God and bless the church as well. The choir would have to begin recording soon as well featuring my singing gift. This is my vision as I see it so far."

"Is that your idea of a vision? Maybe we need to go on to a different point. Reverend Brown, you said you've been a member of your current church for a year now. Why don't we have a reference letter from your pastor?" Deacon Mays wondered aloud.

"Well, he doesn't know I am interviewing for this position."

"Why isn't he aware?"

"Well he thinks I'm moving too fast. He thinks I should wait awhile before I begin leading a church of my own."

Deacon Mays raised his eyebrows and resumed his questioning of Reverend Brown. "Why does he think that? Based on your resume you've been Assistant Pastor of at least four different churches. I'd think those experiences would be some pretty good training."

"I'll be open and honest here. I am an awesome preacher. I sometimes believe I am a better preacher than my pastor is. Personally, I think he may be, well, somewhat jealous. God has moved me along in the ministry a whole lot faster than He's moving my pastor. I've gotten more experience in three years than he's gotten in ten years of ministry." Reverend Brown proudly responded.

"Why do you feel you have more knowledge than your pastor?" Deacon Mays asked. He was beginning to feel this candidate needed counseling.

"Well, all the churches I've been in over those three years have given me a wealth of experience in preaching and teaching. I know I am ready to act as a pastor."

"Uh, Reverend Brown, out of curiosity, exactly how many churches have you been a member of over the past three years?"

"Four. God has seen fit to send me to all these places in a short period because He is doing a quick work in me. You know in this day and time God is doing things faster. The people in these churches have not recognized my ministry so God keeps moving me until someone does."

Elder Howard finally concluded the interview. "Reverend Brown, we appreciate your time, but we need someone who is looking for a bit more than recognition, which you seem to desperately desire. We need someone who sees being a pastor as more than an opportunity to promote his own interests. We need a pastor not some sort of hotshot who can't sit still. Son, please evaluate your attitude. Remember you're nothing without God. On a positive note, I believe with the kind of zeal you have you really will do big things for God one day. This is not the day. You won't have to promote yourself in order for that to happen either. You have to adjust your mindset and redirect your energies. God bless you."

Reverend Brown rose and left the boardroom without a response. This action revealed more to the board members than even his words. They didn't even need to discuss Reverend Brown. He was not an option. They all looked at each other and grabbed the next candidate's information packet. His name was Reverend Mitchell Ross.

Mitchell Ross arrived at Believer's church twenty minutes early. He ran smack dab into a young man who was obviously very distraught. Mitch wondered if he was here for an interview.

"What happened young man? Are you a pastoral candidate?" Mitch asked.

"Well I interviewed for it anyway. I don't think it went very well. If you're interviewing, don't tell them you want to change the church's name. They are very picky about that name," Reverend Brown said as he examined Mitch. Reverend Brown left the building in a noticeable huff. Mitch became concerned. Maybe this wasn't God's idea. Just then, the receptionist came and welcomed Mitch. She told Mitch to have a seat and she would let the board know he was there. Shortly thereafter, he was ushered into the boardroom where the interview would take place.

"Reverend Ross, it's very nice to meet you. I'm Elder Howard and this is our church board. Please have a seat and make yourself comfortable."

"Thank you Elder Howard. Please call me Mitch. This is a very beautiful edifice. How long have you been here?" Mitch said.

"Well Mitch we've been here for about ten years. We feel it has definitely been a blessing both to the community and us," Elder Howard stated proudly. "As you know Mitch, we're interviewing for the role of pastor of this church. We need to get moving on this interview as we have other candidates scheduled."

Mitch smiled and said to Elder Howard, "I'm sorry but I didn't catch your first name. Should I call you Elder Howard?"

Immediately everyone in the boardroom gasped. How dare he expect to call Elder Howard by his first name? Most of them didn't even know what his first name was. Elder Howard wasn't quite sure how to respond to that question. Everyone simply used his title. He pulled himself and his thoughts together and responded, "Well, I don't know why you wouldn't!"

"I suppose I wouldn't unless that was your name. Your parents did give you a name other than Elder I assume," said Mitch with a grin on his face. He enjoyed causing the stern-faced, in control Elder to squirm in his seat.

"Yes, Mitch. My parents did give me a name. It's Eric. I suppose for purposes of this interview only you can call me Eric since I'm calling you Mitch. Why are we having this discussion about names?" Elder Howard said.

"Eric, I feel people of God are very hung up on titles. I understand you are in a position of authority. I think I can respect that regardless of what I call you. I believe the body of Christ should not be a place where people should be position-conscious. There's enough of that going on in the world as it is. I believe there should be structure and lines of authority in place for the sake of order. However, those things should not separate the members of the body in any way. We're all serving the same God, and that's what really matters. What do you think, Eric?"

"Well, Mitch, I guess I never thought about it that way. Let's take this one step at a time here. And remember, we're doing the interviewing," Elder Howard responded.

While this exchange was taking place, Cassandra was taking in all of Mitchell Ross she could. She thought he was a very nice looking man, nice suit, and nice shoes. He appeared to have it all together. She especially liked the way he handled Elder Howard. He brought him right down to earth.

"Reverend Ross, being the sole woman on this board, I'd like to know how you feel about women in leadership in the church?" she asked.

"Well I know some pastors don't condone women in leadership over anything except maybe a women's group or Sunday school. I, on the other hand, believe if God chooses to put a woman in leadership then that's what should happen. After all, He is the creator and we are the creation. We should always do what we believe He wants. My wife has been a very strong support for me. I know she is a woman God has called to leadership. Does that answer your question? Mitch said.

"Did he say wife?" Cassandra thought to herself.

"Yes, you've answered my question. So you don't have a problem with receiving input from any woman?" she asked.

"Well I wouldn't say that. I wouldn't have a problem considering input from you or any other woman in this church as long as it's relevant. But that would go for input from anyone, male or female," Mitch said.

"Well, Mitch, don't you think God placed men in authority in the church?" Deacon Mays asked.

"Yes, I do but I also choose not to limit God. Who am I to say who He can place where?" Mitch responded. He was becoming a bit perturbed at the board's apparent concern over this matter. This couldn't be the prevailing issue for the ministry.

Deacon Mays then said "Okay. I see your point. I'd like to hear your vision for ministry."

"I envision a place where people can come and have encounters with God that will impact their lives in a major way. I'd like to see several different support groups implemented here. There are so many people dealing with so many different issues they need help with. Why shouldn't the church provide those services? The music ministry you have in place here is great. The Bible study you all have in place is good too. We could add home bible studies as well to allow for further outreach into the community. Those would be some of the things I would like to see happen," Mitch responded confidently.

The Board of Directors completed their interviews and decided to meet the next day to discuss their options. Each one felt they would like some personal time to consider the candidates they had interviewed and determine their individual opinions.

Chapter 6

"Where are you going? Don't tell me you're going to another meeting"? Marsha asked Mitch as he readied for a special meeting at the church.

"Marsha, if I am going to effectively lead this church I'm going to have to spend some time doing what pastors do. That means meetings. This should not be news to you", Mitch responded to his obviously disturbed wife.

It had been two months since Mitchell Ross had become the pastor of Believer's Church. He had been meeting with all ministry group heads both individually and collectively along with extensive meetings involving the Church Board, the Deacon Board, and the Trustees. It was obvious he would have to put more time into this than he was required to as Assistant Pastor at his previous church. At least that's what Mitchell thought. He couldn't understand his wife's concern over this. After all, she knew he would be a pastor one day and never seemed to mind.

"I knew this church would require more of your time. But, we haven't even had dinner together in quite some time. You show up in the evenings worn out and tired. You have no energy left for me." Marsha responded.

"Honey, please don't do this. I have to do what I have to do. I'm not just hanging out. I am doing the Lord's work you know." Mitch reasoned.

"Mitch, you have to participate in this marriage. I understand you doing the Lord's work but what about our marriage? What happened to God first, family second and ministry after that?" Marsha stated.

"Okay, Marsha. You're right. What do you say if we sit down right now and schedule a couple of days away for the two of us? No church work and no talk of it either. Me and you and whatever you want to do." Mitch offered.

"That sounds wonderful! Let's make plans for some "us time". I'll even take a trip to the lingerie store for this occasion." Marsha purred.

"Lingerie, huh? I better get my calendar right now before you change your mind." Mitch said as he reached for his planner.

Mitch and Marsha sat down on the chaise in their bedroom and discussed their special time. While Mitch wrote the "special time" in his planner, Marsha was already planning for their time in her mind. The date was set, the plans made and Marsha would get her "Mitch fix".

Chapter 7

Fellowship City was the gathering place for the Christians in the city. It was an alternative to the bars and dance clubs in the downtown area. Fellowship City highlighted comedians, music, book clubs, and other forms of entertainment for the adults. Children who accompanied the adults had their own supervised, age-appropriate Christian activities as well. This was a place where people of faith could fellowship and have some good, clean fun.

Linda and Maxine arrived at Fellowship City together. They had decided to get out of the house and happy to be able to avoid the nightclub scene tonight. Neither of them was in for the sometimes-aggressive behavior of men who often frequented such places. As the two ladies entered the room, they looked around at their surroundings. The multi-level room was stunning in purple with brass accents. All the tables had expensive-looking, purple faux suede chairs. Purple and electric blue brocade curtains covered the stage. The Supper Room was off to the right. This was where the food was set up. The food was very pretty and reminded one of the midnight buffets on a cruise ship with sculptures made out of every type of food imaginable. Everyone visited this room every time they came to Fellowship City. The Word Rooms were off to the left. People could rent these rooms by the hour for Bible studies, meetings, and other such things. The fabric used in these rooms were in a print coordinated with the main room and were equipped with personal computers, a large boardroom table, and dry erase boards. Straight ahead was the area where the children were entertained.

Linda and Maxine headed for a table in the main room. The entertainment tonight would be a Christian poet who both women wanted to hear. Apparently, her poetry was so touching grown men sometimes left the readings crying. If men would be crying, Linda and Maxine had to experience this! As they took their seats, the lights dimmed and the emcee began talking about the entertainment for the evening. After the Christian rappers finished their performance, there was a short intermission.

"Are you hungry? " Linda asked.

"Yes, why don't we get something from the Supper Room. I hear their food is excellent!" Maxine responded.

"If we both leave the table we risk losing it. Why don't I go and get the food and bring it back?" Linda stated as she arose from the table. As she headed for the Supper Room, she had a strange feeling someone was watching her. She glanced around the room and didn't see anyone who appeared to be looking her way.

As he looked across the room, the man couldn't believe what he was seeing. He hadn't seen her in a long time. The gentleman remembered the times they had together and chuckled at how much fun the two of them had in each other's company. He thought about her almost everyday since their breakup. Watching her walk across the room, he wondered whether he should have ever let her go. She didn't ever look the way she did tonight. There was an air of confidence that didn't exist before which was very attractive. He remembered the day he walked away from her for good. He now realized he had been immature, selfish and inconsiderate of her and her feelings. He lost a good woman. He desperately wanted to regain her companionship. However, he knew he betrayed her in a way she might not be able to forgive. He abandoned this woman at a time when she really needed him. What a wimp he was! Today, he would not wimp out. He would not miss this opportunity to speak to her. What did he have to lose? The worse that could happen would be she totally disregarded him and he ended up in the same position he was currently. As he rose to head in her direction, he turned his attention to the woman sitting at the same table with her. He thought, perhaps, she would be a better alternative. He took a deep breath and charted his course. As he approached the woman, he recognized her as

Maxine. Mark got along fine with Maxine while he and Linda were together. However, he knew Linda had probably informed Maxine of everything that had occurred. He wasn't sure what the reception would be like when he finally got to her. He decided to take his lumps. Getting close to Linda was worth it even if the temperature did take a nosedive when he got to the table. Touching Maxine on the shoulder, he positioned himself in front of her so he could greet her face to face. Maxine looked up at the man and squinted as she attempted to recognize whom he was. Maxine knew this face from somewhere. All of a sudden, her face revealed she remembered Mark's face. She responded to his presence with a frown that would send even the most devout Christian to the sinner's bench. Maybe he should have followed Linda to the Supper Room and bypassed Maxine altogether. But, he was committed now so he had to go with the flow.

"It's been a long time, Maxine. How have you been?" Mark asked.

Maxine sat there with her mouth tense and her eyes big and round.

"You do remember me don't you? I'm ……"

"Oh yes, I do remember you. I remember you wined and dined my friend, spent all kinds of money on her and convinced her she should have sex with you. Then I remember she got pregnant with your child and you disappeared. That's what I remember. Actually, I think that's what you should do now. Disappear!" Maxine interrupted. She turned her attention away from Mark towards nothing in particular. It was obvious she had nothing else to say to him. As he considered walking away, Linda returned to the table. It was too late to bail out now. For the first time in many months, he was face to face with the woman who would have been the mother of his child. As Mark looked into her expressive eyes, he could see her emotions change from utter surprise, to joy, to anger and bitterness, to tears. As he watched this happen, he realized how much damage he had done to her. He wondered if he could ever repair the obvious breach between them.

"Hello Linda." Mark hesitantly said to the woman he desperately loved yet deeply hurt.

Linda looked at Maxine who was still obviously upset and announced she forgot chicken wings. She turned and ran back to the Supper Room. He went right behind her. She would talk with him today no matter what.

"Linda, I know I hurt you. I have absolutely no excuse for what I did. Will you accept my apology?" Mark pleaded as he grabbed Linda's hand. "Mark, you will never know how much you hurt me. More than that, you caused harm to come to our child. Even if I forgave you, which I'm not sure I'm capable of, you can't get forgiveness from the baby. So why don't you walk away and leave me alone?" Linda responded.

"Linda don't you think I feel bad about what happened with the baby? Whenever I see babies now I wonder what our baby would have been like. I wonder if he or she would have my nose or your smile. I wonder what kind of person they would have become." He wondered aloud.

"Well, one thing is for sure, our baby wouldn't have been anything like you. I would have made sure of it myself. You can believe that." "Wait a minute Linda. While I'm not trying to rub salt into any wounds, I'm also not about to take all the blame for what happened. You made the decision to have the abortion not me. As a matter of fact, I told you I was dead set against it."

"What was I supposed to do? I wasn't sure what you were going to do. It looked to me like you were running away instead of facing your responsibility."

"What about your responsibility as a mother, Linda? It seems like you took the easy way out too. Bottom line it was your body and your decision. You made the decision that was best for you. Don't try to place your guilt on me." Mark firmly stated.

After their exchange, Linda and Mark stood looking at each other. They each had run out of words. Both realized this event affected the other and they would be tied together forever because of it. Neither was sure what the next step should be. However, they both silently agreed the blaming should stop and the healing should begin.

Chapter 8

"Well, I think we've come to the point where we need to inform the congregation of the changes we're planning," said Pastor Mitch. "It has been a lot of work but the new church organization is complete and I believe God is pleased. What we need to do now is speak with the affected leaders first and then speak to the congregation as a whole. I'm going to assign Elder Howard and Deacon Mays to speak to the leadership during the next week or so. We need to set up a meeting to inform the church body on a Sunday afternoon. Let's do it as soon as possible so we can move on to something else. What do you all think?" Pastor Ross said as he glanced around the room for feedback.

"I agree," said Cassandra "how about next Sunday after the church fellowship dinner?"

"Sister Williams that's not a good date. Sister Ross and I have plans. Can't we do it the following Sunday?" Pastor Ross asked.

"We have our monthly Youth Rock the House on that date. The next open Sunday afternoon is about four weeks from now," Cassandra responded.

"I didn't realize how full our schedule is. I prefer to have it on a Sunday because people usually don't have plans for Sunday afternoon. Well, if we're done by six o'clock it may be okay. But at six o'clock, whether the meeting is over or not, we're out of here!" Pastor Ross stated.

The date was set. Mitch silently hoped Marsha would go along with this and not be too upset because their rendezvous would be later than planned. As the Board members began to leave the room, Cassandra was having her own thoughts. She felt somewhat uneasy which was not good news for those around her. She didn't quite know why but she would find out.

Chapter 9

"Mitch, I know I didn't hear you say what I think I heard you say. We will not be at the church or anywhere else other than the suite I reserved next Sunday night. I can't believe you don't value us as much as you do that church. This is too much!" Marsha responded when Mitch explained the delay.

Mitch looked at her trying to understand why this was such a big issue. They would arrive a few hours later than expected. This was not a big deal. They would still get to spend time together. He stood there watching his wife go through several gyrations clearly designed to let him know exactly how upset she was. He had to decide what the right response was. He didn't want to say something that would re-ignite his wife's anger. Mitch wanted to make sure he said something which would reflect how much he really did value her and their relationship but yet remind her the delay was just that and not a cancellation.

"Baby, our time is of the utmost importance to me. I know church work has taken up a lot of our time. I apologize for that. I am really trying to do the best I can to juggle everything I'm supposed to do. What I really don't understand is why you can't support me in this. What do you want me to do? Put God on hold?" Mitch stated. Why had he said that? Mitch knew Marsha wasn't complaining about his relationship with God. He had done exactly what he didn't want to do…say something stupid.

"Mitch, that is the stupidest thing I think you have ever said. How can you ask me if I want you to put God on hold? You know better than that. However, Pastor Ross, I think you have gotten God and the church mixed up. If you don't get the two untangled in your mind soon, you won't have to worry about our marriage being on your priority list." Marsha responded.

Marsha's comment caught Mitch very much off guard. He wondered if she was really insinuating she would leave him.

"Marsha, obviously you don't appreciate us much if you're going to walk away from our marriage because of my involvement in church work. Are you saying our marriage is in trouble? Have you given up on us?" Mitch asked.

"I'm sorry. Please forgive me for that comment. I really don't know where it came from. I guess I'm just frustrated. We have made so many sacrifices for the sake of ministry and apparently, it has really taken its toll on me. I never thought it would come to this. I only asked for one evening alone with my husband and you agreed. You even promised we wouldn't as much as talk about the church. Now you're telling me I have to make one more sacrifice because of the church and I lost my cool. If you're telling me we'll be out of church by six o'clock I'll go along with that. But, if there is one more delay, we are going to have a problem." Marsha said while drying her tears.

The couple embraced each other and kissed the other's lips passionately. Their love was strong enough to get them through many trials and it would get them through this one…hopefully.

Chapter 10

As the two walked back from the Supper Room, Maxine could see Linda had been crying. She understood completely having known what that snake-in-the-grass Mark had done to her before. What she didn't understand was why the two were walking back together. She assumed Linda would not forgive that so-called man after all she had gone through with him. Mark didn't even deserve to be in the same space as Linda. As they got closer, Maxine caught a glimpse of what she thought was a slight smile between them. She was not going to tolerate that. After all, she had been the one to help Linda pick up the pieces after Mark left her in a lurch. She was the one who had taken care of her when she was too distraught to work for weeks after this event. She comforted Linda during the times when she had encountered the guilt of having the abortion. Why would she let Mark back in her life? She reminded herself she was jumping ahead of herself. She didn't know what happened after the two left the table but she knew she would soon find out.

"I can't believe you would let him get that close to you! He's the same no-good-for-nothing man who left you after his mouth wrote a check that his ..." Maxine started.

"Max! Calm down! Why are you so upset? I know it must be something big in order for you to be standing up in here clowning to the point you're almost cussing. Look at all these people looking at you. Don't embarrass me. Now what is the problem?" Linda inquired.

"What happened between you two back there in the Supper Room?"

"Oh, I see. You don't want me to have anything to do with Mark for any reason. Mark and I briefly talked about what happened between us. It was something that was bound to happen since the issue was never resolved. There is nothing wrong with me talking to him and, just so you know, we'll be doing some more talking. I think we can help each other resolve those issues so we can both move on with our lives. We're not getting back together. We're two people who had a common experience and are trying to get through it together. I'm sorry if you don't agree Max but this is my life and my problem. I choose to deal with it like this and you'll have to get over it. Please understand I don't want us to fight over this. I hope you can find it in yourself to let me handle this my way." Linda pleaded.

Max didn't know what to say. She was virtually speechless. What did Mark say to her to get her to change her way of thinking so quickly? Max quickly assessed the situation and decided she needed to lay low and pretend to go along with this. After all, she had to be close enough to Linda to keep her eye on Mark.

"Okay. Have it your way. If you want to let him slither back into your life then there's nothing I can do about it. Mark, I don't know what you said, but I will be watching you. Linda, you know what Mark is and you know how this whole thing will turn out. But, as your friend, I'll still be there to scrape you up when he messes over you again." Maxine stated with squinted eye and pointed finger.

Chapter 11

Cassandra entered her house in deep thought. As she went about carrying out her nightly ritual, she realized she had a strong desire to write in her journal. She began writing in a diary when she was a teenager. Cassandra stopped when she entered college because she deemed the activity juvenile. However, when the young Christian women's group at the college began touting the benefits of journalizing she had jumped back in wholeheartedly. She actually missed her diary. She really needed it. Cassandra went through some terribly rough times during her college years and journalizing helped her through them. As she reached for the bronze and purple book, tears began to flow from her eyes as she reflected on the incident which had left her feeling so bad about herself and so out of control of her life. It had so affected her that even now she was still feeling the effects. It was the same feeling of being out of control that caused her to cry so profusely now. She pulled herself together and began to put pen to paper.

I feel so unsteady today. I feel like I'm not in control and I don't like this feeling. When a person has been through what I have, you spend a lot of time, effort and thought trying to stay in control of everything surrounding you. I am so sick of men and I'm so glad I don't have one in my life. Those men at the church are enough to make me not want one anywhere near me. They are so chauvinistic it's pathetic. I don't know how they call themselves men of God. The church primarily consists of women and their children, yet they put any man that comes in the door in a leadership position. As women, we can preach down fire from heaven as long as it's from a small podium on the floor strategically placed beneath the level of the pulpit. As women, we bring our tithes and offerings but aren't allowed to handle it once it leaves are hands. All of this while the pastor and his boys sit in the pulpit and "oversee" everything from the "high place". Even those men who show up a few times a year sit in the pulpit while women who are faithful to the ministry for years only have a few options from which to choose. It's utterly ridiculous. It's out of my control. There's nothing I can do about it…or is there!"

She had to map out a strategy to get what she wanted. Yes, she had a new even loftier goal in mind than those before. She had always used her femininity as a tool to get her way. However, Pastor Mitch so far appeared to be unimpressed. He was so enamored with that wife of his and no other woman could divert his attention. Cassandra could not reach her new goal without having him solidly on her team in some way. She didn't know what else to do. As she thought about how things had worked out with Pastor Edwards, Believer's previous pastor, she realized she didn't actually have to "steal" Pastor Mitch's affection. All she had to do was convince others there was something going on, especially the pastor's wife Marsha Ross. She would have to carefully find the perfect time to put her plan into action. Suddenly Cassandra had a brainstorm. Pastor Mitch mentioned something about some time together the Ross' actually scheduled. Cassandra sensed this time was very important to them. Of course, it made perfect sense considering the amount of time Pastor Mitch had been spending at the church. Marsha must be putting the screws to him and that's why this time is so important. She must really want to spend some time with her husband. Cassandra couldn't stand a weak woman who was so in need of a man's company. Why doesn't she realize no man is worth it even if they are men of the cloth? Pastor Edwards was the perfect example of that. Marsha needed someone to show her the light. She would do this not only for herself but also to show Marsha the truth about Pastor Mitch. Everyone would be happy.

Chapter 12

Linda and Maxine returned from the shopping mall with so many bags they both practically fell into the house. As they sat on the couch going through their many purchases, Max turned to Linda and asked, "What's going on with you and Mark lately?"

Linda wasn't quite sure what to say to Max. She didn't want to upset Max with her response but she was tired of avoiding the subject like the plague.

"Max, why are you asking about Mark when we both know you couldn't care less? So what's up with the sudden concern?" Linda asked Maxine who responded quickly.

"Look, I'm just curious. I'm trying to look out for you. Mark certainly won't and you act as if you don't even care enough to look out for yourself. I am your one true friend so I'll look out for you."

"You aren't just being curious. I know you. You don't react like this when you're casually asking. Tell me the truth. What is your real issue with Mark?" Linda was getting somewhat annoyed with Max. She was starting to act more like her mother than a friend does and it was getting on her last good nerve.

"I don't like how he treats you and I don't like how you let him. I've been the one right by your side through this whole ordeal and it seems like you don't value my support at all. Don't think going through all that was a walk in the park for me either. Are you going to let him dog you out again? Because if you are, you need to know you're going down that road alone. I'm not going with you!" Max stated firmly although she knew she could never follow through with such a threat. She didn't want Mark back in Linda's life. She wanted to be the one Linda needed. She wasn't sure how, but she was not going to allow that to happen.

"If that's the way you feel then I'll have to deal with it. As your friend, I would never abandon you if you needed me." Linda said with a quiet resolve. She knew resolving her issues with Mark would be good for her emotionally. She had many unanswered questions for him about their relationship and she needed answers. She also realized she hadn't even dealt with her crisis of faith. How had she become so weak as to allow Mark to cause her to break her vow of celibacy to herself and to God? What had gone haywire in her mind causing her to give in to her flesh?

Chapter 13

Sunday finally arrived. Mitch and Marsha would have their rendezvous. As they prepared for church services as well as their get-away, they both exhibited excitement only paralleled by the days before their wedding. They were both so young and yet so in love then. Neither could wait until their wedding night because they had not been together intimately before that night. It had been difficult to keep themselves out of situations where sexual activity may have occurred when they spent so much time together. As these thoughts went through Marsha's mind, she realized she desired a return to that kind of excitement where their relationship was concerned. She had what she thought were some valid concerns about the direction they seemed to be going in currently. It seemed the church was sapping so much of the energy their marriage once had. If it wasn't a church meeting, it was some troubled parishioner needing the attention of their pastor in order for them to make it to tomorrow. She understood to an extent but she longed for the day when these mature Christians would take more time to seek God to solve the problems in their lives. New Christians she definitely understood. They needed a lot of handholding. But some of these people were mature and yet the nature of their concerns so immature. Cassandra Williams was one of those people. She always insisted she needed to speak with Mitch privately about a "pressing issue". However, when Marsha asked Mitch about the "pressing issue", Mitch always indicated it wasn't really pressing after all. Mitch wasn't concerned about it. Marsha on the other had smelled something rotten. She didn't know what it was, but she knew Cassandra was up to no good. Marsha never cared for Cassandra very much. She always felt there was something very sneaky about her. She would continue to keep her eye on her.

"Mitch, what are you preaching on this morning?" Marsha stated as she broke her own train of thought.

"Honey, I studied all week and haven't come up with anything solid. I'll have to wait to see what comes out of my mouth." Mitch responded as he placed his Bible in his briefcase.

"Well, I see you're ready for church. Have you finished packing for our trip this evening? I don't want to waste any time after the church meeting." Marsha said as she looked around for Mitch's bag he always used for short trips.

"Oh, my bag is packed and under the bed," he said as he retrieved the bag from underneath the bed. He smiled widely at his wife thinking she would be proud of him for packing ahead of time.

"Mitch, that bag looks empty. You need to make sure you have everything you need."

"Marsha, I don't need much for this trip. If you know what I mean." Mitch responded while winking his eye at Marsha.

"You are so crazy and so right. The less the better!" She said as she worked her way over to her husband.

The two looked in each other's eyes and kissed as if their lives depended on it. Each began to embrace and caress the other. Before they knew it they were considering missing Sunday School. Marsha stopped the action leaving Mitch wondering what happened.

"Mitch, we have to go to church. We're leaders and we have to be there. We'll have plenty of time for that later but now is not the time. We both have to get up and get ready for church again." Marsha stated.

"Okay, Marsha. But tonight, it's on!" Mitch stated with much excitement.

"Mercy!" Marsha responded while packing her last few items. They both picked up their bags and headed for the door. Because of that little encounter, they only had fifteen minutes to get to church.

Chapter 14

Maxine and Linda arrived at Believer's Church as the Praise and Worship portion of the service was getting into full swing. They both immensely enjoyed the atmosphere that resulted from this part of the service. As soon as the two women got to their seats and put their Bibles down they got right into the service. They both raised their hands and danced with their feet as the Spirit moved them. Life's issues seemed so far away as they worshipped. Both women needed a break from the daily grind. As Praise and Worship ended, the two women held hands and thanked God for their friendship and for victory in their lives. They hugged each other because they truly loved each other as friends but also because they were sisters in Christ. It seemed natural to them.

What Maxine and Linda didn't notice were the stares from some of the women in the Church Mother's row. These women had been watching Maxine and Linda for months and developed an opinion of the two based on presumption instead of fact. The women noticed both Maxine and Linda abruptly broke off engagements that to these women seemed like loving relationships. The Church Mothers heard men in the church complaining that neither of the women would give them the time of day. They flat out weren't interested in any of them. Then to top it off, the two moved in together and began to exhibit behavior considered inappropriate. Whoever heard of two women holding hands and hugging so openly in the church? What was going on between those two? The church mothers had collectively concluded the women were lesbians. What they didn't know was what to do about it. As church leaders, they couldn't allow this to continue. After all, they had to think about the younger generation who were very impressionable. What were they thinking about this situation? The Church Mothers would take up this cause.

As Praise and Worship ended, the pastor began to move toward the pulpit. As he opened his Bible, he felt the need to speak to the congregation about some of the things on his heart.

"People of God, before I bring the Word of God for today, I want to talk to you about some things which have been weighing heavily on my heart. I am concerned about the lack of unity I see in this body. It seems we pay a lot of lip service to loving each other without ever really, truly exhibiting it to each other or to the world. We all need to understand we're in this thing together and none of us can make it without the other. I've been sensing something that feels like some of us think we're better than others are and I know it's not of God. Some of us are so busy pointing out the speck in other's eyes and not paying attention to the plank in our own. If this church is going to grow and become the body we're called to be, we're going to have to love and respect each other for who we are. We're going to have to cover the shortcomings of others with prayer. We must encourage each other when we're down instead of gossiping about it. We need to speak to each other about the positives and downplay the negatives. If we do these things, we'll begin to notice we are closer and more in tune with each other. That's what we need to happen here. As your leader, I'm going to be the first partaker. I'm going to be more available to you. I'm going to be providing more opportunities for us to fellowship outside of the meetings and worship services. I ask you today to examine yourself and see if there are areas where you can make a difference in this regard. I also ask you to follow me as I follow God toward a more unified body." As Pastor Ross finished, the congregation rose to its feet. They were all in complete agreement. That is everyone except Marsha. She was concerned about the additional availability her husband promised the congregation.

"I can't believe he made those promises without even talking with me. Doesn't he remember what we've been talking about the last couple of months? Did he forget how hard it was for us to plan this short get-away this weekend? Haven't I been telling him I've been missing him?" she said quietly. "I don't know how much more of this I can take!"

Pastor Ross continued, "Thank you for your agreement. I knew I could count on you to be willing to make changes where necessary. Since I feel God has said what He wanted to say this morning, I'm going to dismiss you so we can all come back this afternoon for the meeting. This is a very important meeting and we have to begin on time. We'll be talking about some organizational changes that will affect the way we do things. If you're available, I would appreciate each of you being here this afternoon. If not, we'll make the information available to you next week. God bless you all! Consider yourselves dismissed. Greet your neighbor with a big 'I love you' before you leave."

As Mitch left the pulpit, he looked for Marsha. He noticed while he was speaking something bothered her and he really wanted to know what. He looked over to where she had been sitting and she had disappeared. He decided to greet a few parishioners on his way back to his office. When he reached his office and stepped inside to hang up his robe, he noticed Marsha sitting there with tears in her eyes. As he walked toward her he asked, "What's wrong baby? Why are you crying?" He opened his arms as he approached her but she put her arms up to stop him from embracing her.

"Mitch, do you love me? Do you want to be married to me? If you do you had better make some changes." Marsha choked out through her tears.

"I don't understand what's happening. Tell me what's on your mind." Mitch stated out of concern for the obvious seriousness of the situation.

"Mitch, since you've been pastor of this church you have been spending every moment building this ministry. Don't get me wrong, that's admirable. However, as my husband you have been failing miserably. Our marriage is paying the price for it. "

"Are we still on that kick? I thought we discussed this and had an understanding. Aren't we going away tonight? I know you were disappointed about it being a few hours later than we had originally planned but I thought we were past the delay. Help me understand what the issue is now."

"You stood in that pulpit and promised this congregation more availability when you don't have any extra time to give. You don't even have time for me as it is. I've been complaining about this for weeks and yet you seem to be ignoring my feelings completely. I don't know how to handle this."

Mitch realized he had done exactly what Marsha said. He was overextending himself and in the process sacrificing Marsha and their relationship. The problem was he felt he had to be the one to set the standard. How could he go back and tell the congregation he couldn't do it? How could he make Marsha happy? He realized he was definitely in a difficult situation. He would have to commit this matter to prayer before he lost his marriage.

"Honey, I apologize and ask your forgiveness once again. I will work this out. Please give me some time. Tell me what I need to do." Mitch pleaded with his wife.

"Mitch, I can't tell you what to do. Listen to your heart. I believe you'll come up with the right answer."

Marsha got up and left the room. She felt any further conversation with Mitch regarding this subject would not be the least bit productive. She was much too upset and might say something she would later regret. Walking out of the office area, she decided to head into the ladies room before going any further. She needed to check her make-up.

Entering the ladies room, she acknowledged some of the church mothers who had gathered there. She noticed their talking turned to whispers as she entered. Marsha considered the situation and decided to head into a stall. Once she returned to the basin area, the ladies were still there. Finally, Mother Thomas began speaking to her,

"Sister Ross we need to talk to you about something. We've noticed some things going on in this church and we are sick about it. We feel you and Pastor Ross need to address it. Our issue is, those women are not ..."

Marsha held up her hand toward them indicating for them to stop. The women immediately got the message and left the area with a huff. Marsha knew she shouldn't have handled the situation in that manner. But today, she absolutely didn't have the patience to deal with it. Besides, her husband had stood in the pulpit moments ago and told the people how they needed to handle each other and these Church Mothers still didn't get the point. She would go back to them later and apologize. Now was not the time. She had to get away from the church and the church folk.

In the parking lot, Maxine and Linda were almost to their cars when Maxine heard someone calling her name. It was a very familiar voice but yet she couldn't put her finger on whose it was. Maxine turned around and saw a little lady with a huge smile on her face coming towards her with her arms outstretched. It was Steve's mom, Momma Doris. She was happy to see her as well. This woman had been there for her during the whole engagement breakup fiasco.

"Momma Doris, how are you? How's everything going?" Maxine asked.

"Oh honey, I'm doing good for a little old lady. Baby, where have you been hiding yourself? I haven't seen you in I don't know when." Momma Doris said looking Maxine up and down. "You looking good girl!"

"I'm doing real good. It's good to see you. What are you doing here? " Maxine inquired as she knew Momma Doris was a committed member of the church down the street from her home.

"I came to visit with a friend of mine. She's been inviting me to visit with her for quite some time now. I also thought I might see you here today. You've really been on my heart lately. Aren't you going to ask?" Momma Doris really wanted Maxine to ask about Steve. She wanted to disprove all the rumors her friend Mother Thomas had shared with her about Maxine. She knew Maxine like a daughter and didn't want to believe she had made such a drastic change in her lifestyle. Had her problems with Steve hurt her so badly she would turn to a woman?

Maxine knew Momma Doris wanted her to ask about Steve. She really didn't want to know anything about the man. What difference did it make about what was going on in his life? When it could've made a difference, the jerk hadn't even given her feelings a second thought. If he had told her what was going on, perhaps she could have helped him. Momma Doris had nothing to do with what happened. So out of respect for her, nothing else, she decided to ask about Steve.

"How is Steve doing?"

"Chile, he's doing so good I sometimes can't believe it. He went through a little slump but the Lord has brought him right on out. I know he would love to talk with you. Why don't you give me your number so I can keep in touch with you and maybe Steve can call you as well?" Momma Doris asked and waited patiently for Maxine's answer. She knew Maxine was a Christian and therefore recognized the necessity of forgiveness.

"Momma Doris, I would be happy to give you the number for your use only. I'm sorry but Steve and I have had our last conversation. Can you respect that? " Maxine responded wondering why Momma Doris would put her in this predicament.

"Honey, I know Steve caused you much pain. I won't deny that. I was hurt too. I've never been able to see you two with anyone other than each other. Steve has dated other women since you broke up but they've never really worked out. I know he would like to have another chance with you. Won't you even consider it?" Momma Doris begged desperately wanting Maxine to agree.

"Please don't press this issue. I have absolutely no intention of getting back together with Steve. I don't even think we can be friends at this point." Maxine said and then attempted to redirect the conversation, "I'm sorry for being rude. Momma Doris this is my best friend Linda. Linda, this is Steve's mother Momma Doris."

"It's very nice to meet you Momma Doris. I've heard a lot of nice things about you." Linda responded with a smile while holding her hand out to shake Momma Doris' hand.

"It's funny that in all the time Maxine and my son were together I never heard a word about you." Momma Doris said with her nose turned up and her hand tightly clutching her purse. She wondered if this was "her".

Linda withdrew her hand wondering why the woman refused to acknowledge it. She stole a glance at Maxine in an effort to determine what was going on.

"Momma Doris it was nice seeing you. We have to go now. Bye, bye." Maxine said as she grabbed Linda's arm to direct her to walk away.

Momma Doris knew a good relationship when she saw one and what Steve and Maxine had was a good one. They would be a couple again. She was determined to see them walk down the aisle if it was the last thing she did!

Chapter 15

Eric Howard entered Fellowship City for dinner. He had been dining there alone for the five years since his beloved wife, Eunice, passed away. Since church service was over a little early today, he decided this would be a good place to dine since he could have some good food and good company in a relaxed atmosphere. Today was a particularly rough day for him as it would have been their thirtieth wedding anniversary.

Eric and Eunice had so many plans for "one day" which unfortunately never came. They wanted to go on a cruise but never went because neither was willing to take the time off work. They planned to purchase a chalet in the country as a retreat once they retired. None of the things he and Eunice had desired to do were ever going to happen. Those dreams died with Eunice. Eric decided he would live the rest of his life as if there would be no tomorrow. One never knew when his time would come to meet the Lord.

He was a tall, stocky, bald-headed man women tended to find irresistible for some reason. There's something about a financially stable widower and church-going man who isn't particularly looking for a new wife that somehow sends single women into a tizzy. Eric didn't want another wife. He loved Eunice so completely he didn't feel he had anything left for anyone else. It wouldn't be fair to any woman who would follow Eunice as his wife. However, Eric desired having a companion though. He was seeking someone to share a meal with now and then or to go to functions with. This person would have to understand there would be no romance and no commitment. He wasn't looking for a live-in roommate either. Eric had not been successful in his effort to find this woman. He knew he didn't want any of the women who had been throwing themselves at him. That kind of woman was not attractive to him and they typically wanted more than he was willing to give. So to keep his life free of confusion he avoided them. As he sat at the table trying to decide whether he wanted to have the buffet or order from the menu, he looked up and saw Marsha Ross enter the building. He waved hello to her and continued reviewing the menu assuming Pastor Mitch was parking the car. However, the next time he looked up she was standing at his table.

"Hi, Elder Howard. Did you enjoy the service this morning?" Marsha inquired looking around to see if anyone appeared to be heading toward his table.

"Lord, yes. It was a wonderful service. The Spirit really moved today. I really enjoyed what Pastor Mitch had to say this morning too. Is he parking the car?" Eric asked curious as to why it was taking so long for him to come in.

"No, I left him at the church." Marsha replied sadly. She wished she hadn't left the church the way she did but she needed some time to clear her head. She was sure he was worried about her but she would show up at the church meeting this afternoon.

"Well, Sister Marsha, would you like to join me? I'd appreciate the company!" Eric stated standing to pull the seat out for Marsha.

"Well, perhaps I will." Marsha said feeling a little awkward sitting in the restaurant with one of the church's elders without Mitch being present. She realized she was taking a chance because the church community in general frequented Fellowship City especially on Sunday after church. Seeing them sharing dinner could certainly start tongues wagging. Marsha decided this once wouldn't hurt. Besides, if she was honest with herself, she really didn't want to eat alone. She had already been doing a lot of that thanks to Mitch's absence.

The waitress came to the table to take their orders. Marsha decided to have the buffet while Eric ordered the vegetable platter. As she stood up to head to the buffet, Marsha hesitated as she wondered if Elder Howard would mind her eating in front of him.

"Would you mind if I went ahead and got started?" Marsha asked in an attempt to be considerate. Her stomach rumbled as loudly as she spoke.

"Sure Sister Marsha, help yourself. It won't be long before my meal comes." Eric responded.

Marsha walked over to the Supper Room while Eric stayed at the table. He wondered why Pastor Mitch was not with his wife. He knew they were going away this evening so perhaps he was at the church tying up loose ends to free up his time. For some reason, Eric couldn't shake the feeling that Marsha was saddened about something. He noticed her beeline to the office after service today. She had rushed right past him. From the moment he met her, Eric considered Marsha to be a very classy lady. He had never seen her lose her composure as he had today. It was obvious something really upset her. He wondered if Mitch being at the church while his wife was here having dinner was a result of whatever occurred during service. He wasn't sure how, but he wanted to know what was going on with his Pastor and his wife. As a church elder, he felt he should know.

Marsha returned as the waitress was setting his vegetable platter on the table. As they both individually blessed their food, Pastor Mitch entered the restaurant. He figured Marsha might have come here after he couldn't find her at home or anywhere else she would normally frequent. He looked around and noticed her bowing her head in prayer. As he moved toward the table, he noticed there was a second person at the table. It was Eric Howard. What was his wife doing "breaking bread" with Eric Howard when they obviously needed to talk? He took a deep breath and approached the table. As Eric lifted his head from prayer, he saw Pastor Mitch coming. He nodded at him acknowledging his presence and also to give Marsha a hint someone else was approaching. Before Marsha could catch the hint, Mitch was already standing over her at the table. She didn't know what to say. She hadn't expected him to show up. It was at that moment she realized she had made a poor decision out of anger. Her husband stood there looking at her as if she had stolen something. Marsha felt like Mitch had caught her doing something illegal or immoral and that was not the case. If Mitch could spend his life at the church, what harm was it for her to have dinner with Elder Howard. She was very committed to her relationship with Mitch and had proven it repeatedly. It was Mitch whose level of commitment to their marriage was questionable.

"Hello." Marsha said nonchalantly.

"Hi, Eric. I'm sorry to interrupt your dinner but I would appreciate a moment with my wife." Mitch spoke while never removing his stare from his wife's face. He knew she was upset with him but she had not given him time to fix the situation.

"Hi, Pastor." Eric stated uncomfortably. As he looked at how the two were interacting with each other, he decided it would be best if he removed himself from the situation.

"Mitch, Marsha, please excuse me." Eric walked toward the restroom, which was the only place he could think of to go.

"Mitch, why did you come here? I needed some time to think." Marsha looked at her husband for the first time since he walked up to the table. She noticed he looked as though he was concerned about her. Once again, she felt bad about leaving the church as she had but she wasn't sure how else to react.

"Why would you ask me that question? I didn't even know you left until the church was empty and I still couldn't find you. How did you think I would react?" Mitch asked attempting to hide his anger regarding Marsha's actions.

"I needed to get away from you for a moment to let things cool down a bit. I was very upset and concerned about what I might say or do. I thought it was best," she responded while stabbing a piece of ham with her fork until it broke under the pressure. She then brought it to her mouth and chewed slowly in order to busy her mouth so she couldn't speak.

"Okay, Marsha. I understand and appreciate that. What I don't get is why you left without telling me. I was worried about you. Why couldn't you tell me you were leaving so you could cool down?" Mitch said through gritted his teeth.

"I don't know. I just found myself leaving the church." Marsha responded.

"How were you going to think while sitting here with Eric Howard? How did this happen anyway?" There, Mitch asked what he really wanted to know.

"I didn't know he would be here. I came here to get a bite to eat and it didn't seem to make much sense for me to wait for a table. Elder Howard invited me to eat with him."

"Okay that all seems to make sense. But, we both know this is bordering on being inappropriate. "

"Let's continue this conversation later on. Are you going to stay and eat or what? It seems we're creating a small scene." Marsha motioned over her shoulder at the church folks milling about in the restaurant area.

"I see what you're saying. I'll have a seat for a moment but I don't have much of an appetite. We'll talk about this later." Mitch said while proceeding to sit down in the chair next to Marsha.

When Mitch sat down Eric smiled. He had been watching from the other side of the room. He still wasn't sure about what was happening between his pastor and his wife. It was obviously something serious. He was sincerely concerned on one hand. He didn't revel in anyone having marital problems. He would have taken on all the marital problems in the world if it meant he could still have Eunice in his life. On the other hand, he had been watching how the church was making a turn around and felt now would be a good time for him to take it over. If Mitch and Marsha continued to have problems, perhaps he could become pastor by default with no effort whatsoever on his part. He caught the attention of a waitress and asked her to retrieve his plate and wrap it for him so he could leave gracefully and not have to go back to lions den at the table.

Chapter 16

Activity filled the Believer's Church basement as the members began to gather for the meeting. Everyone was abuzz regarding what was really going to change. People had begun to talk about who they thought would lose their positions and who would replace them. The church mothers were talking about Linda and Maxine as usual.

"I don't know what her problem is. I tried to tell Sister Ross about those women and she put her hand up as if she didn't even want to hear it. She's the pastor's wife. She has to deal with these kinds of things." The ladies surrounding Mother Thomas all nodded in agreement. "But I think she and Pastor Mitch had a disagreement because the first lady looked like she had been crying when she came into the bathroom. That doesn't matter though. Sister Marsha should still carry herself as first lady of this church. I don't know how they did things where they came from but we don't expect our pastor and his wife to act like they do. Pastor Mitch and Sister Marsha are going to have to get with the program." Mother Thomas concluded. The ladies all followed her like ducklings and sat down as Elder Howard called the meeting to order.

Marsha and Mitch also entered in time to hear Elder Howard open the meeting. As Mitch took his seat at the head table, Marsha sat in her usual front row seat. She felt like someone was staring at her, which made her begin to look around the room. As her eyes scanned the people gathered for the meeting, hers met Mother Thomas' eyes. She knew the woman was probably upset with her if the scowl plastered on her face was any indication. Marsha smiled at her and made a mental note to speak with her after the meeting to apologize for her earlier actions. She returned her attention to the front of the room where her husband Mitch was beginning to speak.

"I thank God for allowing me to stand before you today as your pastor and announce the improvements to the way we do things here in this ministry. It's my vision for there to be a specific ministry for each group of people represented in this church. If there isn't a ministry group that interests you, please place a note about it in the suggestions box. It's my desire for everyone to get the ministry needed based on your needs and what you may want to improve about your walk with the Lord. I believe every one of the appointments we'll make today is ordained of God. The first appointment I would like to announce today is for my Co-Pastor. My wife, Sister Marsha, will become the co-pastor of this church. Her role will be to help me to carry on the pastoral responsibilities I have. She is the most logical choice for this role because she is my wife and already works closely with me, but she also has God-given abilities to handle the tasks required of her. I must say I am indeed blessed to have her as my wife, but you are also blessed to now have her as your pastor." Pastor Mitch stated proudly unaware of the body language of his audience.

Cassandra was squirming in her seat. This can't be allowed to happen. She would have to shift her plan into overdrive in order to reach her goal.

The Church Mothers' scowls deepened. How could a woman who was so blatantly disrespectful to the church mothers become a leader in this church? Besides, a woman had never been a pastor of any kind here and they weren't sure they liked her being the first.

Elder Howard smiled outwardly but inwardly was concerned. If Sister Marsha and Pastor Mitch began working closely together, they might work out whatever their problems were. He might not become the pastor as easily as he thought. How could he have chosen Marsha as his co-pastor when Eric had been working faithfully in the ministry for years, well before Mitch and Marsha arrived? The Board hadn't even discussed this part.

The announcement hit Marsha like a ton of bricks. Mitch hadn't said a word to her about this. Was this Mitch's solution to the problems they were having? He should have talked with her about this before he announced it to the congregation. That way he could save himself the embarrassment of having to tell the members he had to change his plans because Marsha had no intentions of being any kind of pastor.

" Additionally, the board decided the Deacon ministry would expand to include Deaconess. The wives of these men have been working alongside them all along but, as a church, we have not recognized what they've been doing. We are now going to do so officially and recognize their ministry. All of you who are wives of deacons please stand so we can briefly acknowledge you right now. Give these women a hand for the ministry God has given them. We'll be speaking with you ladies later to provide some direction as you organize your ministry. We're going to pray for each one of you for the work you'll be doing. God bless you. You may be seated." Pastor Mitch continued.

"Small group ministries are also being organized. We've already prayed and selected the ministry leaders. Elder Howard will head up the group for those who are widows or widowers. We feel this is a unique need requiring special ministry. As most of you know, Elder Howard lost his wife a few years ago. We feel he is qualified to minister to those now living life without their beloved spouses. Sister Wayne will work with those who have children with physical and learning challenges. Her work with her own children and with other youngsters speaks for itself. She is a woman who believes God desires these children to lead full and productive lives, though society doesn't see them that way. If you or someone you know has a child facing Attention Deficit Disorder, Attention Deficit Hyperactivity Disorder, a learning disability or a physical challenge of some sort, please contact Sister Wayne so everyone who needs this type of ministry can get it. Sister Maxine and Sister Linda, I don't see them here, they will be working with our singles ministry. These young women have been faithful to this church for a number of years. They have successfully lived as Christian singles. I've spoken with them and they already have a number of ideas for the singles ministry. I believe this group is going to grow, flourish, and minister to the singles in this church as well as the community. I wanted to highlight those ministry groups. Because the hour is late, I'm going to let you review the information regarding the rest of the groups at your leisure. If you want to join any of these groups please see the respective contact person for more information. There are more changes that will be taking place but these are the first. Let's all stand and praise God for the things He has done in our midst today."

As Pastor Mitch raised his hands, everyone else followed. The praise in the place was exuberant. The people really appreciated the changes they were seeing in their ministry. The newly appointed were excited about the opportunity to exercise their God-given gifts. Pastor Edwards would never have thought about doing anything like that. He always seemed too focused on his own ministry. The people felt like the Dead Sea, always something flowing in but nowhere for anything to flow out. Now they had group ministries where they could spread their wings with the backing of their pastor. God was truly good!

As the last of the people left the building, Sister Cassandra approached Pastor Mitch and Sister Marsha with tears in her eyes.

"What's wrong Sister Cassandra?" Pastor Mitch asked.

"I really need to talk to you about some things that have been going on. I'm so tired of these people I don't know what to do. It's so bad I'm thinking about leaving the Lord." Cassandra said with a straight face that was difficult for her to maintain.

Marsha looked at the clock. It was 5:45. Mitch had promised her they would be on their way by 6:00. She crossed her arms as she waited for Mitch's response. Mitch switched his weight from one foot to the other. He had stolen a glance at Marsha when she looked at the clock. He knew he was cutting it close.

"Sister Williams, why don't you have a seat in my office and I'll be with you in a moment." Cassandra wiped her tears and quickly made her move to the pastor's office before Marsha had an opportunity to change his mind.

"Mitch, you know we should be leaving. Why did you tell her to go to your office? You don't have time for this tonight." Marsha said while patting her feet and clinching her teeth.

"Marsha, I'll be at the hotel in a half hour. Why don't you go ahead and I'll catch a cab when I'm done here." Mitch said hoping Marsha would go along with the program.

"No, Mitch I'm not accepting another compromise. You tell Sister Williams you'll have to counsel her later." Marsha said with such anger Mitch almost didn't recognize his wife.

"Baby, I can't do that. Sister Cassandra is obviously having a crisis of faith. I know what I promised and I know you're upset, but how do I ignore my duties as pastor?" Mitch pleaded.

"You know how to ignore your duties. I'm confident of that. You've been ignoring your duties as my husband for months now!" Marsha responded with a quiet resolve.

"I'll meet you at the hotel in no more than a half hour!" As she fought back tears, she turned and slowly walked out of the church.

Mitch turned to walk toward his office. "Sister Cassandra had better have a life or death problem that must be dealt with tonight." He was growing weary of her apparent need to have access to him at all times.

Chapter 17

Marsha slid under the wheel of her new luxury SUV. They had driven her vehicle because they needed the extra room it provided for their bags. Mitch's two-seater would never work for such an occasion. As she began driving out of the church's parking lot, she thought back on the happenings of the day. She always supported Mitch becoming a pastor. However, Marsha didn't realize she would in effect lose her husband in the process. She and Mitch had vowed before God and the other three hundred people at their wedding they would stay together through anything. She would not allow the idea of divorce to creep into her mind though it was difficult because of Mitch's actions. It felt as though he was effectively divorcing her by his physical and emotional absence from their relationship. They lived in the same house, slept in the same bed, and ate meals at home though not at the same time. However, in all the ways that counted they were leading separate lives.

As she thought back on recent weeks, she couldn't remember the last time they had gone out to eat together. Their favorite restaurant had become accustomed to her coming without Mitch although they would ask about him regularly. They probably wondered what was going on. Saturday mornings had been their official breakfast day. They would go to a small restaurant not far from their home where they served monstrous omelets and a specialty dish Mitch absolutely loved and could only get there. It had gotten to the point Marsha no longer leapt out of bed early enough on Saturdays to even get to the restaurant in time for breakfast. She figured there was absolutely no reason to do so.

As she got on the ramp for the expressway, her thoughts went to Cassandra. She knew the woman was trouble, but she didn't realize until now how much of a problem she was. Marsha thought Cassandra was after her husband who she was sure didn't realize what was going on. Marsha realized she had a decision to make. Either she was going to ask God to help her fight for her marriage or she was going to let the enemy win. She began to pray "Heavenly Father, I come to you now angry and concerned. I am angry because my husband's ministry seems to have overshadowed our marriage. I'm having problems holding on to my faith for our marriage. Strengthen me. Mitch has taken the call to pastor very seriously and has gone in with all he has. I'm angry because he isn't listening to how I'm feeling about this. Father, I ask you today to open his eyes to what this is doing to us. I ask you to show him how to be a pastor and my husband at the same time. Help me to be strong during this process. Cause me to see this situation through your eyes. Help me to deal with my own anger. I turn my concerns completely over to you. Let your will be done in our lives, both Mitch's and my own. Father, help Mitch to remember our vows. In the Name of Jesus I pray, Amen."

As she closed her prayer, Marsha entered the parking lot to the city's plushest suite hotel. She promised herself she was not going to allow Cassandra's actions to upset her. She was going to allow Mitch to do whatever he felt he needed to do. After all, she had already made it crystal-clear what she needed. She resolved to put all her issues and concerns in God's hands.

Tonight she was going to spend time with her husband. Thinking about the candles, negligees, massage oil, and soft music she brought along for the trip re-ignited her excitement. She'd already arranged with the hotel to provide chocolate covered strawberries and chilled sparkling fruit juice. She had also insured that the room was equipped with a huge jetted tub for them to enjoy as well. She smiled as she realized the delay in Mitch's arrival, allowed her time to run the bath, get the music going, and sprinkle the rose petals. The stage would already be set when he arrived. She was determined to trust God with the whole situation and to make this a night to remember.

Chapter 18

Sister Cassandra hurried to get to the office and be seated before Pastor Mitch got there. She had been standing inside the hallway in the office area so she could be within earshot of the conversation between Pastor Mitch and Sister Marsha. She now had bonus information. She knew she had to hold him for at least forty-five minutes in order to insure Marsha was at a brisk boil when her husband reached the hotel. Cassandra positioned herself and completed the unbuttoning of the top few buttons of her beige silk suit coat. She thought this would be the perfect suit for the occasion. During church service, the suit didn't even raise an eyebrow, but with the appropriate adjustments, the personality of the whole outfit could change. The skirt fell a little above her knees and had a split on the side, which would display her shapely legs when she crossed them. The jacket provided just a slit of an opening and converted into a lethal weapon to show the "extent of her giftedness" by unbuttoning it a little.

Pastor Mitch entered the office and looked at his lone female board member. He wondered why the other board members were so negative toward her, now he was beginning to understand. Mitch initially thought it was because they were still fighting the female presence on the Board. The pastor no longer believed that was the case. Cassandra could wear a person out with her neediness! He knew he would sometimes have to deal with parishioners who required a lot of attention. Mitch had prepared himself for that. However, this was beginning to wear on his marriage. He would have to discern when things required immediate attention and when they didn't. It would be hard to change the way he operated. He had a huge amount of compassion for the people who called him their shepherd. However, the sheep would have to learn to get along without the shepherd being within reach 24/7. He sat behind his desk and extended his hand indicating to Sister Cassandra she should begin speaking.

"Pastor Mitch, those men on your board are giving me a hard time. I'm tired of being treated like an outsider because I'm a woman."

"Cassandra, exactly what is the problem?" Mitch asked realizing he could have postponed this meeting.

"They speak to me in a condescending manner. They meet to talk about things they don't want me to hear. They don't respect me at all and I don't understand why." Cassandra choked out through her fake tears.

"I can talk to them Cassandra but I think you need to let them know how you feel first. The Bible says if you have a problem with your brother, you should first go to them and attempt to resolve the problem. It doesn't sound like you've taken the first step to resolving the issue." Mitch said in a pastoral manner.

"I always tell them when they've done something offensive. They simply wave it off as though it's silly. With all due respect, I guess I shouldn't be surprised you don't understand how this makes me feel." Cassandra decided it was time to begin utilizing her bag of tricks. She carefully crossed her legs insuring her split opened enough to show off her pride and joy.

This action was not lost on Pastor Mitch. What was she trying to pull?

"If that's how you feel, why are you here talking to me about it?" Mitch was becoming increasingly impatient with the woman. He would have to suppress his anger. It would not be wise to release it at this time.

"You're a man. You've never had to deal with the prejudice women have to deal with in the church. Because I'm a woman in a position I wouldn't normally be allowed to operate in, I know first hand a problem exists." She said intentionally bypassing his question. She now stood and placed her hands on the edge of her pastor's desk. She leaned over to allow Pastor Mitch a look at her ample womanhood as she moved her face closer to his. She was moving in for the kill. "Acknowledge my call to

the ministry like you acknowledge the call of the men in this church. "
She smiled at Pastor Mitch as she saw his eyes fall on her cleavage.

"I don't understand. What are you are trying to say?"

Cassandra leaned even closer to her pastor's face. "When a man is called to the ministry, he gets certain privileges. He is given ministry opportunities, he's called on to head up things, and he sits in the pulpit. In general, he's not expected to prove himself in the same ways women who are called to the ministry are. I want you to treat me like them. Plain and simple." Cassandra stated emphatically. She then stood up and returned to her chair waiting for Pastor Mitch to respond.

"Sister Cassandra, I'll pray and get back to you on this. I think we should end this meeting." He thought this was the best way to diffuse the situation. He needed to talk to his wife about this. He immediately looked at his watch; he should have already been at the hotel. He could only imagine how angry Marsha would be when he actually got there. Cassandra grabbed her purse and exited the office. Mitch then picked up the phone to call for a cab. He knew he would be at least an hour late once the cab got there and got him to the hotel. "What happened here tonight?" Mitch wondered aloud to himself.

Eric Howard wondered the same thing. He came back inside the church after he saw Marsha leave in tears for the second time today. Mitch was not with her once again. Eric headed to the parking lot to check on Marsha but changed his course once his eyes landed on the only other car remaining in the parking lot...Sister Cassandra's sleek, fire engine red sports car. As he reentered the church, he heard voices in the office area and followed them. He got there as Cassandra made her request, peeked in and saw Cassandra expose herself to Pastor Mitch.

"That woman has no shame." He thought to himself. When he heard Pastor Mitch ending their meeting, he hurriedly moved toward the parking lot in hopes he could get in his car and leave before Cassandra saw him. He had barely gotten his car started when she exited the church. As he rode past her, he pretended he didn't see her. That way, no one would know he witnessed a thing.

Chapter 19

"So, uh, Maxine, what's the problem with Steve's mother? She acted like she had an attitude with me and I've never even laid eyes on the woman before." Momma Doris' actions hurt her feelings when the women met at the church.

"I noticed that but I don't know why she acted that way. I was surprised to see her." Maxine responded thoughtfully.

"Max, what was your relationship like with her? I mean you were almost her daughter-in-law."

"She was always good to me. When Steve acted up, she really helped me a lot. She was very supportive."

"Speaking of Steve, do you ever think about him? " Linda knew Maxine thought about her former fiancé and that was the reason Maxine reacted to relationships the way she did. Someone she loved deeply hurt her.

"No, I don't spend my time thinking about him. Just because you think about Mark all the time doesn't mean I'm thinking about Steve too." Maxine said with conviction.

"I didn't say anything about Mark. We were talking about Steve. Why can't you answer my question?" Linda was growing impatient with her friend.

"The only reason you're asking is because you need someone to justify you getting back with Mark. I'm not doing that. I think we should both leave men alone because not one of them is any good. I'm really surprised you would still want to have anything to do with any man and especially Mark after what happened!" Max spat out.

"For the umpteenth time, Mark didn't treat me right and Steve didn't treat you right either. But, why do you insist on being so bitter about men in general? We can't hold every man responsible for what Mark and Steve did. Living in bitterness and anger can't be fun or healthy for you." Linda said to Maxine trying to help her think past her pain.

"Obviously you'll never understand why I feel the way I do. I thought you would understand because of what you went through. Obviously, you never will. Let's drop the subject."

"How would you react to Steve if you saw him?" Linda asked her friend in one last attempt to get through the hard protective exterior Maxine had developed.

Maxine thought about Linda's question for a moment. Steve popped into her mind quite often because she still loved him. How would she react if she ever saw him? Would she beat him up? No, she couldn't because that would not be appropriate for a Christian. Would she refuse to acknowledge his presence? The truth was Maxine didn't know what she would do and she wasn't sure she wanted to find out. However, she knew she absolutely would not wimp out like Linda.

"I don't think I even need to consider that question because I won't see Steve. I haven't seen him after all this time and I'm sure if we did cross paths, he wouldn't dare approach me anyway. He knows I would chew him up and spit him out. Now, can we get back to working on the singles ministry?" Maxine asked her friend.

"Alright." Linda responded. She made a special mental note to ask God to heal Maxine's broken heart. She also needed to pray for guidance regarding her dinner with Mark tomorrow night. The two decided to get together to talk some more. There were still several issues they needed to deal with so each of them could go on with their lives. Linda realized she needed to face the facts. She actually laid down with this man and got pregnant. This was not supposed to happen. Linda always had good grades, stayed out of trouble, went to college, grew up in church and knew the Bible from front to back. Despite all of this, Linda had found herself a statistic. She had been pregnant out of wedlock. Those around her always spoke of single expectant women as though some sort of disease infiltrated their bodies. Didn't they understand the sickness was sin? The sin was not having the baby out of wedlock but lying down and having sex with someone who wasn't your spouse. Didn't people understand we all have the potential to sin? It's only by the grace of God that some of those pious people sitting in judgment in their church pews hadn't experienced what she had. Quite simply, some of them could appear innocent of this because there wasn't evidence showing otherwise. Her grandmother had always told her "everything glittering ain't gold and everything shouting ain't saved". Regardless, she had let those people and their potential reaction to her pregnancy keep her from having her baby. Linda realized she'd actually allowed them to cause her to compound the sin by having the abortion. How could she have let it happen to her?

Chapter 20

Steve came home from church a little later than usual because of a meeting his pastor had called with the men. When he pulled into the driveway, his nose began trying to figure out what was included in dinner today. He identified the fried chicken, macaroni and cheese and collard greens. Steve thought he also caught a whiff of sweet potato pie as well. He would have to check his predictions when he got inside. He was so happy to be living with his mother. He was good company for her and took good care of her. Steve went to a Christian-based rehabilitation center and came out clean and more grounded in Christ than ever before. The counselors recommended he live with his mother for a while because she provided a stable, drug-free environment for him. Besides, he wanted to make things up to her. He knew he had taken her for the ride of her life. Steve entered the kitchen where his mother was putting the final touches on Sunday dinner. As he looked around the kitchen he realized his predictions had once again been accurate. His mother was bustling around the kitchen taking rolls out of the oven, buttering their tops and placing them on a serving platter. He always enjoyed his mother's cooking. Even after he moved out on his own, he plotted and planned his way to eating at his mother's house as often as possible. She never minded much anyway. Once everyone moved out, she hadn't been able to adjust to cooking for one and usually ended up with more food than she could eat in a week. His thought was he was helping her get rid of all that food before it spoiled.

"Hi Momma." Steve said as his mother took the macaroni and cheese out of the oven and placed it on the dinner table.

"Hi baby. How was service today? It must have been real good because you're getting home later than normal." Momma Doris said to her youngest son.

"Yes, it was very good but we were still out on time. We had a special men's group meeting after service. That's why I'm a little late." Steve replied to his mother.

"That's good. I know you're hungry so why don't you go on in there and change your clothes. Dinner will be on the table by the time you get back." Momma Doris was happy with Steve being home with her as well. Loneliness seemed to settle in since her husband disappeared on her and the kids several years ago. She woke up one morning to an empty bed, closet and garage. At first, she didn't know what to think. Did someone kidnap him? She got her answer a few days later when she received the divorce papers. She never knew exactly what the "irreconcilable differences" were but decided if he didn't want to be with her then she would let him go. They agreed the children should not suffer because of the divorce. He would make sure to stay in contact with them and spend time with them on a regular basis. He did so for approximately three months. Then, as abruptly as he moved out of the house, he seemingly disappeared from the face of the earth. He stopped paying child support for the teenagers he left behind for her to raise. Once the dust settled, she realized she still loved him and missed him immensely. She had to go on though. She had children to raise. She never considered dating because she didn't have time. With all the time she spent working so she could keep her family's head above water and still trying to be a mother to her kids, she didn't have time for anything else as frivolous as dating. So, she didn't date. After a few years, the kids began to grow up and out of the house and eventually she found herself all alone in the house that had once held so many. She began to consider dating but didn't desire the hassle she saw her now grown children going through in their relationships. That's why she was so disappointed when Steve and Maxine broke up. They had such a wonderful relationship and that gave her hope maybe there was a chance for her. She was distraught when her son vanished just before he was to get married. She figured it was because his father left in similar fashion all those years ago and he didn't know how to be a husband. Maybe he thought one day he might up and disappear like his father so he did it before they got in so deep where children may have been involved. Because he was the youngest, Steve took it very hard when his father left. He would mope around and pout most of the time. His whole personality changed. Her once outgoing child had become introverted. When he started disrupting his classes in school, the school psychologist suggested perhaps this was his way of getting his dad's attention. In the past, when there had been a problem, his father had been the first one to get involved. She decided to turn the situation over to God instead of continuing the weekly visits to the psychologist. It wouldn't bring her husband back. What Steve needed was an emotional healing and the only one who could do that was God.

Steve returned to the kitchen with a pair of sweats and a tee shirt on replacing the tailored brown suit he'd worn to church.

"Momma, do you need me to do anything?"

"No, you sit yourself down. Momma has everything under control. I've got some news for you." She said as she set the chicken on the table. She sat down at the table, grabbed her son's hand and said grace.

"Steve, I went to church with a friend of mine today and guess who I ran into."

"Well by the sound of it, it must've been someone I know. Who was it Momma?"

"It was Maxine."

"Maxine" Steve thought to himself. It had been such a long time since he had seen her. He was so ashamed of how he acted with her that he hadn't bothered even to try to approach her again. He'd seen her several times in the mall and the grocery store but never gathered enough nerve to even wave hello. He was sure she hadn't seen him because she didn't as much as sneeze in his direction. His mother had actually seen her and apparently, based on the excitement in her voice, had some sort of contact with her.

"Oh yeah? How's she doing?" Steve asked anxiously waiting her reply. He wanted a blow-by-blow description of what was said and done but didn't want to get his mother too excited. He knew if he let on he was still in love with Maxine his mother would get her hopes up about them getting back together. Although he and Maxine had been deeply in love, he knew Maxine well enough to know she was not the type to overlook what occurred and take him back. She was too stubborn for that. He and his mother would have to accept the fact he and Maxine's love affair ended a long time ago.

"You should have seen her Steve. She looks good and she's still involved in church. She asked about you. I told her you were doing really well. I tried to get her phone number so you could call her but she never gave it to me." Momma Doris said with baited breath. She wanted to see what her son's reaction would be.

"That's good she's doing okay. I never doubted she would do anything else but good with her life. She's a good woman and any man that gets her is getting a jewel."

"You could still be that man. Maybe I could talk to Mother Thomas and ask her to…" Momma Doris began.

"I know what you're trying to do by getting us back in contact with each other. Momma, let's face it. I messed up. So let's not go too far down this road. It will only end in disappointment." Steve lamented.

"Baby Boy I know you messed up too. But I believe Maxine still loves you now. I think you should make a visit to Believer's Church and talk to her about what happened. If you take it slow, you might be able to at least salvage the friendship the two of you had. Why don't you give it a shot?" Momma Doris said. She knew her son needed a little glimmer of hope and she hoped she had given him enough of one.

"We'll see Momma but I don't think so." Steve said with his mouth. With his heart, he pondered actually going to see Maxine. Would she be open to him at all? He might have to find out.

Chapter 21

Mitch arrived at the hotel exactly ninety minutes after he told Marsha he would be here. He was late. He said a quick prayer as he got off the elevator and began to look for their room. Marsha left word with the front desk that she was expecting him. The attendant called the room to let her know he was there and to get the okay to give him the room number. Mitch was nervous. He didn't know how Marsha was going to react to his tardiness. She made it clear this time was of the utmost importance to her and their relationship and he promised he would make it a priority himself. He saw Marsha's face when he had to delay the time because of the church meeting and he was even disappointed with himself for asking her to make the sacrifice. He felt her sheer devastation when they had to delay it for the second time because of Sister Cassandra's problem. Now he was even later than that. As he stood outside of the suite, he thought about how much he loved the woman on the other side of the door. He loved her from the moment he'd first laid eyes on her. She was always by his side just as he'd thought she would be. He didn't want it any other way. Marsha, on the other hand, had made statements leading him to believe she was no longer so steadfast. He decided it was time to go on into the room and take his medicine like a man. He would explain that he was making immediate changes in the way he related to church work. He knocked on the door and heard what he thought was Marsha shuffling around in the room. He stood there and waited. All of a sudden, Marsha's voice came out from behind the door.

"Mitch, is there anyone else in the hallway?" she asked.

"No honey. I don't see anybody." Mitch responded to what he thought was a weird question. As he was pondering the question and it's meaning in his mind, his wife threw the door open revealing a long sheer teal gown with a side split that showed her long legs and the matching teal stiletto healed shoes she wore. He took in the vision before him and forgot he his nervousness from two seconds ago. She smiled at him and asked him through lips perfectly colored with plum lipstick, "Are you coming in?" For the first time that day, Mitch smiled wholeheartedly and entered the room with his wife.

"Marsha, I want to say I am so sorry I'm late and ..." Mitch stated until Marsha lightly placed her index finger over his lips.

"Not tonight. When we planned this we said we wouldn't talk about church folk, church work or anything else related to the church. We'll deal with all that stuff later. This time is about us and nothing else. Now come here, I have something for you. But you have to take your clothes off first." Marsha said to Mitch in a voice slightly above a whisper.

"Why do I have to take my clothes off to get what you have for me?" Mitch questioned as his wife began to disrobe him despite his resistance.

"Mitch, just cooperate. I'm going into the bathroom. When you're finished, you come in there too." Marsha said as she sashayed toward the bathroom. Once inside, she quickly disrobed herself and stepped into the warm scented bubbly water in the tub. She poured Mitch and herself glasses of the sparkling apple cider and waited. She looked up as Mitch slowly and cautiously entered the bathroom. When he saw what his wife had in mind, he relaxed once again and joined her in the tub. He thought about how absolutely gorgeous and sexy his wife was. He realized how much he missed her this way. He hadn't had the time or energy to connect with his wife in weeks. This would never happen again. He reached for the wine glass and sipped of its sweetness. Marsha and Mitch smiled at each other, gazed into each other's eyes and whispered romantic words to each other. Marsha sat her glass down and did something she never done before. Mitch wasn't so sure about Marsha's intentions and attempted to stop her so he could find out what was going on. Marsha, on the other hand, was determined to take their love to another level and it showed in her eyes. He would have to go along for the ride!

Chapter 22

As the sun came through the window in Mitch and Marsha's suite, Mitch began to stir. He took in her glowing face and her hair settled down around her shoulders instead of piled seductively on the top of her head as it was initially. Last night had been wonderful and Mitch was looking forward to the rest of their time. He touched Marsha's arms and she opened her eyes and gazed at her husband. Immediately a smile appeared on her face and she reached over and touched Mitch as well.

"Good morning, Sunshine!" Mitch said as he leaned over to brush his lips over his wife's. Marsha sat up and pulled the covers over her exposed body. Mitch reached over and pulled them back so he could view his wife in the sunlight. Marsha, though a little bashful, decided to let him. He was obviously so nervous and apologetic last night because of the way he thought she would respond. Admittedly, she had been behaving a little unseemly. So, she decided to let Mitch get his eyeful of her. Mitch gazed at his wife and marveled at the fact God blessed him with such a gift. Marsha enjoyed the look in her husband's eyes as he looked at her. She was ecstatic to see he still found her as attractive as he did in the beginning. She was glad they decided to do this and knew it was something they would have to make time for on a regular basis, especially with the church and all. Marsha decided she wanted to be one with her husband once more before they began their day. She stepped over to the CD player and started the music she had picked out for them. She then opened the blinds in the room more fully so the rays from the sun entered the room. She slipped back into bed and leaned over to kiss her husband. Mitch, understanding her actions, eagerly responded in kind. As they held each other in their arms, they both felt life couldn't get any better than this.

Chapter 23

Cassandra grabbed her briefcase and headed out of her door to work. She didn't mind going to work because it got her mind off things. She wondered how her effort paid off last night. Pastor Mitch's face said he was somewhat disturbed by how she handled herself last night. She also saw his eyes fall on her breasts and legs. If she didn't know better, she would have thought her "display" was what made him uncomfortable. Was he attracted to her? She wasn't sure and really didn't care. All she wanted was what she felt was rightfully hers... recognition as a minister in the same way the men were. Cassandra always seemed to be in positions where people didn't recognize her and she didn't know why. However, she knew after the incident, no one was ever going to avoid giving her what was due her. Whatever it took, she would get what she deserved. As she thought back over what occurred earlier in her life, she realized the situation changed her outlook on life completely. She no longer trusted anyone. She made sure to get to them before they had a chance to get to her. As a result, Cassandra never really bonded with people. She was a loner. There were times she became jealous of women who had close relationships with one another. She watched her dorm mates in college as they went out shopping and to the movies together and secretly yearned for them to include her. She knew they wouldn't though. She had told them all she would take no part in that foolishness because none of them could be trusted. As an adult, she now realized shopping for makeup or clothing with them wouldn't have been risky at all. She couldn't have gotten hurt over mascara and eye shadow. She had experienced good solid friendships with men though. She found them to be less of a drag on her. That is until the one man she trusted had spoiled her trust for all men. Now it seemed Cassandra's purpose in life was to make every other man who crossed her path pay for his mistake especially if he didn't give her what she wanted. Pastor Edwards had already paid and now if was Pastor Mitch's turn. If he did what was right, she wouldn't be forced to bring him down. After all, she didn't feel good about bringing these men down. For weeks after Pastor Edwards left, she felt depressed. She hadn't even attended the Board Meetings she'd fought so hard to obtain the right to attend. She didn't understand why she did the things she did even when she didn't want to. She thought of the scripture where Paul spoke about being in the same dilemma. Like him, she typically found herself doing things she didn't want to do and not doing the things she wanted to do. What motivated a person to do something they knew would negatively affect them in the end as well? What made her take herself and Pastor Edwards through those changes? More importantly, why was she willing to go through it all again with Pastor Mitch? Cassandra decided she would do some soul searching after she got her seat in the pulpit. She entered the doors to the bank building and showed her badge to the guard. She got into the elevator and rode up to the top floor. She walked down the various corridors toward her office speaking to her co-workers along the way. As she entered her office, she smiled as she recalled the moment she got her current position. Her then supervisor decided he would rather promote her than to deal with the consequences of the lies Cassandra threatened to tell. He made a humongous mistake by working late in the evening alone with Cassandra in the office. Nothing happened, but, because there was no one to refute her claims, he knew he could end up in the middle of a huge sexual harassment suit potentially losing his job, family and his freedom. Cassandra demanded the promotion that put her in this office with the window and she got it. As she sat down at her desk, she found herself picking up her Bible. She turned to the scripture that crossed her mind earlier on her ride over as well as a few others and read. Cassandra began to ponder the words of the scripture in her heart as she slipped the Bible back into her desk drawer. The Apostle Paul wasn't the only one confused. Cassandra was abundantly confused as well!

Chapter 24

Linda entered Fellowship City and began to look for Mark. The hostess, seeing her looking around, asked if she was looking for someone. When Linda said she was meeting a man named Mark, the hostess led her right to his table. He sat in an out of the way corner of the dining area so they could have some privacy. Mark, seeing Linda approaching, began to smile and waved at her. She was so fine and he still found himself extremely attracted to her. He enjoyed watching the confidence with which she walked; the sway of her hips and the cute way she held her mouth when she was feeling uneasy. He would put her at ease. She would never have to worry about being anxious while in his company ever again. He made up his mind, he was going to get Linda back and having dinner with her tonight was the first step in that direction. He stood and pulled out the chair for her as she arrived at their table. She wore a short-sleeved shimmering royal blue dress with high-heeled blue satin shoes decorated with rhinestones. As she took her seat, Mark got a whiff of her cologne. He smiled as he remembered buying the scent for her. She had fallen in love with the fragrance and taken it for her own signature scent. At least he did one thing right in their relationship. She was still wearing the cologne he picked for her. Mark then took his own seat across from Linda. Each looked at the other not knowing how to begin the conversation.

"Linda, you look beautiful as usual." Mark began the dialog.

"Thank you, Mark. You look wonderful yourself." Linda responded with a giggle.

The silence that ensued between them was deadening. They really didn't know what to say.

"How have you been?" Mark wanted to know if she was as nervous as her body language depicted.

"I'm blessed. How about you?" Linda responded as she settled herself at the table.

"Same here. How's Maxine? Does she know you're out with me?" Mark inquired partially out of curiosity. He knew Maxine didn't want Linda anywhere near him. He was sure Linda hadn't informed her roommate of where she was going tonight.

"Maxine's good and you know the answer to your other question. She really has an issue with you after what happened. I have to admit I sometimes wonder why I'm willing to even speak to you myself." Linda said knowing the ball was rolling now.

"I guess that is a good question. Since I'm such a heathen, why would you even consent to be in my presence? Why did you come tonight?" Mark responded with a few questions of his own. He was getting tired of paying for the same mistake repeatedly. He had to be careful so he wouldn't start believing he was the worst man on earth.

"Mark, I didn't come to argue with you. I'm here to try to resolve some issues within myself about this predicament. I choose to deal with them this way solely because we were in this together. No other reason." Linda stated clearly making the point he could serve no other purpose in her life.

"Why can't you talk to Maxine about this? She's the person closest to you. I think there's another reason you want to involve me in resolving these issues." Mark said with a wink to the would-be mother of his child.

"Maxine doesn't understand number one. Are you saying you aren't willing to be a part of this?" Linda asked.

"I don't mind taking part in this but I think you need to be truthful with yourself. You want to be in my company." Mark hoped he was right. He wanted her to want to be around him.

Linda laughed, "Why would you say that? You know, we need to stop this bantering about who wants who and why. We haven't even begun to discuss what we came here to discuss."

"Okay Linda. Talk." Mark responded

"Don't talk to me like that. I won't allow it." Linda leaned into Mark and spoke with undeniable authority.

"All right, all right. I apologize if I offended you. I'm getting tired of your attitude." Mark confessed his true feelings.

"What attitude?"

"The attitude that I'm totally to blame for what happened and leaves you completely innocent." There, Mark said what he really felt. Now he waited for Linda's response.

Angrily Linda stood up. She looked like she would kill Mark. She appeared to be huffing and puffing like the little engine that could.

"How dare you say you didn't have anything to do with this? Mark how do you look at yourself in the mirror?"

"Yeah, well the real question is how long are you going to refuse to look at yourself." Mark shot back standing as well. He was trying to get back into Linda's life true enough. However, he was not going to do it by backing down to Linda's whims. He would have to risk losing her for good as opposed to losing his self-respect. Linda sensing the ball had changed hands, sat back down in her seat. She had never seen Mark like this. He had spoken to her honestly and with a firm hand. How should she respond to his change of attitude?

"I have absolutely no problem dealing with myself."

"I don't think you have accepted your part in what happened. I think you want to blame it all on me." Mark declared.

"Well I think you're saying that because you can't handle the truth. I only had the abortion because you didn't want the responsibility of being a daddy. If it weren't for your unwillingness to step up I would have had a baby and not an abortion." Linda countered.

Mark reached across the table to hold Linda's hands as he carefully formed his next comment.

"Linda, how did you feel about the responsibility of being somebody's mommy?"

Linda's composure broke as the flood of emotions flowed like water breaking through a dam. Mark got up from his chair and moved to Linda's side. He held her close and allowed her to cry on the new custom-made suit he purchased for this occasion. He didn't like having to say what he said, but he felt Linda was completely missing the point. He knew his actions weren't the best but he never told Linda to terminate the pregnancy. By performing his disappearing act, he led Linda to believe he didn't want the baby. This assumption was somewhat true. The timing wasn't the best. However, he would have dealt with the consequences of his actions. He hadn't had the chance to tell Linda this before she informed him she was having the procedure done. The fact remained…whether he wanted the baby or not, Linda had total and complete control over what happened. She could have had the baby with or without him.

"Linda, let's go to my place. I know we haven't eaten yet but I think we should do this in a more private setting." Mark proposed.

Linda got up and grabbed her wrap without even thinking about it.

"You're right. I don't want people to see me like this." Linda said while wiping her eyes.

"We'll drive your car. I'll get my car later. I don't think you should be driving." Mark responded as he threw a tip on the table for the waitress since they had taken up her table and not ordered anything.

"Let's go." Mark said as he lightly touched Linda in the small of her back to direct her from the building.

Chapter 25

Linda immediately noticed the changes that had taken place in Mark's condominium since the last time she had been there. The living room held large blue leather furniture sitting on dove gray carpeting. Two huge floral arrangements adorned end tables flanking the sofa. A chair sat in front of the sliding glass door leading to the balcony. Next to the chair was a tall, silver reading lamp standing on the floor. Contemporary art by a local artist whose work Linda immediately recognized covered the walls. Mark directed Linda to have a seat on the couch as he took her wrap.

"Would you like something to drink?" Mark asked in order to be polite. He really wanted to ask for a kiss. However, he knew that would have to come later...much later.

"Actually, I would really like some water please." Linda responded. Mark returned with two bottles of water. Opening them, he gave one to Linda and immediately took a drink from the other. The two seemed awkward again. Mark decided to deal with the problem directly so they could get past this as soon as possible. He wanted to get on to possibly making up.

"Linda, I want you to know I understand the pain you must have gone through during this whole process. I don't understand why you felt I didn't want you or the baby at all." Mark asked already knowing the answer.

"I felt your actions said you washed your hands of the situation which left me to make a decision." Linda said as the tears began to flow once again.

"I'll be honest with you, I really didn't know what to do. I didn't want you to have an abortion though." Mark responded.

"Well what do you think I should've done?" Linda asked looking Mark directly in his eyes.

"As I said, I didn't know what to do. However, what you should have done was follow your heart." Mark said while gently holding Linda's hand.

"Mark, my heart said I shouldn't have broken my promise to be celibate until I got married. If I had kept that commitment the pregnancy never would have occurred." Linda dropped her head in shame. She had let herself down.

"I have to take some of the blame as well. I should have respected your stand for Christ." He sincerely wished he hadn't put her in the position he had. He had pushed her to make a decision he hoped would be contrary to her vow of celibacy.

"More than that, Mark, I should have respected my stand." Linda admitted her own fault in this regard.

"Why did you choose abortion Linda?" Mark really wanted to know.

"I didn't see another way. You seemed to lose interest in me once I was pregnant. I didn't think you wanted the baby."

"All of the reasons you gave me are all about me and what you thought I wanted. What about your feelings?" Mark asked as he moved closer to Linda. He knew if she really answered truthfully, there would probably be another flow of tears.

"I always dreamed of having children with my husband by my side in the delivery room coaching me through the delivery. He would cut the umbilical cord. We would share tears of joy, as we both looked into the eyes of our child for the first time. We would name him or her together and raise the child in a Christian home. Having a child out of wedlock with an uninterested person was not a part of the vision. I couldn't bear not living my dream." Linda said as she stared off appearing to be looking at the sad ending of an extremely enjoyable movie.

"Linda sweetheart, are you listening to yourself? Let me ask you something. What would you have done if I said I wanted you to have the baby, but you and I would only be friends? We wouldn't get married, but we would work everything else out like visitation and child support. Would your decision have been different?" Mark proposed. Linda thought for a moment. How would she have felt?

"I would have felt rejected." Linda responded.

"Would you have had the baby under those circumstances or not?" Mark cornered Linda. He really wanted her to accept responsibility for her actions. As Linda thought about the scenario Mark laid out, she knew the answer. It was a difficult pill to swallow. Once again, she began to cry. Why had Mark pushed her so hard? She tried to burrow her face in Mark's chest so she could avoid actually answering the question. Mark held her up with his arms so she could not do so. She knew he wanted her to answer. Why couldn't he accept he was wrong and leave her alone? She didn't want to face the facts.

"No" she sputtered, as she broke down further. Mark still held her up by her shoulders. He pressed Linda further.

"Was this all my fault?"

Linda pulled herself together enough to be able to answer Mark. She sat straight up and readied herself to give the confession of her life. She looked in his eyes and answered him.

"No, it wasn't all your fault." Linda once again broke down in tears. This time Mark allowed her to burrow her face in his chest. Mark knew the discussion still wasn't over. But he believed if he didn't get Linda to face the fact she made her decision based on her own needs they would never resolve the issues they both had. Linda stopped crying for a moment and looked at Mark once again. She saw the tears forming in his eyes.

"What are you crying about? I admit you weren't totally at fault." Linda angrily asked Mark.

"In all this everyone forgot this was my child too. A child I'll never see. A child I'll never hold in my arms. Don't you think I may have some pain to work through as well?" It was Mark's turn to get some things off his chest now.

"Mark, you didn't have to lay your body on that table knowing full well what was about to happen. You didn't have to sign paperwork to authorize strangers to bury your baby's remains. You didn't have to lay up nights crying because you felt so guilty for having done something like that. You don't have to live your life looking over your shoulder hoping no one would be able to look at you and know what a terrible thing you did." Linda spoke strongly to Mark now. There was no sign of the bawling woman who was sitting there just two minutes ago.

"I'll tell you what I have done. I've laid up nights wondering how I could have allowed this whole thing to happen. How could I let you get rid of my own flesh and blood because of poor timing? You'll never understand how helpless I felt not being able to stop this from happening. I hated you for a long time because of your decision. You never asked me what I wanted. You told me what you were going to do. Neither of us wanted to have the baby and we didn't want to put it up for adoption. I realize that didn't provide a solution to the dilemma. However, Linda if I had known you were seriously considering terminating the pregnancy I would rather have had the baby and raised it on my own. I've always wanted to be a father. I always have. I beat myself up for months trying to reconcile how I let you get rid of a child of mine knowing I wanted a family." Mark responded.

"That's why you treated me the way you did afterwards?" Linda asked now understanding some of Mark's actions back then.

"Yes, that's why. You aren't the only one who has dreams. As far as I'm concerned, you stomped on mine. I know you don't realize this but I really loved you. I know seducing you was not a very good approach to getting you to feel the same way about me. I won't ever do that again. I gave you all the jewelry and flowers because I wanted to show you how I felt about you. Those things were from my heart. Making love to you was wonderful. When you became pregnant, I was a little shocked. At the same time, I looked at that child as a reflection of our love for one another. When you got rid of it, I felt you crushed any hope I had for our love to grow. What reason would I have to continue to hang around?"

Mark's honesty was making Linda uncomfortable. She never even considered the termination would have affected Mark in any way. Once again, she had been selfish and self-centered. She hadn't taken into consideration this was Mark's baby too and he had an emotional connection to him or her regardless of how he acted in response to the news. It had been unexpected. Neither of them was trying to make this happen. They were both in a state of shock. They each made decisions without slowing down and attempting to think clearly or consulting the Lord. Once she really thought about it, they really hadn't even had many face-to-face conversations about it. Mark was right. They both contributed to the outcome. Looking at Mark, she saw his lip begin to quiver indicating the dam was about to break in his emotions.

"Mark, come closer. It's my turn to comfort you." Linda said as she scooted closer to Mark who immediately laid his head on her shoulder and began to weep. Linda found his ability to maintain his manhood while being emotional to be endearing. Who wouldn't love this man? She was beginning to feel something for him all over again. She quickly snapped herself out of it. She absolutely couldn't ever fall in love with him again.

Chapter 26

Mitch and Marsha sat on the couch in their suite as the waiter set up the food they ordered for dinner. The two decided to stay in for dinner tonight because they had been running around all day long. Once they pulled themselves away from bed, they went to lunch at a new restaurant they both wanted to try but hadn't had the time. After lunch, the couple went to the Mirage Mall. Mitch and Marsha held hands as they walked through the mall. Marsha purchased a few suits for upcoming occasions. Mitch had been happy just seeing his wife happy. He didn't realized how unhappy Marsha was until now. He saw the contrast between her recent behavior and how she was acting now. Marsha was like a child at Christmas being around him. It made him feel so good about making the time for them to be together. He enjoyed watching her trying on suit after suit because it gave him more opportunity to just look at his wife. The way the various ensembles fit her body had given him a virtual visual smorgasbord. Next came Mitch's opportunity to shop. He definitely had a shoe fetish and his favorite shoe store had opened a branch in this mall. As he tried on pair after pair of shoes, Marsha helped him pick out the styles and colors he was missing from his shoe wardrobe. After choosing ten pairs, Mitch gave himself permission to buy five. It had been so long since he had time to go shoe shopping he'd forgotten how much he enjoyed it. As they walked past the Suit Closet, Marsha decided she wanted to buy her husband a suit just because. She pulled Mitch into the store ignoring the look of confusion on his face.

"This is the last place I need to be. You know I only come in here when I am looking to buy something. I can't come in here and browse." Mitch stated while attempting to pull his determined wife out of the store.

"Will you just pick out a suit? It's my treat." Marsha asked as she snuggled against her husband. She knew he wasn't expecting this and neither was she.

"Marsha, let's do this later. We've already spent a small fortune on what we have in our hands." Mitch responded.

"Let me do this for you." Marsha pleaded. Mitch knew he couldn't deny her this. That's when he allowed his eyes to begin to roam and start the process of picking out a suit. Mitch and Marsha both left the mall skipping. They each enjoyed their impromptu shopping spree.

After the waiter had been tipped and left the room, Mitch blessed the food. The two ordered Chicken Marsala with fettuccine noodles, garlic bread and antipasto salad. As they began to eat their meal, Marsha brought up what she promised they wouldn't discuss…church stuff.

"Mitch, I know we said we wouldn't discuss the church but I need to ask you something." Marsha said as she took a bite of her salad.

"Okay. But remember, you wanted to discuss it and I didn't bring it up." Mitch stated.

"I've enjoyed this get-away immensely. I feel we've reconnected and that's what we desperately needed. I've enjoyed every minute of being in your arms and being in your presence. I'm concerned this is a temporary thing and we'll go back to the way we were before we came here." Marsha said with a sincere concern for her marriage as well as herself personally.

"I've enjoyed this mini-retreat as well. You're right. I think having this time together strengthened our marriage. I understand your concern about what things will be like when we go back home. All I can say is I am committed to making some changes so we can keep the momentum going. You have to remember I am a pastor and have a lot of responsibility for the ministry. That may mean there will still be times I'll be away more than you would like in order to take care of things. One of the reasons I want you to be my assistant is that we'll be together more while we're working. Also, you'll be able to handle some of the things I would normally have to deal with which means I'll have more time available." Mitch explained hoping his wife would agree with his thought process.

"I'm glad you brought that up, Mitch, I didn't like how you announced my new role without discussing it with me. Did it ever occur to you I might not want to be your assistant pastor?" Marsha asked.

"Honey, after you disappeared from the church, I tried to formulate a strategy to handle things at church and at home. I thought this would be a good solution. I thought maybe you would develop some church-related interests of your own which would help in filling up your time." Mitch responded sensing a negative undercurrent he couldn't quite understand.

"Do you think because I don't have a job outside of being your wife and taking care of our home that I'm unhappy about you being away all the time?" Marsha asked.

"Yes, I think because you don't get out and socialize much, you get lonely. When that happens you look for me to eliminate the loneliness. I can't always be there to entertain you."

"So what is that supposed to mean Mitch? Are you saying I need to get a life?"

"That's not exactly what I said although that would be another way to put it."

"Okay Mitch. I will get a life but it won't be in the way you want. See, I don't have a desire to work in the ministry. I will gladly continue to help you the way I always have but I won't take on dealing with the board or those deacons. I believe my place is to take care of you. I'm contributing to their care by doing that."

"Well I thought…" Mitch began.

"You thought instead of asking me and knowing what I would like to do. My heart is to minister to the women in our church. God has given me the vision for a ministry called Heart to Heart to minister to the unique needs of women. We'll discuss all kinds of women's issues and provide help and support to those who need it. That's what I want to do." Marsha said.

"That's a wonderful idea. I hadn't even thought about anything like that. You go ahead and do that. Let me know what you'll need and we'll get the ball rolling to make it happen. This will definitely give you something to do." Mitch was relieved. He wouldn't be under so much pressure from his wife.

"Thanks for you support but I resent the fact you think I need something else to do so I won't expect so much from you. Regardless of what I do, it doesn't excuse you from being around. You are still my husband." Marsha explained to her husband.

"Okay honey. You're right. I'm working on it. Please be patient with me. God is not through with me yet!" Mitch responded. The two ate a few bites of their food during a long pause.

"Mitch, can I ask you what Cassandra wanted?" Marsha asked her husband. Mitch had hoped Marsha would forget about that situation. After all, they'd had a wonderful time together and he promised he would modify his behavior as best he could.

"Marsha, it turned out to be nothing really." Mitch answered while preparing to take a drink of his lemonade.

"Well, what was it?" Marsha asked desiring to know if her hunch about Cassandra was right.

"Honey, I need to talk to you about what happened but let's not do it tonight. We'll have plenty of time for that once we get back home. Okay?" Mitch asked.

"No dear it's not okay. This situation seemed to appear out of nowhere on the night everyone knew we were going away. I think I have a right to know what was so important." Marsha stated laying down her fork. She wanted to give this her full attention.

"Marsha, please don't do this. It'll only upset you. Why can't we let our last few private moments pass in peace?" Mitch pleaded with his wife who had now pushed her seat away from the table. He recognized the stance she now took. She was digging in and there was no way he was going to get around discussing Sister Cassandra's escapades tonight.

"This sounds serious if you think I'm going to get upset which is even more reason for you to tell me now." Marsha said.

"I promise you, I'll tell you tomorrow morning when we get home." Mitch utilized his last ditch effort to persuade Marsha to wait.

"Mitch, honey, absolutely not. I won't wait until tomorrow. I want to know now." Marsha was serious and Mitch could tell. He decided he would tell her before things got bad. He laid down his fork and brought his glass to his mouth to alleviate the dry mouth sensation he was experiencing. He knew he would have to tell his wife. Really, he wanted to. Somehow, he thought he had some time before he would have to tell her, which would allow him some time to figure out exactly how to give her the news. He took a deep breath and decided to open his mouth and spill it.

" Cassandra feels she's been called to the ministry." Mitch began.

"What's so serious about that?" Marsha asked.

"She wants to be acknowledged as a minister which would mean a lot of adjustment." Mitch continued.

"Okay, though I'm not sure she's really called to that area, I don't see the problem here." Marsha was puzzled.

"Oh, I know she's not ready for that type of ministry now even if God has called her." Mitch stated with a certainty.

"Why Mitch? Is it because she's a woman? I thought you were passed that Mitch." Marsha responded.

"Marsha, I've never seen that in action and I'm not sure if I want to be the first. I do know one thing though, Cassandra is not the one to break the ministerial glass ceiling and that's a fact." Mitch stated hoping she would understand.

"I understand. Perhaps this "Minister Cassandra" thing needs to go before the Lord. I'll grant you that. But why won't you be the first?" Marsha asked.

"I've seen what having women in leadership can do. Those brothers are already deeply upset about having to deal with Cassandra on the board. They're not used to having a woman's point of view to consider.

I'm not sure if I want to further rock the boat." Mitch responded before he considered his words. He could already see Marsh gearing up for her response.

"I'm a woman. Yet you're willing to allow me to be your assistant pastor, co-pastor or some kind of pastor." She stated while obviously laying in wait for his response.

"You're my wife and you're able to perform the role because of your place in my life. You know having a woman minister is controversial. I still hold to the tenants of our former church, which does not allow for female ministers. While I don't completely agree, I'm having trouble getting past it." Mitch replied knowing he had given the wrong answer.

"That's totally chauvinistic and completely contradictory. What's the difference between me and any other woman? You don't even have to answer that. I'll do it for you. There's absolutely no difference except I'm your wife. On top of that, even in our former denomination you had the freedom to do what you wanted in that area anyway. If we were still in that organization and I become your assistant pastor, what would have happened? You know the answer…absolutely nothing. Now let's get back to Cassandra. What happened?" Marsha asked redirecting their attention to the subject at hand.

"Marsha, she intentionally exposed herself to me. I believe this was supposed to somehow motivate me to decide in her favor. That's never happened to me or to anyone I know and I don't know how to handle this." Mitch said as he placed his head in his hands.

"She did what? Mitch, you must be mistaken. Did she flash you or did you catch an accidental glimpse of something that made you a bit uncomfortable."

"You're not listening to me. She did it intentionally."

"Okay, exactly what did she do?"

"She crossed her legs without even trying to cover them. I believe she must've unbuttoned her jacket a little because it sure wasn't that way before I got to the office. While she was telling me what she wanted, she stood up and leaned over so her bosom was almost in my face. If I didn't know better, I thought I saw a grin on her face as she did it. Make no mistake about it, she was attempting to seduce me."

Marsha began to do the deep-breathing exercises she learned in her stress management class. She knew Cassandra was trouble but didn't expect her to try to steal her husband away from her. Now she understood why Cassandra always had a reason to spend extra time with her husband outside of Board meetings. She wanted Marsha's man and Marsha wasn't about to let it happen.

"Mitch, let's go home now. I need to lay hands on Sister Cassandra right now. I bet after I get through with her she won't ever even think about looking at another woman's husband let alone try to get with him." Marsha stated as she rose to gather her things in preparation for leaving the hotel.

"See that's exactly why I didn't want to tell you right now. Now the rest of our evening is ruined." Mitch responded while trying to corral his wife into his arms.

"I had a wonderful time but it's time for me to handle my business with that so-called woman of God. Our time isn't ruined but her time will most definitely be as soon as I get to her. Now come on Mitch. Let's do this." Marsha said as she tussled with Mitch.

"Woman, I am not about to let you go after Cassandra. You are a pastor's wife and this is not how a godly woman handles herself in situations like these. Cassandra might be devious but you're not. We're going to handle this the way that will most glorify God. Now settle down and let's talk about this." Mitch said as he grabbed Marsha firmly about her shoulders. Marsha stopped and unwillingly gave him her attention. She knew he was right but the sheer power of her emotions had taken her down a path that mirrored her temperament in younger days. She had never taken anything off anyone then and before she knew it that side of her had resurfaced. She really wanted to beat the woman down but decided it wasn't an appropriate response. She consciously chose to join her husband in seeking a godly solution. She then allowed her husband to guide her to the sofa in the room. She sat down and looked her husband in the eyes.

"Mitch, you know I love you and support your decision to pastor Believer's Church. I know being in this position can make you even more attractive to other women. I don't know if I can deal with this kind of blatant disregard for me as your wife and for our marriage in general. I can't deal with women being in your face all the time, flirting with you, and now exposing themselves to you. I overlooked a great deal of it, but I won't any longer. If I don't stand up and let it be known their behavior is unacceptable, I don't think you will. I have been telling you for months Cassandra had something up her sleeve but you didn't listen. Instead, you kept trying to figure out how you could provide me with more to do so I wouldn't be on your back about your time away from home. I wondered why you would do that and the only reason I can think of is because you get something out of these women chasing you. That would certainly explain why you aren't bothered by the lack of time we spend together. I mean if you can get attention from the women at the church then you don't need me."

Mitch looked at Marsha. He couldn't believe what she was saying. He really didn't know how to respond however he knew he absolutely had to.

"First of all, I never even noticed women all up in my face the way you say they've been. If it did happen, and I didn't respond, it's because I didn't realize what was happening. Second, I understand you have a problem with Cassandra. I have to say I don't understand your insecurity where she is concerned. If you feel someone is acting out of line with me then you are well within your rights to say something about it. The two of us can handle it together. But, you can't have a problem with every woman in the church because not all of them are after me. Some of them have legitimate business with me. You have to get to the point where you can tell the difference between the two. Now, as far as me getting my kicks from the attention these women supposedly give me, you couldn't be further from the truth. I can't believe you would even fix your mouth to say that. I would much rather be spending time with you doing whatever than dealing with parishioners on any level. However, it is part of what I do and you have to figure out how to deal with it. Let's find out what the Lord wants us to do about Cassandra." Mitch regained his composure. He was actually outraged about Marsha's allegations. However, he knew if he responded based on how he felt nothing would be resolved, and the ground they gained during their get-away would be lost.

"I guess I can't pluck her hair out one by one huh." Marsha chuckled as she settled back into her seat. "I'm really sorry about what I said and the way I acted. I was reacting out of the emotion of it all. What do you think we should do?"

"Well, I don't know if confronting her right now would do any good. I'm going to pray that God deal with her about her actions. I won't ever meet with her alone again. I want you to be with me whenever the two of us have to be together." Mitch began.

"Oh, you don't have to worry about that. I will not allow any further displays of Miss Cassandra's body to you. I think we need to confront her though because if we don't she'll continue to do things like that. If she can't do it to you then it will be other men in the church." Marsha pointed out.

"Marsha I really don't want to disturb things too much. I'm willing to make it policy that we should always have chaperones when there are one-on-one meetings between people of the opposite sex. That should solve the problem of her doing this to other guys. As far as this ministry thing, I won't tell her I don't think she's ready to be a minister but I will tell her I believe the timing is off." Mitch stated.

"Mitch, why do I get the feeling you're trying to avoid speaking with Cassandra at all costs?" Marsha inquired.

"Honey, I'm not trying to make this situation any less serious than it is. I think if I attempt to confront her, she'll just deny the whole thing happened. What purpose would that serve?" Mitch asked his wife.

"The Word says we are not ignorant of the devil's devices. Why should we act like we are? She knows exactly what she was doing and so do you. If you uncover her then she'll have no other choice but to repent and change her behavior. Having chaperones only prevents future problems. I think you need to deal with what she did the other night." Marsha said as she leaned over toward her husband to show her interest. She really hoped Mitch would decide to do the right thing. Being a woman herself, Marsha knew the thought processes some women had. If Mitch didn't say anything, Cassandra would think he enjoyed it and was willing to see the exhibit again. Was his hesitance to aggressively deal with the situation a sign that he did enjoy what he saw? Marsha would keep her eyes and ears open and her knees bent on this one.

Chapter 27

"Hurry up, Steve. We're going to be late. I don't like to be late for anybody's church especially one I'm visiting."

Momma Doris was bustling about her house trying to get her son from in front of the mirror and out the door. The two were attending Believer's Church. Steve said he wanted to go because he heard such good things about the pastor over there. Momma Doris grinned as she thought about the real reason Steve wanted to go. He wanted to see Maxine and Momma Doris was not going to leave this meeting to fate. She had to make sure Maxine's "friend" would not pose a problem. She felt it would only be a matter of time before her lovebirds got back together.

"I'm ready. Momma, you know you don't have to miss your own church service to go with me."

Steve tried talking his mother out of accompanying him to the church for a few days now. He didn't know why he even told her he was going. That was a mistake on his part. He wanted to see Maxine again alone and without his mother's interference no matter how well intentioned. He also didn't want his mother to make any more out of their meeting than there was.

"Honey, you know I like to go over and visit with my friend when I can. Besides I already told her I was coming and she's expecting us." Momma Doris explained as she turned off her oven, made sure her pots were covered, and headed toward the door.

As Momma Doris and Steve entered Believer's Church, the newly assigned greeters embraced them. They received hugs from at least three or four people, literature about the church, and cards, which once filled out and turned in, entitled them to a free book or cd of their choice. As they completed their visitor cards, Steve began to look around the lobby to see if there was any sign of Maxine. Just as he decided she must already be in the sanctuary, he heard her laughter. It had been quite some time since he heard her laugh but it still made his heart dance. He smiled and turned around to see where she was. His eyes met hers as if planned. He felt his palms getting sweaty and his breathing speed up. He tried to move his feet so he could get closer to her but they wouldn't cooperate. By this time, Momma Doris noticed the two had seen one another and gave her son a push that sent him flying toward Maxine. Maxine couldn't help but laugh as she saw what happened. She figured Momma Doris would bring Steve here. Part of her wanted to see him, part of her didn't. She still remembered the pain and embarrassment she felt when she had to cancel their wedding. The memories made her want to slap Steve so hard his head snapped. However, she knew this was not the place. Before she could form a plan for how to handle Steve, he was in her face thanks to his mother.

"Hi Maxine, it's so good to see you." Steve said as he prepared his arms to embrace Maxine. Maxine extended her hand toward Steve only allowing him to shake her hand. She wanted it to be obvious there was nothing more between them but friendship.

"I'm glad to see you today too. Service is starting so we'd better get inside." Maxine responded while in motion toward the sanctuary.

"Maxine, maybe we can talk after service. Would that be okay?"

"We'll see. But, I'm really not sure we have anything to talk about." Maxine caught Linda by the arm to let her know she was ready to go in.

Mother Thomas' eyes rarely missed anything and they didn't miss Maxine turn down a sincere attempt at reconciliation from Steve so she could be with her "girlfriend" Linda. She was not going to allow this sort of thing to go on one more day. Since the First Lady of Believer's Church wouldn't initiate correcting this situation, Mother Thomas would bring the problem up to Pastor Mitch herself.

"This has to stop today!" she spoke to no one in particular. She greeted her friend, Doris and her son Steve and they all walked into the sanctuary together.

Chapter 28

Sunday Worship Service was now over and Cassandra knew it was time to make her move. She headed toward Pastor Mitch's office to find out what he was going to do about her request. When she got to his door, she noticed his wife, Marsha, was in there with him along with Elder Eric Howard. Cassandra stepped into the office to make her presence known.

"Hello, everyone!" Cassandra spoke to all who were in the office. Cassandra saw Marsha glance at her husband with a look that held a message Cassandra couldn't quite interpret.

"Hi, Sister Cassandra. What can I do for you today?" Pastor Mitch asked.

"Pastor, I need to speak with you in private if at all possible." Cassandra stated while looking at Marsha and Eric.

"I was leaving anyway." Elder Howard said. "See you later Pastor. Bye Sister Marsha."

"Take care Elder." Pastor Mitch responded as he and his wife waved goodbye to Elder Howard.

"Um, Sister Ross, would it be too much to ask for you to let me have a few moments of privacy with my pastor?"

"Yes it would be way too much to ask." Marsha sat down in a chair near her husband's desk. "Don't mind me, I'll be quiet as a mouse." Marsha responded crossing her legs and making it clear she wasn't going anywhere.

"I need to speak with you privately. Would you please ask your wife to leave for a few moments?" Cassandra pleaded. She couldn't figure out why Marsha was being so uncooperative. She never had a problem like this with Marsha before and she didn't know why it was happening now.

However, she knew Pastor Mitch would not allow his wife to stay and hated she would have to witness him put his wife out of the office.

"Cassandra, what do you need?" Pastor Mitch stated much to Cassandra's surprise.

"It's of a private nature, Pastor, and I would prefer if we could speak alone." Cassandra said, her voice revealing the potential for tears. Tears always worked for Cassandra. Surely they'll move Pastor Mitch.

"I'm not going to insist Marsha leaves. Feel free to discuss whatever you need to." He responded.

Cassandra now felt she was in a fix. She knew Marsha wouldn't allow her to use her secret weapons if she needed to.

"Well, Pastor Mitch, if you insist. Not too long ago I met you with about my call to the ministry. I wanted to check with you to find out what you decided. Have you had time to pray about it?" Cassandra asked while being very conscious of her body language. She would normally be more seductive in her actions but with Marsha in the room, she couldn't take that chance.

"Yes, I have Cassandra. I'm not second-guessing your calling but God hasn't shown me yet. You have to remember I am accountable for what happens in this church and I have to make sure I only do those things I believe are God's will. I'm sorry but we'll have to wait until God confirms that He has indeed called you. I'll be the first to acknowledge it. Until then, we're going to have to wait." Mitch said with his eyes firmly planted on Cassandra's eyes. He felt it was important for her to understand he took God's calling seriously and it was well beyond her flashing her flesh.

"I have to say I am very disappointed in your decision. I heard God plainly say He was calling me. I don't know why you refuse to accept that. I guess I'll be going. Thanks for your time." Cassandra felt dejected. As she turned to leave the office, she had a brainstorm that gave her hope. "Before I go, can I ask you one thing?"

"Sure." Mitch responded.

"Are you turning me down because I turned you down the other night?" Cassandra said as firmly as Pastor Mitch had been when he refused her.

Marsha stood up, walked toward Cassandra and stood precisely two inches from her face.

"What are you trying to say?" Marsha asked Cassandra through clenched teeth.

"I'm sorry you have to find out this way Marsha. When Pastor Mitch and I met the night he sent you ahead to the hotel, he came on to me. I came to tell him God called me and he attempted to kiss me. When that didn't work, he tried to touch me in a very intimate way. He said if I didn't go along with it, he would never allow me to walk in my calling. That's the real reason he's denying me. Pastor Mitch, I hate to do this, but if you think you can get away with this, I have no other choice but to inform the Board about what happened. Marsha, I'm sorry to have to tell you this but I think you need to know." Cassandra spouted off her words with a newfound energy. She was back in control of the situation.

Marsha lifted her hand to slap Cassandra's face but found it suspended in mid-air by her husband.

"Cassandra, leave my office right this minute." Mitch yelled at Cassandra who scurried out willingly.

"See Mitch, if you confronted her like I told you to, we wouldn't be in this situation. Now what?" Marsha said through tears.

Before Mitch could answer, they heard Mother Thomas yell "What?" Mother Thomas almost instantly appeared at the door to Pastor Mitch's office. She looked as if she had seen a ghost.

"Pastor Mitch I came in here to tell you about a problem in this church and I find out you got more problems than that. I promised myself I was going to tell you this today and I'm going to do it. Those women you put over the Single's ministry are gay. That's right, they're lesbians and this church needs you to step up and handle this situation. If you don't, this church will be on its way to hell in a hand basket. Now what are you gonna do about that?" Mother Thomas said with her hands on her ample hips.

"Mother, are you talking about Maxine and Linda? They're not lesbians! What makes you think that?" Mitch asked bewildered as to what was breaking out in this congregation. No wonder their former pastor left!

"Pastor Mitch, it's as shocking to me as it is to you. The two of them are too touchy feely with each other to begin with. Then they're always together skinnin' and grinnin' all up in each other's face. Neither one of them has a man and don't look like they want one. They got each other and that seems good enough for them." Mother Thomas had her pastor's ear and she was sure he would bring this circus to a halt.

"Mother Thomas, none of what you've said makes these two women gay. I think you should be sure about what you're saying before this goes any further. I don't expect you to spread this around the congregation." Pastor Mitch demanded of Mother Thomas.

"I don't take this lightly Pastor and I know what I sense. These women have ungodly affections toward each other and I'm sure of it. Everybody else in this church sees it and I'm surprised you don't. If you hear about this from anybody else, I didn't tell them. They seen it with their own eyes." Mother Thomas explained.

"If that 's true, why are you the only one who said anything about it? If this has been going on all this time, why haven't you said anything before now?" Pastor Mitch argued.

"Pastor, as a church mother it's my place to say what needs to be said. Other folks are sometimes scared to speak up and I'm willing to step in and do it. I tried to point this situation out to your wife but she didn't want to hear it. She held up her hand as if to tell me to hush my mouth. Sister Marsha was very disrespectful to me and I don't appreciate it. So I'm telling you because your wife didn't take it seriously. I take my position on the Mother's Board very seriously and I think the two of you should too as leaders in this church." Mother Thomas stated in a rather presidential tone.

" I apologize for disrespecting you. Mother Thomas I was under a lot of stress and didn't mean any harm. Please forgive me. But, you have some nerve coming in here spewing these accusations with nothing more than a hunch as evidence. I know those two young women love the Lord. I don't believe they're going to live any type of lifestyle that doesn't glorify God. Now, Mother Thomas, if you will excuse us we are once again under stress. Can you please leave us alone for a few minutes?" Marsha responded. She thought her husband looked like he was about to lose his cool. This was by far the worse thing they'd dealt with as pastors and these situations were going to be challenging.

"You two are always under stress. I heard about this thing with Sister Cassandra and Pastor you should've known better. That woman is definitely the kiss and tell kind. Now I understand this is a whole lot for you to deal with at once but you have to get right with the Lord and do what you have to do. The Mother's Board fully expects you to handle this situation with those two or we're going to take our tithes and go somewhere else where the pastor is a true man of God. God won't put more on you than you can bear. I'm leaving but I believe God's going to help you do right thing." Mother Thomas turned on her heels and left.

Mitch closed the office door along with the blinds in the office. He turned around to find Marsha falling apart at the seams. He walked over to her side and held her in his arms. He wanted to fall apart too but someone had to keep a cool head. He didn't know what to say to Marsha so he remained silent. He prayed silently that God would show him what was going on and what he should do. He sensed there was an undercurrent of something he couldn't quite put his hands on. When he had some time later, he would spend time with the Lord to find out.

Chapter 29

Maxine and Linda walked toward the parking lot after church was over. The service was good but they were ready to head home. They heard the rumblings of the controversy over Pastor Mitch and Sister Cassandra and decided they wanted no part of it. Neither believed it so they felt it was not for them to stand around and gossip about. Suddenly, Steve appeared in front of them.

"Maxine, I'm glad I caught you. Can I please talk to you for a minute?" Steve said while trying to catch his breath. Maxine was surprised. She thought he had been long gone from the church.

"Steve, do you remember Linda?" Maxine said through her surprise.

"Hi Linda, how've you been?" Steve said glad to see Maxine was at least entertaining his conversation.

"Hey Steve. I'm blessed. Maxine, I'll wait for you in the car." Linda said as she headed toward the car.

Linda got into the car and turned the key to put the windows down and turn on the CD player. As soon as she settled back into the seat, she saw movement and was startled as she realized someone was standing near the car. She looked up and saw it was Steve's mom, Momma Doris. She barely even acknowledged Linda when she met the woman weeks ago. What could she possibly want now?

"Hi. Do you remember me from before? Maxine introduced us. I'm Momma Doris, Steve's mother" Momma Doris inquired.

"Yes," Linda responded, "I remember you. What can I do for you?" Linda asked.

"I'm glad you asked. I'll be quick and to the point. I need you to step aside and let my son and Maxine get back together." Momma Doris said conspiratorially.

"I'm not sure I understand. Why do you think I'm in the way of Steve and Maxine getting back together?"

"Oh, I think you understand why. I know about you two and your relationship. I think it's appalling you would want to keep those two apart so you can continue doing what you're doing."

"Ma'am I don't have anything to do with who Maxine sees. If she wants to get back together with Steve she will…if not, she won't. But either way, I don't understand why you think I want to keep them apart." Linda was confused. She really didn't know what this woman was trying to say. She looked past the woman to see if Maxine was looking in their direction hoping to get some back up. Unfortunately, the two were walking toward a bench near the church.

"I can see you aren't going to cooperate so I'll say it. I know Steve hurt Maxine and she turned to you for comfort. Honey, it's not right for the two of you to be lovers. The Word of God says so. You and Maxine need to stop it before you end up in hell. If you turn your back on this lifestyle now Maxine can learn to love men again. I believe you'll be able to as well. Steve and Maxine belong together." Momma Doris blatantly said to Linda.

"You think we're lovers?" Linda asked.

"Baby, I know you are. My friend Mother Thomas told me that a while ago. I didn't believe it until I saw you two together for myself. God can restore you and He's able to deliver. All you have to do is ask." Momma Doris said in a comforting manner.

Angrily Linda looked at the woman as she stood there and so easily made an accusation that she and her best friend were lesbians.

"In the first place, I can't believe you have the nerve to think that. In the second place, Steve went off somewhere doing drugs. You know that's why they broke up." Linda almost screamed at the woman. She had never been so offended in her life.

"Chile, I know why they broke up. I was as brokenhearted as anyone was. I know Maxine, she's a forgiving woman, and I'm sure she has already forgiven Steve. They were once very much in love but now she's cool towards him. That's because of you. Why else won't she give him the time of day?" Momma Doris calmly stated.

"Not that this is any of your business but Maxine is not as far down the road to forgiveness as you think. She can't even think about Steve and what he did without getting angry. That's why she's being cool as you call it. Now, if you don't mind, I think you need to leave me alone." Linda stated and turned up the volume on the radio.

"Think about what I said. Don't be a fool. She will leave you and return to Steve and then you'll be all alone. Have a blessed day!" Momma Doris backed away from Linda and returned to her car. She looked toward Maxine and Steve wondering what the topic of conversation was. She didn't stare so the two could have some privacy. She'd wait until she and Steve were on their way home to find out about their chat. Momma Doris looked at Linda once more and thought about how that "hussy" refused to admit what was going on. She would be in big trouble if she thought Momma Doris would let her stand in the way of true love.

Chapter 30

"Maxine, I've really missed you." Steve lamented.

"How's that Steve? You had your drugs to keep you company." Maxine spat back at him.

"Is that what you think? Drugs could never replace you! I love you!" Steve said as he tried to convince Maxine he was sincere in his affections.

"Save it Steve. You have no idea what love is so you could never love me." Maxine said bluntly to her almost-husband.

"I know I hurt you. I apologize for everything. I take full responsibility for what I did. Will you forgive me?"

"Steve, I forgave you a long time ago but that has nothing to do with how I feel about what you did. I don't even want to sit here and talk to you. I won't be rude and walk away from you like you did me. If you don't have anything else to say this conversation is over." Maxine said as she stood to walk away.

"Um, I really wanted to have a chance to talk to you." Steve said.

"Well we've talked." Maxine shot back and began to leave. "Goodbye Steve."

"Don't go. Maxine, do you think I could have your phone number so I can call you later. You seem to be in a hurry and I don't want to hold you up. There's more I'd like to say." Steve lied. There wasn't anything else to say but he couldn't bear to see Maxine walk out of his life without being able to contact her.

"You had every opportunity to talk to me but you chose not to. Now you have things to say. I think what you did spoke volumes and I don't think there's anything else to be said." Maxine's words were like venom. They hurt Steve deeply.

"Can you honestly say there are absolutely no feelings left? I refuse to believe you don't feel anything." Steve pleaded with Maxine to search her heart and be honest. He could still feel the sparks between them when they were close to each other. He was sure he'd seen Maxine react to it by moving away from him enough so her body wouldn't be so close to his.

Maxine wished Steve hadn't asked that question. She was aware of her feelings for him. She wanted to feel nothing but contempt for him but for some reason couldn't.

"I'll give you my number Steve. But, you need to understand we are only friends and that's all we'll ever be. The time is over for us to be anything more. Here's my card with my home number on it. I have to go. Goodbye." Maxine walked away feeling somewhat upset. She resigned herself to the fact she still had a weakness for the man. She didn't know why she couldn't be mad at him.

Steve smirked as he watched Maxine walk away. He knew he pushed a major button when he confronted Maxine about her feelings. She always tried to be hard but he knew she was a "softie" on the inside. At least he could contact her now. He believed he had his foot in the door. There was hope.

Chapter 31

Elder Howard printed the final financial reports for the month and turned the lights off in the business office. He put the reporting together monthly for Pastor Mitch as requested. He almost forgot to do it today in his haste to leave so Cassandra could talk to the pastor. He walked down the hallway toward the pastor's office. When he got to the office, he saw the blinds and the door closed. He thought the pastor had already left. He opened the door to the office to find Pastor Mitch and Sister Marsha in each other's arms. They were both obviously upset. He wished he had at least knocked before entering but it was too late for that now.

"Please forgive me for barging in. I didn't know you were still here. I came to bring you the reports for the month." Elder Howard said as he quickly slid the reports on the desk and prepared to leave. He looked at the couple and sensed something was very wrong. "Is everything okay?" Elder Howard asked sincerely.

"Elder, you're chairman of our church Board so you're going to be hearing about this anyway. Please, shut the door and have a seat." Pastor Mitch said as he pointed to a chair sitting in front of his desk.

Elder Howard wondered what could possibly have happened between the time he left them in the office and now. It had only been a matter of twenty minutes or so…thirty at the most. He thought back and remembered Cassandra was in the office when he left. That could only mean Cassandra was up to her old tricks again. He made himself comfortable in the chair and braced himself for whatever was to come next.

"Elder Howard, some things have happened that Sister Marsha and I are going to need your help in dealing with. In fact, we are going to need the full support of the Board in order to get this church back in order. We also need you to be discrete as these issues are very sensitive. Others are already aware and probably spreading the word throughout the congregation. Do I have your support?" Pastor Mitch asked.

"Well, yes, as much as I can support you without knowing exactly what you're talking about." Elder Howard responded.

"Mitch, why are you even honoring this mess with any discussion at all? That's all it is…a big mess!" Marsha asked her husband before he spilled the beans about the occurrences of the day. "If you talk about it you're implying it's worthwhile. Plain and simple, none of it is worth any discussion. Let it drop. It'll die. That's all we need to do." Marsha stated.

"Honey, I don't think we should ignore what's going on especially considering the entire membership will probably know by the end of today. If we don't address it at all people will begin to question our leadership. A leader doesn't sweep controversy under the rug. We have to address it. I think we need to do it as a united front in order to stop anyone's idea they can split leadership…."

" Excuse me, but will one of you tell me what's going on? You asked me to be here and now you're shutting me out." Elder Howard interrupted.

"I'm sorry Eric. Let's get back to the point. We have two situations we need to deal with. The first is Sister Cassandra has accused me of coming on to her sexually. One night she came in here and asked me to acknowledge her call to the ministry. During the discussion, she did things like showing her legs and pushing her breasts into my face. I believe she did that in order to seduce me into doing what she wanted. I asked her to leave saying I needed to seek the Lord for an answer to her request. When I told her today I couldn't do want she wanted, she accused me of making sexual advances toward her and denying her request because she wouldn't respond to them. I need to say this allegation is false and I am very disturbed by what this allegation may do to everyone involved. I wish I hadn't allowed myself to meet with her alone. Maybe then this wouldn't have happened because there would be witnesses. I have seen churches split because of the turmoil caused by things like this. I don't want that to happen here. The other problem we have is Mother Thomas seems to think Linda and Maxine, our new Single's ministry leaders, have been exhibiting lesbian tendencies. She doesn't have any proof except they are 'touchy feely' as she calls it. I don't believe there is any truth to this but Mother Thomas is insisting something be done about it or she will leave and take the entire Mother's Board with her. Now, I'm not concerned about them leaving. If that's what they decide to do, I can't stop them. However, I don't want them to cause a bunch of ruckus on their way out." Pastor Mitch explained.

"Wow, pastor, you've said a mouthful." Elder Howard said as he shifted in his chair. He mulled the situation over in his mind carefully considering what his next words should be. Should he tell his pastor he did in fact have a witness? He would hear him out first.

"What do you have in mind for handling these problems?" He asked Pastor Mitch.

"I haven't really had time to think about it. I'm going to spend some extended time in fasting and prayer to hear God clearly about this. I think we need to confront this immediately. Maybe there should be some sort of hearing or something so everything can be brought out in the open." Pastor Mitch said as he pondered what might be the plan of action.

"Pastor Mitch it's interesting that you would suggest a hearing because I believe that's what our church bylaws say should be done. In fact, I'm sorry to say, it's going to be necessary for you to step down temporarily while we go through this process."

"Why is that necessary? I mean we all know this didn't happen the way Cassandra says it did." Marsha spoke up.

"I won't step down regardless of what the bylaws say. I am the pastor of this church and I'm not going to be treated as some sort of pervert because Cassandra says I acted like one. That will not happen." Mitch angrily responded.

"I don't see where we can do anything differently. We set this up years ago when we founded the ministry. Because we don't have denominational ties, we had to come up with some sort of process for accountability." Eric Howard stated.

"Who would lead this ministry? I mean we can't leave the church without leadership." Mitch asked.

"The Board would actually lead the church but as it's chairman I would be expected to actually be the interim pastor." Eric said.

"You mean to tell me that because Cassandra made these allegations, she would automatically become an even larger role in the leadership of this church. Eric, you can't tell me this is appropriate. That would mean any board member would be able to make an allegation about the pastor and then basically take over his job." Mitch was agitated now. "There is no way this is going to happen. I am still accountable to God for the leadership of this ministry and I will not idly sit by and see it destroyed by some manipulative woman like Cassandra. We'll have to find another way to deal with this." Mitch stated decisively.

Eric Howard hadn't thought about this as a possibility in his quest to unseat Pastor Mitch and become pastor himself. That would have been too obvious for him to do anyway. It didn't matter who did it, he knew this was his opportunity to make his run. He now had the answer to whether he should make what he witnessed in Pastor Mitch's office that night known. He may have to take this secret to his grave.

"We don't have to allow Cassandra to stay on the board while this situation is being resolved. I believe it's totally within our discretion to release her during this process if we choose. In fact, I think we should do so immediately. We wouldn't want her to be in a position where she could potentially be harassed again now would we. The Board is all men you know. It would be good to protect everyone involved. We'll take that route where Cassandra is concerned. What are you going to do Pastor?" Eric asked.

Chapter 32

Cassandra walked into her abode with very conflicted feelings. One the one hand, she felt as though she was floating on air because of the victory she felt was imminent after she threatened Pastor Mitch. On the other hand, she felt somewhat melancholy. It made her feel bad when she had to go to such lengths in order to get people to do what they should do willingly anyway. The turmoil inside of Cassandra was overwhelming and she collapsed on her couch and cried. After what seemed like hours, Cassandra got up and went to her bedroom to retrieve her journal. She began to write about the situation and what she felt about the happenings of the day.

I cannot believe Pastor Mitch refused me. I don't know why I failed. He obviously doesn't know who he's messing with. I really don't feel right about lying on Pastor Mitch but he gave me no choice. It was clear that he wasn't going to move me into my seat in the pulpit and I couldn't let that slide Why is it so unbelievable God would call a woman to the ministry? What is it about my feet that would defile the "Holy ground" of the pulpit if they would dare to touch it? Why couldn't he go along with the program? All he had to do was what I asked. I wonder what he'll do now. Obviously, he'll have to leave the church because surely the Board won't let him stay after all this comes out. Once he leaves, maybe we'll get a pastor who will see things my way. What happens if he doesn't leave? I don't even want to think about that. All I do know is that I used my last tool and I'm no closer to getting what I wanted. I'll have to stay positive. What do I do about the pain in my heart? How do I stop acting the way I act? I know there is something at work in me I can't control. It's like the things I do happen before I can catch them in time to stop them. I feel bad but not bad enough to stop it. I have no other choice but to continue handling things the way I do. God, please help me to understand the war going on inside of me!

Chapter 33

"She said what?" Maxine yelled as she and Linda began to talk about the events in the church parking lot.

"Steve's mother said Mother Thomas told her we were lesbians. She thinks I'm the reason you and Steve aren't together." Linda stated.

"This really ticks me off. This is none of that woman's business. If Momma Doris knew what was best for her she would stay out of it. As for Mother Thomas, well, she's plain wrong. I thought she was supposed to be all holy and everything. Why is she in the middle of this? She must have a little undercover stuff going on herself. What would make either of them think that?" Maxine angrily wondered aloud.

"She told me she didn't believe Mother Thomas until she saw you and I together for herself." Linda answered calmly. She knew Maxine would blow up when she heard what happened and now she was trying to keep her calm. She had to tell her because she felt her friend needed to know.

"Look, I loved Steve and was ready to be his wife. He messed everything up. You and I were friends even then. So why wasn't anyone suspicious at that point?" Maxine asked in a loud voice.

"Maxine, do you think it's because we live together? I mean that's the only thing different now." Linda asked her friend. She was trying desperately to make sense of these accusations.

"We live together, big hairy deal. That doesn't automatically imply anything. That's one big jump in logic there. These people obviously don't have anything better to do." Maxine said as she continued to analyze the situation.

"Max, calm down. I'm trying to figure this thing out. Steve's mother said she didn't believe we were lovers until she saw us. What did she see? For that matter, what did Mother Thomas see?" Linda said.

"You know what. I refuse to get into offense over this situation. I'm going to approach this situation differently than I would normally. I'm going to let this be their issue and I'm choosing to ignore it. The problem is while we may choose to overlook it others may not. If I know Mother Thomas, she has already told all the Church Mothers and that means by next Sunday the whole church will know. That's another issue".

"I hadn't thought about that." Linda said as she began to ponder this revelation. She realized it was always difficult to shake her insecurities arising from what others thought of her. This would not be an easy thing to walk through. "I can't face all those people knowing what they think about me. I don't think I'm going back for a while. Maybe this is God's way of moving me on to something better. We do sometimes get too attached to churches and pastors anyway." Linda said in order to justify her desire to avoid the situation.

"I know you Linda. You're making excuses so you can avoid facing this head on. What if Jesus had decided to take the easy way out and avoided the cross because it would be too painful? The Bible says we too would face persecution so this should be no surprise. I think we ought to go right back to that church like we've always done. I refuse to run and hide. We are not going to justify these rumors running from their accusations. But, it won't be the same if I'm the only one facing the music. Are you with me or shall I bear this cross alone?" Maxine asked her friend as she grabbed for her hand.

"What you said makes a lot of sense and for once I agree with you. I'm going to operate out of faith instead of fear. You're right, we don't have anything to be ashamed of. Now, let's go shopping. I want to look good when we walk into the den of lions next Sunday." Linda said as she lifted Maxine's hand in victory. The two women broke out in laughter as they grabbed their handbags and headed for the door. Before reaching the door, the phone rang. The two looked at each other as if to identify who would answer it. They each looked at the phone as it rang and looked back at each other once again. As if communicating through their facial expressions, the two continued toward the door.

Chapter 34

Elder Howard waited patiently as Linda and Maxine's phone continued to ring. He thought they would have been home at this time but was obviously wrong. When the voice mail system came on, he wondered if he should leave a message or call back later. He decided he should leave a message letting them know he wanted to speak with them.

"Greetings Linda and Maxine. This is Elder Howard from Believer's Church calling. Would one of you call me back at home when you can? This is regarding some church affairs that I need to discuss with you both before next Sunday if possible. Hope you're having a blessed day! Goodbye."

Elder Howard put the receiver back on the cradle. The events that transpired at church today were overwhelming. It was more than he had ever seen happen at one time in any church setting. In difficult times like these, he could always count on Eunice to hold him up. She was a powerful prayer warrior and he always benefited from her crying out to God. This was a new predicament for him. Going through rough times was not something he normally did alone. Now he had no choice.

He thought about the situation with Mitch and Cassandra and wondered how it would turn out. He realized he was being selfish in thinking about how hard this was going to be for him. After all, he wasn't directly involved but only called on to help handle the fallout. He thought about Cassandra and how she always seemed to be at the crux of most of the problems occurring at the church. She obviously had issues she was trying to work out in an inappropriate manner. He wondered why Mitch put himself in the position he had. Did he actually have an attraction for Cassandra?

He knew what he had seen that night would exonerate his pastor. Did he miss anything? Perhaps some signals Mitch sent made Cassandra think he wanted her in some way. Knowing Cassandra and how she tended to operate he doubted that very seriously. Who would risk losing a woman like Marsha for the likes of Cassandra? He gasped as he thought about how this was taking its toll on Marsha. She was the only innocent one in this. He thought back to the dinner the two of them almost had at Fellowship City and how concerned she was about her marriage and how the church had affected it. This has not been a very good experience for her. Mitch should thank God for a woman like her. He should not take her for granted. God knows if Eric had a woman like her in his life, he would never treat her that way. After losing Eunice, he learned little things make a big difference. Flowers for no special reason, spending the night at a hotel just because, having dinner out at a four star restaurant, those were things he now knew were important to women. How he wished he could go back and do some things over again. However, that was impossible. Eunice was gone and he couldn't bring her back. It wasn't too late for Marsha though. Maybe he could help her out. Be a support for her. While everyone is focusing on Mitch and Cassandra, they would all probably forget Marsha. I won't forget her. I'll make sure she has a shoulder to lean on.

Chapter 35

Momma Doris worked feverishly in her kitchen to get dinner on the table as she had for years and years. She had a new pep in her step now that she had gotten Linda straight and Maxine and Steve were getting back together. That's all she wanted now…to see Steve and Maxine happy together.

"I feel like Simeon in the bible. I'll be able to die in peace once my Steve and Maxine are married." she said aloud because it sounded too good to keep in her head.

"Once your Steve and Maxine are what?" Steve asked as he walked into the kitchen and overheard his mother's words.

"Oh, honey it's okay. You don't have to pretend with me. I know you and Maxine are back together now. Have you two set a new date for the wedding?" Momma Doris said while seemingly walking on air toward her bewildered son.

"Momma, Maxine and I are barely talking. I mean she isn't even sure she's willing to be my friend at this point let alone being my wife!" Steve stated firmly to his mother. "I knew you would take anything you thought you saw or heard about me and Maxine and run with it before the play was even called!" Steve continued. "Don't you get it? I messed up Momma. I caused some damage I might not be able to fix. I don't know if it can ever be repaired." Steve lamented.

"But I saw you talking and…" Momma Doris began.

"Momma, you're a Bible scholar right? You remember the story about Jesus' friend who had died, been buried, and was stinking by the time the Savior showed up? What was his name?" Steve asked.

"His name was Lazarus. But what does that have to do with you and Maxine?"

"Lazarus' condition seemed impossible right? I mean anyone who has been dead for so long they're beginning to smell, even from behind that huge stone they placed over the grave opening, must have been irrecoverable. There didn't seem to be any way he could be raised from the dead." Steve explained.

"Yes, honey God is the God of the impossible. Jesus did raise Lazarus even though it seemed impossible." Momma Doris countered.

"Well, my point is that the relationship between Maxine and I is deader than Lazarus was. It's been stinking for a very long time. There may be no resurrection." Steve stated matter-of-factly.

"God is the same yesterday, today and forever and He's no respecter of persons. What He's done for others He'll do the same for you." Momma Doris sang.

"That's nice rhetoric Momma. It looks good and it sounds good but it's not reality in this situation. It'll take more than some nice sayings to get Maxine back." Steve was convinced this situation was hopeless.

"But, son that's what I've been trying to tell you. There's more working in your favor now. I've seen to it!" Momma Doris said with conviction and excitement not missed by her son.

Steve walked closer to his mother with alacrity. He was both curious and excited himself.

"What are you talking about Momma? Tell me!"

"Sit down and let me tell you what I did for you." Momma Doris sat down and waited for Steve to follow suit, which he did immediately.

"Okay Momma I'm sitting. Did Maxine say something to you I don't know about?" Steve asked now adding caution to his list of feelings.

"No, I didn't talk to Maxine. I went to the source of the problem. Linda. I let her know that she had to let Maxine go so you two could be together. She wasn't real receptive at first but I think..." Momma Doris said to her son proudly.

"What do you mean Linda has to let Maxine go?" Steve's caution rose. He had a bad feeling about this but he would wait to hear exactly what his mother had to say.

Momma Doris leaned in to her son. She wanted to be close enough to comfort him when he found out how Maxine had run into the arms of a woman because of their breakup.

"Baby, you know you hurt Maxine really badly. We talked about that a few minutes ago. When we get hurt, we start looking for something to ease the pain. Some people turn to drugs and alcohol. Some turn to God. Some even turn inward and isolate themselves. But honey, Maxine looked for comfort in a way different from drugs, alcohol, isolation or God." She paused wishing she didn't have to tell him this. It might cause him to feel more guilt than he already did.

"Momma will you please get to the point?" Steve asked anxiously. The waiting was particularly hard for him especially since this concerned the woman he loved.

"Maxine and her friend Linda are more than friends. They're roommates if you get my drift." Momma Doris looked at Steve sideways with one eyebrow up and one down. Steve was confused and becoming irritated.

"What's wrong with Maxine and Linda being roommates? They've been friends for years and decided to share a place together. What's the big deal about that?"

"Stevie, it's what they do in that place they share together! Now do you understand?" Momma Doris asked hoping against hope he would completely understand.

"No Momma I don't understand and I'm tired of playing this game with you. I feel like we're in the middle of a game of charades with all the clues you're giving me. I'm going to my room. Let me know when dinner's ready." Steve sighed and got up from the chair. Seeing Maxine and having to work so hard to get close to her was challenging at best. Now his mother obviously had some information that she wanted him to guess and he'd had enough.

"Maxine and Linda are lesbians. I told Linda she was living a life of sin and she had to let Maxine go, repent and ask for forgiveness. I think she's going to do it after seeing you two together today. I pointed out how much you two are still very much in love with each other. Anyone would have to be blind not to see it." Momma Doris had finally gotten it out. She stuck her chest out with pride. She knew her son would be proud of her.

Steve stopped dead in his tracks. He wasn't sure if he really heard what his mother said. He slowly turned around and looked at her mother. For a moment, he felt as though his heart would jump out of his chest. Steve knew he heard correctly but wanted to confirm it.

"Momma, what did you say about Maxine and Linda?"

"Honey, I know it's hard to believe but it's true. Maxine and Linda are lesbians."

"What makes you think that? They've been friends forever. Even while Linda and I were engaged."

"Look dear. Mother Thomas told me about this a while ago. I kept it to myself until I could have a chance to see it for myself. I saw it and I took care of it for you. Now you need to forget about their relationship and go on with your relationship with Maxine. That's what you need to do."

"Momma, I never thought I'd be saying this to you. You need to learn to mind your own business. You're wrong about Maxine and Linda. I don't want to hear anything more about it."

"I know you're not getting angry with me! And I know you're not using that tone of voice with me!"

"If you had spent more time minding you and Dad's business, he would still be here with us. You didn't do it then and you're not going to do it now."

Momma Doris reached up quickly with her right hand and stung the side of Steve's face. How dare he speak to her this way? What does he know about her marriage to his father?

Steve took several steps backward because of his shock. Then he took as many steps toward his mother as were necessary to almost touch his nose to hers. He opened his mouth to speak but instead found it full of sobs. As he released the tears that went with them, his mother put her arms around him to comfort him. As soon as she got her arms around him fully, Steve jumped and moved away from her. He didn't even know her anymore. She may have completely ruined his relationship with Maxine and she was slapping him?

"Momma, don't ever touch me again. You're dead wrong and I won't forgive you for this. I've been thinking lately that it's time for me to move out of here anyway. Now I'm sure it's time after what you've done. Tonight I'll grab enough to get me through a few days. I'll have all of my things out by the end of the week."

"No, Stevie. You can't leave. I mean, where will you go? How will you make it? Please don't leave. I promise I'll leave this thing with you and Maxine alone. Okay?" Momma Doris pleaded with her baby boy. The last thing she wanted to do was push him out of the house.

"It's too late Momma."

Before anything else could be said, Steve ran up the stairs two at a time. He had to hurry up and get out of the house before he said or did something more he would really regret. Besides, he was a grown man living with his mother. It was way past time for him to move out on his own. This time he hoped his life outside of his mother's house would include Maxine. As he exited the house, all he heard was his mother's cries. This was one time he couldn't comfort her. She would have to get comfort from the Lord.

Chapter 36

Mitch and Marsha sat lounging in their Master suite. Mitch sat on the leather chair with the vibrating feature turned to full blast. His head was down and his eyes seemingly stared off into space. Marsha sat on the edge of the bed reading her Bible. This scene played out in their home on many occasions. Yet, something was very different about this time. A blanket of tension had settled there. It was nothing they couldn't work through and eliminate if they wanted to. What was there to say? Marsha felt if Mitch had spent more time with her when she asked, there would not have been an opportunity for this to happen. Mitch thought Marsha was sitting there reading her Bible looking for a reason to start an argument. They both would rather pretend this very sensitive predicament never happened. However, it was the subject of each of their thoughts.

"I think I'll turn over and go to sleep. Good night Mitch!" Marsha said to create a feeling of ease in the room. Mitch's head popped up and he looked at Marsha. He saw the beauty of the woman he had loved for so long he couldn't remember a time he didn't. As he looked a little longer, he also saw the pain that was so evident on her face. Was him becoming pastor really worth it?

"Marsha, before you go to sleep, can we talk for a minute?"

"Yes. What do you want to talk about?" Marsha asked as if she didn't know.

"How are you handling what's going on?" Mitch wondered while at the same time thinking he wasn't sure he really wanted to know.

"Well since you asked, I think Mother Thomas is trying to maintain a certain level of control in the church. She sees those two young women as threats to her kingdom. For some reason she feels her way of doing things is the only right way and anyone who doesn't follow is dead wrong. The problem is her expectations are unrealistic and she'll be disappointed for the rest of her life. You need to talk to Linda and Maxine to get their side of this. Then you need to get Mother Thomas back in her place. The church mothers should nurture and support not control and tear down. If this church is going to prosper, we can't allow this spirit to continue to operate. I think…." Marsha continued.

"What about what Cassandra is saying? You do believe I didn't do it don't you?" Mitch interrupted. After a long pause, Marsha replied.

"Mitch, all I know is you spend a lot of time at the church."

"I'm asking if you believe me when I say this didn't happen?" Mitch repeated trying to get to the root of the issue.

"Let me put it this way. Do I think you propositioned Cassandra? No, I don't. Do I think you have given her and others reason to believe you'd be available no matter what? Yes, I believe you have. She knew all she had to do was whimper and you would come running."

"A pastor is supposed to care for the flock. What do you expect me to do?"

"I realize you have a shepherd's heart and you really care about the people. It's one of the things I love about you. As my husband, you're supposed to care for me too."

"You think I don't care for you because I postponed our plans for an hour or so?"

"I think you felt her needs were more important than mine or ours for that matter. She knew that too and used it to her advantage."

"I don't get your reasoning."

"Think about it. Everyone in the church knew about our plans weeks ahead of time and that includes Cassandra. I believe she intentionally requested time with you at that particular moment in order to set this whole thing up. She knew I wouldn't be happy about it, which is a separate issue. She also knew you would adjust however you had to in order to see to her needs. That's the problem." Marsha concluded her speech. She laid her head back on her pillow with her hands behind it as she waited for Mitch to continue the conversation. After five minutes, it was apparent he didn't have anything else to say so she went to sleep.

That night Marsha had a disturbing dream. She saw what she believed to be a young Cassandra kissing a man older than her. She couldn't quite see his face but she wondered if it was her husband. It was obviously an intimate moment and she wondered why she was privy to it. She saw the man touch Cassandra in places that were off limits in purely plutonic relationships. What she remembered most about the dream was the look on Cassandra's face. Her expression said she was forcing herself to enjoy a horrible encounter. As Marsha wrote about it in her journal the following morning, her interest was further piqued about what she was supposed to learn from the dream.

Chapter 37

"Hello." Cassandra groggily said into the phone.

"Good morning sleepy head." Cassandra's mother sang with enthusiasm. "Wake up!"

"Momma? Is that you?" Cassandra inquired as she sat up in bed.

"Yes it's me honey. Are you doing okay? You've been heavy on my mind these last few days and I wanted to call and see what's going on. You know, a mother can always tell when something is going on with her children no matter how old they are. Even if you lived on the other side of the world, I would know about it. So tell me what's happening with you."

"Okay I'll be honest with you."

"Well chile spit it out so we can get you through it. Me and the Lord."

"I'm going through some things I seem to repeat over and over again; things that really hurt me. I don't know why I keep doing it. I want to stop but can't."

"What is it you keep doing? You can tell me." Her mother pleaded.

"Momma I really don't want to tell you. I'm ashamed of the things I do. I'm not the daughter you think I am. I'm scandalous."

"Uh huh. God revealed something last night but I didn't understand it. You need to tell Momma what it is you're into."

"Momma, I lied on someone and because of it a marriage and a church are in trouble."

"Who did you lie on and what was the lie?"

"I lied on my pastor. I had to Momma. He wouldn't put me in my proper place in the church."

"That's why you lied on him? Because of a position in God's church?"

"Yeah." Cassandra responded weakly. She hadn't thought about it that way before.

"What did you say about him?"

"I said he came on to me and when I didn't respond to his advances I said he decided not to give me the position."

"Baby girl, tell me what really happened."

"I told him God said I should be recognized as a minister. He said he had to pray about it. When I asked him the following week about it, he told me it wasn't going to happen. That's when I told his wife he had tried to get with me."

"So what you're telling me is that you hurt him because he didn't give you what you wanted."

"Men don't treat women right in the church and I intend to help God get this straight."

"Honey, you're right about the way women are treated in some churches. Women can be as anointed as any man. I believe God places His call on the lives of the people He chooses whether they are male or female. However, God will fix that in His own time and He does not need your help. He will most certainly deal with men who choose not to yield to Him in this area. However, my dear child, you can't appoint yourself to do what God hasn't asked you to do. Even if God told you He would use you to help bring women into their rightful place, He certainly didn't want you to lie in order to make it happen. God will place you in situations so people can hear His voice on this issue. I'm sure He didn't tell you to make things happen. "

"I know Momma. I feel greatness inside of me Momma. I really believe I can help the church. I just need for Pastor Mitch to see that."

"This isn't about Pastor Mitch. This is really about that man you got involved with in college."

"Who? Are you talking about Pastor DeWayne? What does this have to do with him? We were only friends."

"Honey, I know you were more than friends with him. Like I said before, a mother always knows."

Cassandra paused for a moment to ponder what her mother said.

"Momma, I've got to go. Thanks for calling and I'll talk to you later. Love you!" Cassandra said all the while moving her finger closer and closer to its intended destination, the off button. She began to think back to DeWayne and their relationship. She had always looked up to him and thought he was an outstanding spiritual leader. When he addressed the congregation, all eyes were on him. He was an amazing orator. Cassandra always admired him and considered him a very handsome and sexy man. The guys from the university she went out with were so immature compared to DeWayne. She always made sure she went to Bible study whenever she could to be in his presence. She desperately wanted him to notice her but it appeared he didn't even realize she existed. That's why it was such a surprise when he approached her after church service. He asked her to his office so he could tell her about a special assignment God had for her to do. She never got to the assignment God had for her. However, she did fulfill Pastor DeWayne's assignment for her.

Chapter 38

As the Believer's Church Board members began gathering, Cassandra stood in a corner away from everyone else. She didn't feel comfortable with them. There appeared to be a lot of whispering going on. Since she wasn't privy to the information, she had to assume it had something to do with her. Mitch probably convinced "his boys" she was lying. She knew she had to put on a good show to sway their opinion. Since Mitch wouldn't be there, it seemed an easy goal to reach. As Eric Howard began to look around as if he was going to call the meeting to order, Cassandra moved toward her seat.

"Gentlemen and Cassandra please bring your minds in and let's begin the meeting. We've got a whole lot to deal with as you might guess but if we start now we might not have to meet about this again." Eric stated with a lack of excitement in his voice. He wasn't very excited about having to handle this mess. He wanted it resolved smoothly and without incident. Everyone took their seats and looked toward Eric for direction.

" People of God, we have received some very serious charges against some of our church leaders. It deeply concerns me as an elder and a member of this glorious church for all these years. Some members of Believer's Church think we have lesbians in leadership. I assure you it wasn't my idea to put these people in leadership. It was something our beloved Pastor Mitch did. He's responsible for..."

"What exactly am I responsible for Eric?" Mitch said as he entered the room. It was obvious from the reaction of those in attendance his presence was not expected.

"Pastor Mitch. I didn't expect you. Why are you here?" questioned Elder Howard.

"Why wouldn't I be here, Elder Howard? I wouldn't miss this meeting for the world. Now what was it you were saying I was responsible for?"

"Uh, well. We were about to talk about Maxine and Linda. You know, what Mother Thomas said about them." Elder Howard offered as an excuse.

"Oh I get it, you were trying to make it clear you weren't involved in putting them in leadership. Well, I will completely admit I did it. I decided to put them in oversight of the singles ministry. Does that solve this issue?" Pastor Mitch stated with aggression that was unseen up to this point.

"Well, it probably doesn't make things any better. I didn't want anyone to feel bad about it if they did feel responsible for the appointment." Elder Howard breathed a silent sigh of relief. He felt he effectively handled this situation.

"I don't think this issue is the highest priority considering what else is going on." As Pastor Mitch made this statement, he glowered at Cassandra. He never thought he could hate anyone, especially anyone whose soul he was to oversee. But, Cassandra had pushed Mitch to his limit. He could now understand the hatred people had for other people. He could see it clearly.

Cassandra saw the look on Pastor Mitch's face. She could almost read his mind. It was obvious her pastor couldn't stand her. She knew she had to think of something to keep the debate from knocking on her and Pastor Mitch's problem.

"Who's a lesbian?" was Cassandra's best effort at deflecting the attention. For the first time since she could remember anything about herself, she really didn't want to be in the spotlight.

"No one. I'm glad you're here because I want to talk about what you said I did."

"We can't talk about that Mitch. Not while the two of you are here. We haven't even begun the investigation." Elder Howard shot back.

"What investigation? There was no one here besides Cassandra and I. She says something happened. I say it didn't."

"Pastor, we can't forget about it and assume nothing happened based on your word only."

"That's exactly what should happen because nothing happened and Cassandra knows it."

"Cassandra's a godly woman. She's been a member of this church for years and her reputation is unblemished." Eric stated with a calm resolve.

Everyone had a sudden coughing spell and reached for their water glasses. No one in attendance at this meeting believed this to be true. Cassandra looked at Elder Howard while at the same time wondering what his angle was. She didn't think he could be trusted.

"Well Eric I'm not going to argue that point with you. Only God knows what's in her heart and I'm not going to get into judging here. I don't care about you all investigating. I'm concerned about your demand for me to step down because someone accused me of something. That's what really bothers me."

"I can't help what the church documents say. You have to step down until this is resolved. The church will be in good hands while you're away. I'll see to that."

"While I'm away? I'm not going anywhere Eric. So I know it'll be safe because I don't plan to miss a beat. Whatever your bylaws say is irrelevant. I'm the pastor here and that's the way it's going to stay as long as God wants me here."

The room went silent. Cassandra wished she could melt into the walls and out to her car. Mitch was wondering how Eric Howard was going to respond. The board wondered why this whole thing was becoming a mountain when it was really a molehill.

Deacon Mays decided to take the reins before things got too far out of hand.

"I want to make sure I've got this straight here. Elder Howard you want Pastor Mitch to give up the pulpit while we decide if Cassandra's story is true. Pastor Mitch, you say you won't step down while we're looking into this. So we have a deadlock here." Deacon Mays assessed. "I think there's a way around this. I remember a team working on those bylaws and I think there are some considerations in there which might allow us to make an exception here."

"What do you think Cassandra? You brought this complaint. What do you think should happen? Do you think he should be relieved from his duties as pastor until this issue is resolved?" Elder Howard questioned hoping Cassandra would give the right response.

Everyone in the room turned to face Cassandra. She liked to be the center of attention but only when she could control it. She looked into the eyes of everyone present in an attempt to determine what they were thinking. She wanted to speak but the words wouldn't come. She gulped and opened her mouth to speak. Instead, she passed out.

Chapter 39

Linda rushed from her office after working only a half-day in order to meet Mark at Fellowship City. She hated hiding this from Maxine but she wouldn't understand. Linda had come to the realization she still had deep and abiding feelings for Mark. Regardless of the hatred Linda felt toward Mark during the ordeal, she knew now she still loved him. It became clear to her what she really felt was the pain of Mark's abandonment. She approached the entrance to Fellowship City and before entering, stood on her toes and looked through the front windows to see if Mark was there yet. Linda wanted to make a grand entrance. Therefore, she couldn't enter first. When she didn't see Mark, she assumed he was running a little late. She placed her heels back on the ground, releasing her weight from her toes and her position became a flat-footed stance. She turned around to head back to her car to wait and immediately ran into the body of the man she loved. His face was about six inches from hers; so close, she could feel the force of his breath on her face. Mark moved closer to see if what he was sensing was true. When his lips touched Linda's he knew he was right. She did still have feelings for him. The two kissed each other so passionately it was as though they were alone instead of standing directly in the public view. As their embrace relaxed, Linda smiled at her long-time love. Mark took Linda by the hand and led her into the restaurant. He was so glad he had arranged with the manager to surprise Linda as she had never been surprised before. The hostess took the two to their reserved, secluded and candle-lit table and they sat all the while never taking their eyes off each other. For weeks, Linda and Mark had been seeing each other clandestinely. Not only had this allowed for them to attend counseling to resolve the issues surrounding their child, but it had also provided each with an opportunity to reconnect with the other. Absolutely no one, including family and friends, had any idea about the rebirth of their relationship.

Mark spoke first. "Linda you are looking absolutely exquisite tonight. I didn't think you had any room for improvement."

"Mark tonight is special. Special in ways you don't even know yet."

"You're on the money there. It is a very special night."

"Hello, I'm Devon your waiter. Can I get the two of you something to drink? Would you like to order an appetizer? The beignets are excellent tonight." The waiter said interrupting the flow the two had achieved.

"Um, yeah we'll have the beignets. Can we also have a carafe of your sparkling peach sensation?" Steve crooned to the waiter while keeping is gaze on Linda.

"Yes sir, I'll get it right out to you." The waiter walked away leaving the two in almost complete solitude.

"Mark, thank you for helping me resolve my issues, you know, about the baby and all. I feel like I've taken a load off. You know, we can only carry so much before we end up collapsing. I want you to know I appreciate your support."

"Although I'd like to take the credit for helping you, I was there to get some help for myself as well. It seems society understands the effects of abortion on women but has never even thought about the effects on men. While it's true the mothers are the ones who actually go through it, fathers have to deal with the loss as well."

"Mark, don't go there. I've already repented to God and you for making the decision without regard to God's law or your feelings. Again, I'm sincerely sorry."

"Here's your appetizer and your peach sensation. Are you two ready to order?"

"Linda do you know what you want?"

"I'll have the Orange Roughy with a side of Au Gratin potatoes and Collard Greens."

"I'll have the Pork Chops with Macaroni and Cheese and Collard Greens as well."

"Thank you. I'll put your order right in."

At that precise moment, the spot light hit the stage and music began playing. It was an upbeat, jazzy medley of well-known Praise songs. As the crowd began to notice the music, they began to sing the words and Fellowship City became a church. The Master of Ceremony came to the stage and introduced the entertainment for the evening. It turned out the performance tonight would be by a rapper/musician who had founded the band that played the medley in the introduction. As Junior Jesus hit the stage, the crowd went wild. He rapped and played the keyboard throughout the entire show. On cue, he stopped and looked toward the booth where Mark and Linda sat. Mark inconspicuously nodded toward him. Junior Jesus and his band, led by the bass guitar, went into an R&B-style groove. Junior Jesus began a rap based on the love exhibited in the Song of Solomon. While some seemed offended, others were encouraging him to continue.

Chapter 40

Steve initially planned to grab a bite to eat at Fellowship City but quickly changed his plans when he saw Linda and Mark in front of the restaurant. Maxine was nowhere in sight which inspired Steve to seek her out. He would eat later. He wanted to re-ignite the fire like Linda and Mark apparently had.

Steve approached the house with the address that matched the one he'd found on the Internet for Maxine. As he stood in front of the home, he imagined living there along with her. It didn't even matter to him if Linda and Mark lived there too. It would mean the world to him to be able to wake up to Maxine every morning. He would relish the opportunity to hold her in his arms as she fell asleep each night. This dream was far-fetched he knew, however, he had hope. After all, there had to be a reason why she re-entered his life. Steve decided now was as a good a time as any to see where this relationship could go.

Steve carefully pulled the doorknocker from its bed and pushed it back again so it made enough sound to alert the inhabitant. He stood there trying to compose himself so he would have something meaningful and logical to say. Steve thought about how much he hurt Maxine. Quickly, he realized there was nothing he could say or do to change things. Before she could come to the door, Steve turned and ran away from the house to avoid Maxine finding him there. As he reached the sidewalk, Maxine opened the door and saw him. Steve knew he couldn't leave now. Maxine did something he never imagined; she waved him in. Steve immediately retraced his steps right back to her front door. In an unforeseen occurrence, Maxine kissed Steve as passionately as she had during their relationship. Steve lost himself in her love. She would never get away from him again.

Chapter 41

Mother Ilene Thomas made her way from her bathroom to her living room. It had been so long since her home held anyone beside herself. She never bore any children and her husband had long since left. After twenty-five years of marriage, Buddy turned out not to be the man she thought she married. Ilene always knew there was something different about her husband. He always had very close relationships with men. The intensity of his friendships with men easily rivaled the intensity of their marriage. What had really broken the camel's back was when she came home early from church and caught him in a compromising position with a man who lived a few houses down from them. She knew right away that these two had feelings for each other and her marriage was over. Ilene wanted to maintain the illusion of her marriage so the church people would never have to know how much of a fool she was. Here she was a saved Christian woman with a husband who liked men and women equally. That would never play out the right way in the church. With that in mind, she decided to stay in her farce of a marriage. However, Ilene sentenced Buddy to sleep in the cold damp basement. Mother Thomas had chosen to use their guest room for her nightly accommodations. After all, she couldn't sleep where she had seen Buddy with his "friend". She did have some pride left.

It was exactly one month later when she came home from a revival and noticed Buddy's things were missing. She went to the basement to find everything he had there was gone as well. At that moment the phone rang, she struggled to rush up the stairs and made it on the fifth ring.

"Hello." Mother Thomas said to the person on the other end.

"Hi, it's me, Buddy. Ilene, I saw you coming in from church and I wanted to let you know I moved out. I can't take it anymore. We don't love each other no more and I know you know it. There ain't one good reason for us to keep pretending. I moved down the street. I'll see you sometime out in the yard."

After he spoke, Mother Thomas didn't say a word. Her worst nightmare had become a reality. She no longer had the façade of a marriage to cement her standing in the church. She slowly hung up on Buddy and their relationship. She had to let Buddy go. He no longer wanted her.

Once Buddy got the divorce and the man he wanted, Mother Thomas had a few gentlemen callers. She even liked a few of them. Ilene was never able to trust them. If any of them had close male friendships, she became very suspicious. Her mind always went back to Buddy and his "friends". She couldn't bear the embarrassment and humiliation as she had before. She sabotaged her relationship with every one of her suitors leaving her all alone with her memories.

Chapter 42

Junior Jesus walked closer to the edge of the stage. He turned toward the band and gave them the signal to bring the music down a notch. As the band did so, Mark squeezed Linda's hand to let her know he cared for her and to get her attention. At the precise moment Linda's eyes landed on Mark, the lights dimmed in the entire dining room except for a spotlight that found its resting place on the couple. Mark took his cue and began to tell Linda how much he loved her.

"Linda, I truly can't find the words to express how I feel about you. During the time we were apart I thought of you every day. I regretted the day I thought I lost you for good. I'm so sorry for being the wimp I was then. I want you to know you're looking at a changed man. I know what it's like to be without you. No other woman can bring out the best in me like you. No other woman has my heart. No other woman is more important to me than you are. You are my world and without you, I am nothing. I was never so miserable as I was when we were apart. Now you're back in my life. I'm so grateful to you for allowing it to be so and to God for causing our paths to cross. I knew then God was giving me a second chance at being with you."

Linda's eyes began to mist. Mark had no idea how long she had been waiting to hear those words from him. Though his abandonment did hurt it did not decrease her love for him.

Mark began to ease down on his knee. As he did so, the restaurant filled with the comments of those witnessing this very tender moment.

"I refuse to mess up this opportunity. I promise I will always be there for you no matter what. I promise you will never have to wonder about my love for you. I vow to make sure that my love is obvious for the rest of our lives. Will you please honor me by spending the rest of your life with me as my wife? I will not let you down."

The patrons of Fellowship City awaited Linda's response with baited breath. Linda's mouth began to open however it seemed her words refused to approach and exit her mouth. Honestly, she didn't know what to say. She did love Mark, but she wasn't sure this was the right time for them to enter into a marriage. They had only recently gotten past the issues surrounding their breakup. Was marriage the right thing to do at this time? Linda didn't think so. However, how could she say that to Mark without embarrassing him in front of all of these people? She decided to respond affirmatively but explain her reservations to him later. The fact was she would marry him but not now.

"Mark, we've been through a lot with each other. I mean there were some hard times. There were good ones too but the hard times were especially difficult. In spite of it all, we still love each other. That's the sign of a really strong and solid relationship. I know we can make it together because of all we've been through. It would be my honor to be your wife. Yes, I will marry you."

Junior Jesus and the witnesses congratulated the newly engaged couple. Junior Jesus and his band completed the song as Mark and Linda kissed each other as though they had just said, "I do".

Chapter 43

"Maxine, I've always loved you and I never wanted to hurt you," pleaded a repentant Steve.

"Steve, the fact of the matter is you were obviously too deep into your addiction to show me any kind of love. I won't say you didn't love me but it was sure hard to tell by your actions. I had to believe you loved me by faith because you were too afraid to show your feelings for fear you would be hurt," countered an angry Maxine.

"You're right as always. I'm not trying to start an argument here but you weren't there for me either."

"How was I supposed to be there for you when I couldn't find you?"

"You didn't understand how I was feeling. I had lost my job, which meant I couldn't take care of you. I couldn't pay you back for the truck, I couldn't pay for the house you wanted and I couldn't even buy you the ring I wanted to give you. Do you have any idea what that does to a man when he can't provide?"

"No, I don't know that does to a man. Do you know what it did to me when you left? There was no explanation or no 'it's me and not you' speech. To top it all off, you took what we had saved and did only God knows what with it. What happened to you Steve?"

"Like I said I was ashamed because I had to depend on you. I started smoking a little weed with my friends to feel like I was a real man. The first time I did it I realized I didn't hurt inside, at least not while I was high. When I came down, my problems were right there waiting to remind me how sorry of a man I was. I kept doing it because I felt like I was okay as long as I was intoxicated. I knew I couldn't live like that forever and be married to you. Either I could feel bad about who I was as a husband or I could avoid dealing with reality. I chose to stay inebriated so I could numb my pain."

Maxine believed Steve's explanation. He was being honest with her. She didn't know what she was supposed to do with the information now that she had it.

"How is that supposed to make me feel, Steve? How am I supposed to feel knowing you left me because of your stupid pride."

"See, I was trying this honesty thing and look what it got me. I came here to tell you how sorry I am about how things went down. I wanted to see if there was a chance for us to at least think about a relationship."

"I don't know about that. But, there's another problem. For some reason, your mother has the crazy idea that Linda and I are lesbians. She believes that's the reason you and I broke up. Well somehow, it got back to leadership at the church and now there are questions in people's minds about us. That means everybody knows and there's no telling what they're thinking! Did you know about that?"

"Yeah, I heard."

"You know that was way out of the line don't you."

"I moved out the moment I found out what my mother said. I let her know I didn't appreciate it. I don't know what got into her. I always took full responsibility for us breaking up. I never wanted there to be any misunderstanding about why we aren't together."

Maxine was impressed. She knew Steve was really close to his mother and defended her constantly. She suspected he knew about his mother's thoughts on her and Linda's relationship. She assumed he would support his mother by making excuses for her as he usually did. However, since he didn't react in that manner, she had to assume he was really maturing. Steve didn't know it, but the points were adding up in his favor.

Chapter 44

"Look baby I know it's past the time that I was supposed to be home. If you'll be a little more patient, I promise I'll be there in exactly one hour."

"No you look! I'm tired of sitting here alone. Since that stuff happened at the church, you're there more than you were before. I don't believe your promises anymore because they've been broken every day this week!"

"I know honey. I do. I understand you're angry. You have to understand my ministry is under fire here. They're trying to suspend me and I refuse to go down without a fight. Why can't you see that? Why are you being so unreasonable?"

"Unreasonable? Who's being unreasonable, you or me? You think it's reasonable for your wife to be alone while you're out with your other woman?"

"Other woman! I know you're not talking about Cassandra! Good Lord you should know better than that!"

"No, this really has nothing to do with Cassandra. The other woman in your life is Believer's Church, your ministry and anything or anyone related to it."

"Woman, are you crazy! You know this is something I have to do."

"Quite frankly, I'm tired of even talking about it. It doesn't do any good anyway. Do whatever you want. I'm done with it."

Marsha hung up the phone. She really didn't understand how Mitch couldn't see her point. When she thought about it, last year she had gone to visit some family in California and he called her every day trying to talk her into coming back early. Apparently, he missed her. When her flight landed, he was at the gate waiting for her with a bouquet of "welcome home" flowers. He even took the next day off to spend with her. It seemed their marriage suddenly took a turn for the worse when Mitch accepted the role of pastor at Believer's Church. What was supposed to be a tremendous blessing had somehow become a curse. She never saw him anymore and it wasn't okay. Apparently, he saw it as completely acceptable when he was the one who was unavailable. This was not going to work.

Marsha read an article in a magazine she picked up and realized her stomach was growling. Why wait for Mitch when it wasn't clear when he was coming home? Marsha placed the magazine on the table and slipped on her shoes. She glanced into the nearest mirror and found her face, which she'd made up to perfection in anticipation of the time she and Mitch were supposed to spend together this evening. Grabbing her purse, she made an instant decision to do more by herself since it appeared this was their new normal. Spending time with her husband was becoming foreign to her.

"Fellowship City here I come!" Marsha could already taste those fried shrimp.

Chapter 45

"Sir, how many in your party?" the hostess asked.

Eric looked around the restaurant for the face he wanted to see. He had been coming to Fellowship City most nights this week looking for her. He made sure to be there when he knew Mitch would be working late. Marsha typically found her way to Fellowship City when that happened. Realizing she wasn't there, but sensing she would be, Eric decided to get a table for two.

"I'd like a table for two please but, I only want it set up for one." As the waitress led him to his table, he recognized he couldn't seem too presumptuous. That's why he wanted to appear as though he planned to eat alone. He sat at the table and began to look over the menu. He had a taste for something different tonight. Something perhaps he had never tried. Placing the menu back on the table, Eric began to notice the size of the crowd tonight. This was an unusual number of people for a typical weeknight. He assumed there was something special scheduled that had all the people here tonight. At that moment, his eyes finally landed on the object of his search, Marsha had entered the building. He thought about what his next step should be. Should he wait to see if she perhaps noticed him and asked to join him? Maybe he should go to the door and offer her a seat at the table with him. She sat down on a bench in the waiting area. Apparently, there was a short wait for tables now. He decided to go to her, acknowledge her presence, and ask her if she wanted to eat with him.

Eric moved toward the bench where Marsha sat. He noticed the sad look on her face. It wasn't sadness so much as a look of fatigue. Marsha looked as though she'd had enough.

"Hi, Sister Marsha. How are you?"

"I'm blessed Eric. How about you?"

"I'm blessed as well Marsha. Why haven't they seated you?"

"It seems there aren't any tables available right now. I'm waiting for one to open up."

"Why wait? I've already been seated at a table and there's room for one more unless Mitch is coming."

"Mitch is still at the church," Marsha snapped letting Eric know there was trouble on the home front.

"Well, what do you say? Two saints can sit and break bread together."

"Well, I wanted to be alone with my thoughts tonight. I've got a lot on my mind and I probably won't be good company."

"If you change your mind I'm sure the waitress will tell you where I'm sitting. Have a nice dinner Marsha."

Eric began to move toward his table. Before he got past the hostess stand, Marsha apparently reconsidered.

"The wait is fairly long and I guess it wouldn't hurt to have some company. Is your offer still available?" Marsha really didn't want to eat alone even though she did have things on her mind.

"Come on sister. You can sit with me. In fact, it would be my honor."

When the two got to the table, Eric helped Marsha with her coat, pulled her chair out for her, and then seated himself. About the time the silence became awkward, the waitress approached to take their orders.

Chapter 46

"Steve, I have to admit I'm glad you came by."

"I wasn't sure if I would be welcome. I'm glad I came by too." Steve said with a smile on his face bigger than he'd had in months.

"Well, take care Steve. Again, I'm glad we talked. It helped me understand things a little better." Maxine began to move toward the door, hinting the visit was over. She cared about Steve, always had. As sincere as she was about understanding him and the things that happened, she still wasn't completely over the hurt and pain she had suffered because of his actions. She wasn't sure what Steve thought the result of their talk was going to be. She knew, however, they weren't on the same page about the outcome. That was obvious after looking at the smile he had on his face. That smile still caused her knees to buckle. She would've given him the world if she could have.

"Whoa! What do you mean take care?" Steve interrupted Maxine's train of thought. What he heard was "see you later!" What he wanted to hear was "baby I love you and I want you back in my life!"

"I mean it was nice seeing you and clearing the air. What else did you think it meant?" Maxine responded. She realized quickly this was not going to be easy.

"What? Are you asking me to leave?" Steve questioned.

"Well the visit is over isn't it?" Maxine shot back.

"Yes, this visit is over. What about next week or next month?"

"What do you mean, Steve? Don't beat around the bush!" Maxine's frustration was showing. It was obvious he was going to push her to her limit. This was definitely a different Steve. The old one would have let this go about five minutes ago. The new Steve didn't look like he was even close to running out of steam.

"I thought things were back to normal," Steve mumbled as he moved seductively toward Maxine who promptly backed out of reach. Steve tried once again to move toward Maxine. This time Maxine didn't move. He got close enough to her to see the different colors swirling through her lipstick. He saw her lip quiver slightly which he knew was her body language indicating she was somewhat afraid. Steve felt he had come too far. She kissed him when he first arrived. He now wanted to return the favor. He wrapped his arms around Maxine and pulled her so close he was able to feel her heartbeat. When she didn't resist, Steve decided it was time to move toward her lips. When he did so, he saw the familiar lip quiver but didn't let it hinder him. He barely got his lips to hers before she began to speak.

"Steve, I know you're sorry and everything. But, you broke by heart into a million pieces. Each one of those pieces still loved you but they were also full of pain. Not only did you hurt me but you also embarrassed me. I had to cancel all the wedding plans. I had to tell everyone I didn't know why we weren't getting married. You don't regain trust in a person this quickly. You just don't! Not with one conversation and an apology! And for you to think my pain is so quickly resolved hurts even more!" Maxine yelled showing the true depth of her feelings for Steve.

"What do I have to do Max? I don't even know why I try. I don't even think you're really all that hurt. Your love for me, if you really do, should cause you to be able to get over this." Steve struck back.

"Oh, you know it hurt me. You don't want to deal with the consequences of your actions. So instead, you're trying to make it my problem. As for what you can do, you can back off. No promises about what will happen between us. If you still really love me, you'll wait for me as long as you have to!"

"Alright Maxine, we'll do this your way. But you should know I'm not giving up easily." He kissed Maxine on the forehead and left. He wasn't sure about what was going to happen, but their relationship was not going to die because he gave up on it.

Chapter 47

Mitch walked into the kitchen from the garage. The garage that usually held Marsha's car when he came home no matter how late he had been gone. He knew he had been away a lot lately but he felt Marsha should have understood the call of God on his life. They had discussed it at length before they got married and she knew it was what formed a major part of his destiny.

"I don't know why this woman is giving me such a hard time God. I obey your word and I believe I'm doing your will. Why is she being so difficult? She has everything a woman could want!"

"Except she doesn't have you!"

Mitch was sure of what he heard God say but didn't think it made much sense considering it was His call he was pursuing. For that reason, he decided to ignore what he believed he heard and move on to the real issue at hand. Where was Marsha? It was a little after ten o'clock and his wife wasn't where she supposed to be at this time of night.

Chapter 48

"I really enjoyed dinner tonight, Eric. It was really a nice show too." Marsha said as Eric helped her with her coat.

"Yes it was Marsha. You know, God's anointing was all over those singers. I thought we were going to have some church up in here!" Eric responded happily.

"I thought so too. Maybe we can get them to come to Believer's for a mini-concert sometime soon. It would really help to uplift the congregation after all this mess is over with."

"I'll certainly mention it to the board and you mention it to Mitch and we'll see what we can do. It might do us all some good to get this situation off our minds. Of course, there's never anything wrong with praising God." Eric seemed to sing. He was so excited Marsha had spent some time with him this evening. He could hardly contain it.

"That's the truth. Well, thanks again for a fun evening Eric. I hope I won't be spending so much time alone. No offense but I could certainly have enjoyed my husband's company tonight. I'd better be getting home. Good night, Eric."

"Good night, Marsha and I didn't take offense to what you said. I'll see you soon." Eric said the expected sentiments because they were expected. What he really felt was he had to keep Mitch busy so he wouldn't have time to spend with his wife. He wasn't interested in Marsha as an intimate partner. He enjoyed her presence and it didn't hurt that she was gorgeous as well. He cared about her in the way a man should about a woman whether she was his or not, protective and concerned.

Chapter 49

Linda and Mark barely made it into Mark's apartment before their lips connected. Once inside, Mark began to touch Linda in an uncomfortable manner. Mark noticed her stiffen and wondered aloud " What's wrong baby?"

Linda backed away from him and looked him straight in the eyes. She knew why it made her uncomfortable but she wasn't sure she could or should tell him at this point. She quickly decided she needed to make her position clear so Mark wouldn't have to wonder what was going on with her. After all, she had accepted his marriage proposal.

"Mark, you remember how we got into this mess in the first place. How we ended up in a sexual relationship?" Linda asked cautiously. She didn't want to bring about the wrong response. Yet, she wanted to be completely honest.

"Yes, I remember. One thing led to another and we ended up in bed. That's normal. What's the problem?"

"Well, you should also remember it was not my desire. I always wanted to save that part of myself for my marriage."

"We're about to get married. I don't understand what you're trying to tell me."

"I have to be honest. I'm not sure we really are getting married. It doesn't feel right."

"But you said…"

"I know I said yes. I wasn't sure then but I didn't want to embarrass you. Mark I do love you deeply. I probably never stopped. I don't see going into a marriage without the benefit of being sure. I don't want to fall back into bed with you, even though I really want to, until I'm your wife. I assure you I am still committed to this relationship and I will definitely contemplate your proposal."

Mark fell into the nearest chair, feeling dejected. One hour ago, he had been so sure he would spend the rest of his life with Linda. She had said yes.

"Linda I really don't understand what's going on here. You say yes and it really means no?" Mark paused for a moment to regain his composure. He looked up, spoke through his tears, and said, "Okay, I'll accept what you're telling me But don't expect for me to back off."

Linda walked straight to Mark and lowered herself onto his lap. "I don't ever want you to back off." She passionately kissed Mark again to make her intentions clear. She slowly arose and headed to the door. She opened it and blew a kiss to Mark before she exited. She wanted to leave things the way they were for awhile at least until she could prep Maxine. She would have to warm her up to the idea of the renewed relationship with Mark anyway. She also needed some time to think. Though she forgave Mark and was still intensely in love with him, there was also a part of her that was unsure about the long-term security of their relationship. He abandoned her at a time when she really needed him. Would she be able to trust him not to do it again?

Chapter 50

Marsha pushed the automatic garage door opener and hoped Mitch wasn't home yet. She didn't know why she felt like she had to sneak. She had simply gone out to get dinner. Maybe the closeness she felt sitting there with Eric caused her to feel guilty. Perhaps it was because she wished she'd been experiencing that closeness with her husband. However, he wasn't available. It wasn't her fault. She had to eat regardless of who sat at the table with her. She also had to begin to live her life. Besides, Mitch was at the church all the time doing whatever he felt was necessary. She didn't know what that was but she wondered sometimes. He on the other hand never had to worry about what she was doing or where she was. Maybe it was good for him to miss her sometimes. Suddenly, she realized she had done nothing wrong and if she had dinner with Eric again, it shouldn't be a problem. As Marsha reached her conclusion, she looked up and saw Mitch's car in the garage. She pulled into the garage, gathered her purse and exited the vehicle. Before she stuck her key in the lock, she took a deep breath and said a brief prayer for peace and restoration in her home. After her prayer, she entered and turned on a light so she could see. Immediately she noticed Mitch sitting at their dining room table. He looked somewhat angry and perplexed at the same time.

"Hi Mitch. Is everything alright?" Marsha asked sincerely concerned.

Mitch didn't respond right away. He turned his angry and perplexed-looking gaze toward her. Neither of them moved. Marsha was actually afraid. She wasn't sure she had ever seen Mitch this way.

"Where have you been Marsha? Do you know what time it is? It's way past the time you, a pastor's wife I might add, should be at home."

Mitch's stare seemed to bore holes in Marsha's resolve to build a life outside of her marriage.

"What time did you get home? I waited for you so I know it was well after the time you promised to be home. Since I've decided to get a life so to speak, this will probably happen more often. By the way, I don't appreciate what you're apparently trying to imply when you said I should've been home before now. I'm a grown woman. You have no right telling me when I should be home just because I'm a pastor's wife. Now if you'll excuse me, I'm tired, I'm heading up to bed." Marsha moved toward the stairs to the upper level of their home.

"Wait honey. Let me talk to you. I'm sorry. You're right about being a grown woman and I had no right trying to tell you when you should be where. Honestly, I think I was a little thrown when you weren't here like you usually are. I'm sorry about not being around very much lately. It has to be hard on you and I never looked at it from your point of view." Mitch spoke in a whisper. He felt he scolded and found guilty.

"Yes it's hard. I'm struggling. I'm constantly looking for things to fill this void and yet I still feel empty. I've accepted every apology you've offered but what I want even more is to have you back as my husband. I miss spending time with you. I miss laying in your arms at night and late into the morning. Can you remember the last time we even ate dinner together?"

"It's been a while. By the way, you never told me where you were."

"I went to Fellowship City to have dinner," Marsha quickly stated deliberately leaving out the part about Eric.

"I feel really bad about you having dinner alone. I promise things will get better..."

"I didn't have dinner alone. It turns out Eric Howard was there as well and offered to let me sit at the table with him so I wouldn't have to wait for one. I thought that was nice of him."

"Yeah, that was real nice of him. Marsha I'm going to stay here for a little bit. I'll be up in a few."

"Okay, good night." Marsha went up the stairs to her haven. She had never seen Mitch act in that manner. He really didn't seem like her husband.

Mitch sat at the table thinking. He noticed Eric wasn't at the church tonight. Someone said he had a schedule conflict. However, that obviously wasn't the case. He'd had dinner with Mitch's wife. Now Mitch began to wonder what was really going on. Marsha seemed to be different. He decided he indeed needed to take better care of his marriage. Otherwise, Eric could step into his shoes and they might fit.

Chapter 51

"I sure hope those women don't show their faces today. It wouldn't be right." Mother Thomas sat on the Mother's row in the church waiting for the morning worship service to start. "God don't like that kind of ugly you know. They on a express train to hell I'll tell you."

Linda and Maxine sat in Maxine's car in the church parking lot. They decided that despite what people thought about them they would show up to give God the praise regardless.

"Max, are we doing the right thing?" Linda wondered.

"Absolutely. Why shouldn't we hear the word? Huh? Think about it. Who needs church more than some women like us anyway?" Maxine said with a laugh in her throat that soon escaped into the open through her mouth.

Laughingly Linda replied, "Let's go!"

Both women exited the car and looked to the other for support. Maxine signaled with her hand for Linda to put a smile on her face. They both walked toward the church with their heads held high and a confident stride.

Linda and Maxine entered the building and began to acknowledge some of the Believer's Church members as they did every Sunday prior. Every other time the response was positive. People always seemed happy about seeing them. Apparently, there had been a change. Their brothers and sisters in Christ were ignoring them. Some at least acknowledged their presence with a half-smile but no one spoke to them. It seemed as though they were attempting to respond without anyone else knowing about it. To make matters worse, they were laughing and talking with others. They were obviously ignoring them. It seemed as though they thought what they were doing was okay. Were Linda and Maxine supposed to accept this?

"Linda, keep walking. We really don't come here for them anyway." Maxine whispered in an attempt to encourage and refocus Linda who was standing in the foyer of the church with her mouth hanging wide open.

"I thought they loved me with the love of the Lord. I can't believe this. How could they believe all of those rumors? They should know me, the real me, by now!"

"Girl you can't depend on these people to do anything but be people. The only one you can depend on is God. Remember the word says He never changes. Other stuff around us is subject to change but never God. Now let's go to our seats. I don't want to miss one moment of Praise and Worship." Maxine said through clenched teeth so the others didn't know what was going on.

Chapter 52

Pastor Mitch and Marsha arrived at church in time to see Elder Howard getting out of his car with his robe over his arm. He smiled and seemed to poke his chest out as he moved through the parking lot greeting arriving members. Marsha wondered what was going on. Eric didn't sing in the choir and he wasn't the pastor.

"Why does he have a robe?" Marsha wondered aloud.

Mitch had wondered the same thing but quickly realized the answer, "I think he believes he's the interim pastor. That means he thinks he's going to preach this morning and that's not happening."

Mitch exited the car and quickly headed toward Eric. Marsha prayed all the way up until Mitch and Eric met face to face. At that point, she wanted to be aware of what was going on.

"Good morning, Mitch. I'm glad you're here to support me today. It's been a long time since I've brought the Sunday morning message but I believe I have a word from the Lord. That gives me all the confidence I need to squelch these butterflies I have fluttering in my stomach."

"Elder Howard, what do you plan to preach about today?" Mitch asked with a bit of obvious sarcasm.

"I'll let that be a surprise. By the way, do you have the key to your study? I need to get in there and settle myself before it's time for me to minister." Eric asked trying to peg Mitch's reaction.

"Sure, I have the key. Why don't I escort you there?"

"God bless you Mitch. Thanks for being so understanding."

Mitch and Eric headed into the church toward the pastor's study. Mitch stepped to the door and opened it with the key. The door swung open and Mitch stepped away so Eric could enter first. Mitch then noticed Marsha standing near the church's entrance they normally used and motioned toward her with his hand to give him a few minutes. Marsha was obviously unsure about what was going to happen and she really didn't want the two of them to be in that room alone. However, she felt peace in her spirit and walked to another office close-by to wait for the outcome of the confrontation she sensed was getting ready to happen. Mitch entered the office after knowing Marsha was okay and shut the door behind him.

"Mitch, this is a nice office man. Did Marsha decorate it for you?"

"Cut it Eric. You and I both know you're trying to force your way into being the pastor. You have a lot of nerves showing up here with a message and your robe. I didn't even know you had one."

"I didn't have one until now. I felt I needed it so the people would see me as a pastor even if it might be temporary."

"Might be temporary? Eric you are not the pastor of this church. As far as I know, you've never been. So I guess I'm not going to argue about how temporary it is or isn't."

"You heard what the bylaws say. You know you can't pastor this church right now. I didn't create those rules. Our church fathers did. If you don't like what they say you are certainly welcome to try to get them changed. However, today you're required to let me preside over the service. If you'll excuse me, I have to prepare for ministry. Pray for me." Eric seemed to dismiss Mitch. Mitch stepped outside of the office door searching for strength and wisdom for this situation. He got none. He made his way to the office where he knew Marsha was waiting. He entered the office. Marsha stood upon seeing his face. His countenance was dismal at best. Mitch closed the door and went to Marsha. Before he could open his mouth to tell her what was happening, he broke down and sobbed. Marsha stepped close enough to him to embrace him. She let him cry on her shoulder as he had so many times before. She didn't see it as a feminine act. Actually, she thought Mitch was stronger because he would cry when he was distressed. Which is apparently what he was experiencing …pain.

Chapter 53

Deacon Mays and half of the Deacon Board headed toward the pastoral study inside the administrative wing of Believer's Church. One of the deacons had gone to the study that morning, as was his custom, to see if Pastor Mitch needed anything. When he arrived at the study this particular morning, Elder Howard greeted him instead of Pastor Mitch. With a notebook and Bible in tow, Elder Howard asked the deacon for a glass of water with lemon and a towel to help with the sweat he believed he would shed while ministering. Without a word, the deacon turned, left the study and headed toward the room where the deacons were preparing.

"Lord have mercy on us today!" he said as he entered the room, "Elder Howard is in Pastor Mitch's office acting like he's the pastor. I don't know what is going on in his head. What are we going to do?"

"I thought he might try something like this. Where's Pastor Mitch?" Deacon Mays asked already moving toward the study.

"I don't know. I didn't see him or Sister Marsha."

The deacons arrived at the door to the study concerned, angry and somewhat out of breath because of the rush.

"Y'all let me talk. I think I can get to the bottom of this." Deacon Mays stated with authority and confidence.

Before anyone could knock on the door, Pastor Mitch and Marsha stepped out of the office where they had been asking God how to handle the predicament. They were peaceful and even smiled at the deacons who were obviously there to help them. They waved the deacons into their retreat and after everyone entered, they closed the door.

"Let's let him do his thing today." Mitch stated calmly.

"Do you two know what's going on because we still don't have a clue?" Deacon Mays asked.

Pastor Mitch spoke first, "Well you remember when the subject of the bylaws came up? You know, the part about me having to step down as pastor until this whole Cassandra problem is taken care of."

The deacon board collectively nodded indicating their remembrance of what Pastor Mitch was saying.

"Think about it. When we last met, we never told him we weren't going to handle things that way. He thinks he's stepping in for me while the investigation takes place."

The deacon board said in concert, "Oh!"

Marsha spoke up and said, "Instead of telling him and maybe causing a scene, we believe it would be wise to let him do his thing today. We can handle this later. The congregation doesn't even have to know what's going on. Whoever is running the service today can just say he's bringing the message and Mitch will resume his duties next Sunday. "

"I really don't want to give him any type of foothold but I love this church enough not to send it through any more turmoil. I agree with Marsha, let's get through today and deal with him later." Mitch agreed.

Deacon Mays lowered his head and closed his eyes as if in meditation. He stood silently for what seemed like several minutes. Suddenly, he raised his head and began to speak.

"I'm not sure that's the right thing to do. He might get the idea he can do whatever he wants. I think he needs to respect authority like everyone else."

The accompanying deacons began to talk amongst themselves. They were obviously in agreement with Deacon Mays.

"I repeat, I don't want to do this either. I think you all would agree that the congregation probably knows what's going on. Things are a little awkward as it is. I'm not sure talking to Eric is going to change his mind. We would probably have to physically force him to do what we wanted and I don't think any of you are willing to cause that kind of trauma to this ministry. I don't know what else we can do." Having said his peace,

Pastor Mitch allowed himself to drop into his chair. Visibly tired, he looked at the people around him. He loved being their pastor. Though it was challenging in the beginning, the group was finally beginning to mesh. Now that they had come into agreement with the vision, Elder Howard decides to pull a trick like this.

Again, Deacon Mays communicated his unwillingness to accept Pastor Mitch's arrangement. "Pastor, why don't you let me talk to him? I'll be clear about where we stand and tell him he has to forget about this idea he has about taking your place. If after I speak to him he doesn't comply, then we'll go along with your plan. I don't appreciate what Eric's trying to do here. Whether you all are behind me or not, I'll see to it he will meet with harsh consequences for the choice he made today. I promise you that."

Once again, the deacons spoke as one, "Yeah we need to handle this. Who does he think he is?"

"Well, someone better move now. I hear him leaving the study and heading toward the sanctuary." Marsha said softly.

Everyone except Mitch and Marsha moved quickly toward the door of the office. Whey they got out into the hall, all they could see was the movement of Elder Howard's robe as he went around the corner toward the sanctuary.

"Eric!" Deacon Mays called out.

Elder Howard turned around and looked at his friend. However, with a wave he kept moving eliminating any possibility of someone trying to talk him out of this. Deacon Mays turned around and saw Pastor Mitch and Sister Marsha standing behind the crowd of deacons holding hands in solidarity.

"Pastor, I tried. Let's have a word of prayer."

Chapter 54

"I can't believe those lesbians showed up today! I guess they need to Jesus too!" Mother Thomas spoke as Linda and Maxine stepped inside the doors of the sanctuary and moved toward their normal seats. The other church mothers glared at the women. They couldn't believe they had shown up today either.

At that moment, Pastor Mitch and Elder Howard met each other once again in the pulpit. Elder Howard had apparently waited out of reverence for the opening prayer before entering the sanctuary. After all, he didn't want to disturb the congregants by walking during the prayer. They would be shocked soon enough anyway. As the two men headed into the pulpit area, it was obvious to those who were observant there was tension between them. To those whom missed the tension, it became very clear there was a problem when each went to sit in the largest pulpit chair at the same time. Pastor Mitch gave Elder Howard a subtle nudge that Elder Howard immediately returned. The gasps of the congregation caused by the arrival of Sister Cassandra Williams upstaged the pulpit drama.

Dressed in pink from head to toe Cassandra was a vision of loveliness. The soft pink two-piece skirt suit had a slight metallic silver design swirling throughout the long sleeves and knee-length skirt. Obviously, cleavage and legs were unnecessary today and it showed in her wardrobe choice. The outfit was complemented by silver sheer hose and silver and pink shoes made from the same fabric as the suit. Diamond solitaires, set in silver, on the neck, wrist and ears completed the ensemble. She looked around at the members and noticed while most were obviously upset about her being there, some were just as obvious they were happy about her presence. She acknowledged those in the latter group with a simple "Praise the Lord" and continued on to her seat.

Cassandra's attendance in church today was not lost on Mother Thomas and the rest of the Mother's Board.

"Well we got us a regular three ring circus here today. One ring for the 'pink lynx' that just walked in, one for the two lesbians and one for the so-called pastor who's obviously going to bring the word. If I had known all of this was going to be going on I would have sold tickets and made popcorn." Mother Thomas remarked while chuckling at her own humor. As expected, the rest of the Mother's Board followed suit.

Pastor Mitch took the opportunity Cassandra's entrance provided to sit in the "big chair". Elder Howard, realizing he was not going to win the battle over the chair, sat in the next available chair. With everyone seated, the praise and worship team stood up to lead the people into the presence of God. The team members stood behind their microphones and the musicians were standing with their instruments.

As the praise began to flow, Maxine began to dance in the aisle. She knew people were watching her but so what? If they realized how good God was they would be wearing out the carpet too. All of a sudden, Maxine felt an urging. She knew she was holding some anger towards Mother Thomas however, she felt it was justified. She really didn't want to do it but she felt led to go to Mother Thomas. She didn't know why God would lead her to do that. There was nothing for her to say to the woman. Mother Thomas had intentionally attacked Maxine and Linda with her lies. Maxine decided God would have to send someone else. This time, she would tell God "no" and deal with the consequences.

All of a sudden, Mother Thomas began dancing in the aisle and bumped into Maxine. She seemed as surprised to be in the aisle as Maxine was she was there. The two women stopped dancing before the Lord and began to stare at each other. Finally, Linda, unsure about what her friend might do, came into the aisle and looped her arm through Maxine's arm. In an instant, Maxine knew Linda heard from God as well. They both knew what they had to do.

"Mother Thomas, we need to tell you that what you have accused us of was very hurtful. It's also untrue. We have forgiven you and are continuing to pray for you." Linda declared.

"Mother, we don't know why you said those things but we forgive you. God bless you." Maxine added after she realized she had no other choice. She meant it though she didn't want to say it to the woman who was intentionally trying to tear her and her friend's reputation down.

Mother Thomas heard what the women said and felt something stirring on the inside of her. Something she hadn't experienced in years. She wasn't quite sure how she should react. The women seemed so sincere and returned to worship, dancing joyously. Mother Thomas remembered when she was so joyous. She remembered when her salvation was a source of bliss. She realized her joy had disintegrated and she hadn't really been happy in years. However, these women needed to know they were the ones who needed forgiveness.

"Sisters" Mother Thomas began, "I want you to know you need to be seeking your own forgiveness. Homosexuality is not acceptable to God and it's not acceptable to me. I don't know why you're forgiving me. I haven't done anything but try to save your life from the pit of hell. What did I do to you that you need to forgive me for?" Mother Thomas questioned Linda and Maxine who kept on praising the Lord in dance. When Mother Thomas realized they were done with the conversation she stated, " I thought you two would see it my way." Little did she know it was God who was nudging her to repent for her being so judgmental.

Chapter 55

The deacon board came to the front of the church to facilitate taking the tithes and offerings. After the prayer, the ushers began to direct the people from their pews to the front of the church to give. Pastor Mitch took this as an opportunity to speak to Elder Howard regarding what seemed to be the "hijacking" of the pulpit this morning.

"You are out of order!" Mitch whispered so only Eric could hear him.

"I don't know why you're still fighting this Mitch. We have to do what the bylaws say. You're the one who put yourself in this predicament." Eric countered glad he had the church's foundational documents behind him.

"You're so busy talking about what's supposed to happen and you don't even realize the board decided there isn't a need for a temporary replacement for me."

"What are you talking about? The bylaws clearly state that …"

"That's right. I'm keeping my position while we go through this farce of an investigation. The board doesn't support what you're doing and if you decide to go through with this anyway, there will be consequences. If I were you I would get up, go to the back and remove your robe. If you decide to come back to the sanctuary you'll sit with the rest of the church officers." Mitch decided to give Eric one more chance to fix his mistake.

Eric thought about the situation. He had no warning the board found a way around the bylaws. He might've done something different if he knew. However, since they didn't inform him of their decision, he wasn't sure there should be any repercussions because he followed protocol. If he decided to go ahead and preach his message, he didn't know what would happen. If he backed down, he felt they would always feel they could push him around. With the offering almost complete, he needed to make a decision quickly.

Marsha, noticing the brief but intense conversation between her husband and Elder Howard, began praying immediately. She didn't know exactly what her husband said, but she knew by the expression on his face he wasn't wishing Elder Howard well. She thought Mitch was convinced God wanted him to allow Eric to do whatever he needed to do and deal with him later. Obviously, that was no longer the case.

Marsha was concerned about what was happening. She looked around the congregation to see if she could see any sign they had noticed the conflict. As her gaze flowed over the people of God, her eyes landed on Sister Cassandra. Immediately, her mind went back to the dream she had about Cassandra and the man. She remembered the look on Cassandra's face in the dream because it was very similar to the look she had on her face that very moment. Though this woman had caused her and her husband a tremendous amount of pain, she felt strangely led to pray for her. Marsha closed her eyes and prayed that God would heal this woman emotionally and spiritually. She asked God to bring her to a place of repentance so Cassandra could be all God called her to be. Marsha also made sure she forgave Cassandra for the lies the woman told on Mitch. Marsha completed her prayer in time to see the deacon rise from his seat to introduce the speaker for the morning.

"My brothers and sisters, this is the day that the Lord has made. Let us rejoice and be glad in it. God has given us a beautiful morning today. What we need to remember is regardless of what happened this morning before you got to church, God is worthy of our praises. Despite what has gone on since you got to church, God Himself made this day. He knew before the foundation of the earth what you were going to face. Our Heavenly Father knew all of the problems you would have to deal with today. He was aware someone was going to do something sure to upset you. That stubborn child of yours wreaking havoc in your house this morning was no surprise to God. The fact you wanted to stay home today instead of coming out to the house of God was not lost on Him. Whatever is going on, God tailor-made this day. In spite of it all, God still expects you to rejoice. Rejoice because your name is in the Lamb's book of life. Rejoice because of the Blood. Rejoice because God is able handle all of the problems you could ever face. Somebody ought to say amen!"

"Amen brother! Preach!" responded the congregation.

The congregation's mouth said "Amen" but their faces said "huh?" Elder Howard was wearing the loudest and most colorful robe ever made. It was red white and blue. The left side was blue with a red sleeve. The right side was red with a blue sleeve. The sleeves were huge like someone had blown hot air into them and it almost appeared Elder Howard could end up flying away. Inside each sleeve were several pleats with the colors of the rainbow in the middle. As if that wasn't enough, there was a huge white tassel on the front and one on the back of the robe. It was truly a work of art. Elder Howard picked up his bible and his portfolio. Oh no, this wasn't a regular bible. It was the most humongous bible anyone had ever seen. It was only rivaled by Moses' tablets in size. The portfolio was red patent leather, obviously to coordinate with the robe. It was really quite a sight and it didn't get past the eyes of Mother Thomas and the Mothers Board.

"What is that get-up he's got on?" Mother Thomas asked her fellow Mothers Board members.

"What are you talking about?" Mother Young asked squinting her eyes trying to see the "get-up" Mother Thomas saw.

"What's wrong with you? You blind or something?"

"Now I'm not blind! Why you so mean? You know everybody don't see as good as you. Don't forget you and I both had cataracts. Your surgery must have been better than mine." Mother Young quipped in an attempt to get Mother Thomas straight.

"I'm not gonna argue with you this morning. I'm talking about Elder Howard. He looks like a patriotic peacock up there." Mother Thomas chuckled.

Deacon Tom finally finished his exhortation and turned to face Pastor Mitch to find out whom he should introduce. Mitch, in turn, looked at Elder Howard to see what his intention was.

"What are you going to do?" Pastor Mitch asked after leaning over toward Elder Howard to keep the conversation confidential.

"Mitch, I prepared a message and I believe God meant for me to deliver it today. I know you don't want me to do this. I'll just have to deal with whatever happens after I'm done. Now, excuse me, I have to minister to God's people." Eric stood and grabbed his huge bible and portfolio and headed toward the pulpit. He moved in a quick and decisive manner so Mitch couldn't fight him anymore on the subject.

"I want to present to you, Believer's Church, our very own, Elder Eric Howard. Please welcome him with a warm handclap."

Elder Howard looked around the sanctuary and noticed Marsha praying, the deacon board staring holes through him, and the rest of the congregation looking at him as though they were wondering why he was there. He decided to place his things on top of the pulpit but quickly noticed there wasn't enough room. He decided the only thing he could do without was the portfolio so he sat it in his chair, took his notes out and positioned them on the pulpit. Then he bowed his head in personal prayer. All of a sudden, he raised his arms to his side so fast it caused a slight breeze to stir and threw his head back as if to look towards heaven. The congregation let out a collective gasp. The Mother's Board collectively shook their heads in unison. He eased his arms down to his side slowly and then brought his head down as well.

"Good morning brothers and sisters." Elder Howard began in somewhat of an English accent. "I'm blessed this morning. God is an awesome God. He has blessed me to be standing before you this morning as your interim pastor. I'm sure Pastor Mitch will return as the full time senior pastor very soon. Until then, I'll be in charge. Therefore, while we are going through this process, you will call me Pastor Howard and you can contact me with any pastoral issues as you deem necessary."

Mother Thomas couldn't hold her peace any longer and yelled out "How did you get to be the pastor? I don't know what's going on but you are not my pastor and never will be. Don't you ever forget it!" As was their custom, the Mother's Board all agreed with Mother Thomas by nodding their heads.

Deacon Jones stood and made his discontent obvious, "Eric you've been an elder all this time and you seemed to be happy. What's going on? You're acting like you done lost your mind!"

Elder Howard began to sweat because of the effort required to maintain his composure. As he looked around at the faces of the people around him, he realized there were no supportive looks coming from anyone in the sanctuary. He thought the congregation would accept him in this role because they all knew what Sister Cassandra accused Pastor Mitch of doing. Elder Howard anticipated the congregation would be appreciative that Pastor Mitch was not in control right now. Nonetheless, they would have to get over it. Regardless of what Pastor Mitch and the rest of them decided, he fully intended to be pastor as long as possible.

"I'm not going to explain what's going on." Elder Howard said obviously losing some of his confidence and his accent. "I don't think it's appropriate for me to talk about it right now. So, why don't we just put this issue for now and enjoy the word God gave me for today. Okay?"

"Mothers, let's get out of here. I refuse to sit up in this church building and deal with this mess. If we go now, we can make it to my sister's church across town to sit in a real service!" Mother Thomas gathered her things and began to move out of the row. She noticed the rest of the Mothers Board weren't moving. Once she gave them the "eye", they all immediately began to gather their things and stood up as if to wait for further directions. When all of the Mother's were ready, Mother Thomas led the way as the group moved toward the door and left.

Suddenly it seemed the rest of the church's inhabitants emerged from the shock of what was going on and began to leave as well. Some left quietly while some left with shouting and yelling. Before long, the sanctuary was empty except for Pastor Mitch, Sister Marsha, the board and the deacons. Eric didn't even had a chance to start his sermon. Worse than that, he didn't know what was going to happen next.

Pastor Mitch stood and began to applaud Elder Howard. "Bravo Elder! Did you mean to clear the temple?"

"Mitch, you know that's not what I meant to do. I don't understand what happened. I believe I heard from God and got a word from Him for today. Then everything fell apart." Elder Howard dropped into the nearest pulpit chair and dropped his head into his hands. There was so much riding on him ministering today.

"Eric, here's the problem." Mitch sat down in the chair next to Eric and leaned forward with his elbows coming to rest on his knees. "This is not your time. You want it to be your time really badly but you have to wait on God. You also can't push yourself into the place you want. God will place you where He wants you in His own time. You have to trust God and wait on Him. He'll bring it to pass when you're prepared and when the people are prepared to receive you. Today wasn't that day Eric. I think it's apparent based on the outcome."

"But God spoke to me. He's the one who gave me this message and told me to preach today." Eric replied in tears.

"It may have been your mind telling you exactly what you wanted to hear. Is it possible you mistook your own mind for the voice of God?"

"I guess when you look at what happened it could have been my will and not God's. But why did God give me this message?"

"Elder Howard, what was your message about?"

"I was going to talk about authority. I wanted the people to understand that authority comes from God. Since I'm the interim pastor, I wanted them to see it was God who put me in this position so they would have to accept it."

"I think God was trying to speak to you about authority. What you've done here is you've usurped my God-given authority. God desires us to do things decently and in order. You were clearly out of order. That's why God didn't bless it."

Eric sat there and thought about what happened for a few minutes. He really messed up. He realized he may not have heard from God and had definitely walked outside of His will on this. Not only had he disappointed God he had disappointed himself as well. However, he could reconcile with God and he would eventually forgive himself. Eric knew his problem was with the deacons and the others who were standing around waiting to pounce on him in his weakness. The elder lifted his head and began to look at their faces. His eyes landed on Marsha. He had done what he promised himself he wouldn't do; that was to make Marsha sad. She was due an apology from him. The next time he saw her alone he would give her a personalized apology. Everyone else could wait. Eric knew he was in big trouble.

Deacon Mays took this lapse in the conversation to speak. "Elder Howard I am really surprised and disappointed in you. You have been in leadership in this church since the beginning and you should have more wisdom than you exercised today. The board will meet Tuesday afternoon to discuss what the penalty for your actions will be. Please don't attend because the board needs to be able to talk freely and make a decision that is not influenced by your presence."

"Brothers, I apologize from the bottom of my heart for what I've done. I never meant to hurt this ministry. It would be like me doing harm to myself since I'm a part of this church body. I'm asking for your forgiveness. I simply made a mistake like the rest of you have at one time or another, " pleaded Elder Howard. He was really begging to hold onto the only meaningful thing he had left in his life. Working in the church, after the death of his wife, became his lifeline.

"You should have thought about that before you pulled this trick," responded Deacon Mays. "You have caused a huge amount of confusion today. Your mess sent every member of this church home or to another church. We don't know who came today with a serious concern or problem and went away unchanged. I consider that justification for a serious consequence."

"Okay let's stop the debate. Eric, everything Deacon Mays said is true. We don't know what the full impact will be yet. This could be very problematic. However, I pray God will restore anything that was lost today. On the other hand, I'm reminded of a scripture where Jesus spoke to the crowd who wanted to stone a woman who made a mistake. He challenged them to look at themselves before they judged her. He was trying to teach them that none of them was without sin. He let them know the only way they should be so willing to punish this woman's sin is if they were without sin themselves. Jesus, the only one who was sinless in the crowd, showed mercy and released her from the punishment due her." Marsha, who understood exactly where her husband was going with this, joined Mitch.

"Men of God," Marsha began "we need to remember God loves us all even though we make mistakes too."

Mitch continued, "Here's what I feel led to do here. I don't think we can ignore what happened. I believe each of us should go home and seek God about a resolution. I want you all to extend the grace to Elder Howard you would want extended to you. Everyone, you're dismissed and we'll gather together again on Tuesday to deal with this."

Marsha rushed to catch Eric to speak to him about all that had transpired. When she finally caught him she said, "Everything is going to be okay. Don't you worry."

"Thanks Marsha. I don't think everyone else feels that way but I'm glad you do. Pray for me." Eric smiled as he spoke. He appreciated her support considering she was going through so much.

Though Marsha's show of support was the right thing to do, Mitch didn't like it. He thought to himself "she should be supporting me and there she is having his back." He wondered, once again, if anything was really going on between the elder and his wife. Noticing the closeness developing between the two gave Mitch a bad feeling. He would continue to keep an eye on this relationship to ensure that everything was as it should be.

Chapter 56

"Hey, Linda. How are you?" Steve asked hoping to enter the house where Maxine and Linda lived.

"Hi Steve. I'm doing really well. I haven't seen you in a while." Linda wondered how Steve found out where she and Maxine lived. She also silently prayed Maxine wouldn't put up a huge fight when she found out Steve was there.

"Is Maxine home? I would really like to see her."

"Yes she's here. Let me see if she's available."

"Linda, before you get Maxine, can I ask you something?"

"Sure."

"Is Maxine seeing anybody? I'll be honest with you. I really want to get back together with Maxine. I never stopped loving her and I'll do anything I can to get our relationship back."

"Look Steve. I can't say what you should or shouldn't do to get Maxine back. All I can say is that you hurt her badly. I don't know if Maxine can get over what happened enough to allow you back into her life."

"I didn't mean to put you in a bad position. I saw you and Mark the other day outside of Fellowship City and you two looked like you got things back together somehow. I thought you might be able to give me some advice about what I could do."

"Whatever you do don't tell Maxine about seeing me and Mark together. She doesn't know about that yet and I want to tell her when the time is right." Linda whispered her request to Steve. She really hadn't planned on telling Maxine about her renewed relationship with Mark so soon and now she had to worry about whether Steve would tell her out of desperation trying to get Maxine back. Somehow, she had to change the subject and hope Steve wouldn't tell.

"I will tell you this much. I know Maxine loves you. I don't think she ever stopped either. Maxine isn't going to be willing to open herself up to you very soon because of the pain you caused her. But let me tell you something you may not know. Once Maxine loves you, she always will. Regardless of how you treat her she will always love you. She keeps up this hard exterior to protect herself. If you can hang in there, you will probably get the response you're looking for. I think you're a good brother and I know you really love my friend. I want you to know I'll be praying for you. I'll go to get Maxine for you." After hugging Steve, Linda walked away from him in order to see if Maxine would come out to talk to the man who was trying so hard to win back her love. How romantic she thought.

"Max, I want you to take a deep breath. I need to tell you who's in the living room waiting for you." Linda was so excited that Maxine didn't know if she could really take knowing who was there to visit her.

"Alright girlfriend. Who is it?"

"It's Steve."

"Okay, tell him I'll be right out. I need to freshen up a little bit."

"Is that all? I can't believe that's the end of it! What's going on?"

"Okay, I'll be honest with you. I've seen Steve since we saw him at church. He actually came over here and we talked. I figured he would come back. He has become a very determined person since we've been apart. I don't know what I'm going to do about it yet so don't even ask me."

"Say no more. I'll tell him to make himself comfortable." Linda responded with the hope that Maxine would be as lenient with her once she got up the nerve to tell Maxine about Mark. "

Chapter 57

Fellowship City was standing room only after church. People were milling around outside, leaning against the wall and the planters at the curbside outside of the restaurant.

"Babe, let me go inside and see how long we'll have to wait to get in here," Mitch said as he worked his way through the crowd. He really didn't want his wife to have to prepare dinner today after all that had transpired at church.

"Honey, you know we won't be able to get in soon. Look at all these people. Why don't we go home and I'll just whip something up. We'll probably get to eat sooner that way." Marsha wasn't sure why she sensed desperation in her husband's voice and even more so in his actions. She quickly decided to follow along and allow her husband to run the show.

"I don't want you to cook today. I want to be able to relax and have dinner with my wife. Is there anything wrong with that? You wait here and I'll go inside and talk to the hostess. There's no sense in both of us wading through this sea of people. Okay?"

Before Mitch was done with his statement he was already well into the crowd. Once inside, he headed for the hostess and asked her if she had any tables for two available soon. Her response was that it would be at least an hour before anything would open up for his party. Eric sat witnessing the conversation between his pastor and the hostess. He wasn't sure if he wanted to get involved and ask Mitch if he and Marsha wanted to join him at his table. Initially he had no intent of even making his presence known. However, when he remembered how Mitch stood up for him and didn't attack him, he thought differently. He also thought about Marsha and his attachment to her and quickly decided to ease Pastor Mitch's nerves and offer them a seat at his table.

"Hi Pastor Mitch. I overheard them say you won't be able to get a table for a while and I thought that maybe you and Marsha might want to sit with me. There's plenty of room and I would enjoy your company. Actually, let me buy you and Marsha's dinner. It would be my honor." Eric was being as sincere as possible. However, looking at the expression on Mitch's face didn't reveal any appreciation at all for his sincerity.

"Brother let me be frank with you. I know you and my wife have developed a friendship of sorts and normally that wouldn't be a problem. But, it occurred to me you might want to be more than friends. You seem to always be available to her and I'm not sure how that happens so often. I get the feeling you set it up somehow. I want you to remember Marsha is my wife. So no thank you. We'll either wait for our own table or we'll go elsewhere." Mitch then turned to leave Fellowship City.

"I thought we were okay, you and I. At church you seemed to be on my side!"

"I was being a pastor then. Now I'm being a husband. God bless you, Eric. I'll see you after the meeting Tuesday."

When Mitch got outside, he grabbed Marsha's hand and quickly led her to the car. After all, he didn't want her to see Eric Howard and start the questioning him right there on the spot. He never imagined he would be fighting so much in one day. Actually, he never thought he would be fighting for his marriage.

Chapter 58

"Hey baby!" Linda cooed into the phone after she heard Mark answer the phone.

"Hi. What can I do for you?" Mark wasn't prepared to hear Linda's voice when he answered the phone. He was still angry with her because of how she handled his marriage proposal. He hadn't planned to talk to her until he decided what his next step would be.

"You can tell me what's wrong with you."

"Look Linda. I really don't want to talk to you right now. Can you respect that? I need some time."

"Time for what Mark? You came back into my life, I gave you my heart, and now you want space? What's going on?"

"I feel like you played me. You accepted my proposal in front of all of those people. They think we're getting married. They don't know you turned around and told me something different. That's unfair to me because now I have to explain this every time someone asks me about it. I don't even understand it fully myself. What do I say to them?"

"Is this about what other people think? This is my life we're talking about and all you're thinking about is what other people think."

"That's who you were thinking about! By the way, it's my life too! You think you're the only one whose heart is in this? You know what? You don't think about anybody else but yourself. How do you think I feel? Huh? Well, since I know you didn't think about me, let me tell you. I feel like my heart has been pulled from my chest and stomped on with no regard for how badly it would hurt. That's why I can't talk to you right now. So since I've answered all of your questions Linda, I need for you to think about my needs right now and say goodbye." Mark was angrier than he even thought. He hoped he hadn't come down too hard on Linda but she needed to understand he had feelings too. He had handled her delicately with her when they were working through their issues about the baby but that was over. This situation did not require the same care. He would deal with any fallout later. Now, he had to think about his own feelings.

"I'm sorry to bother you. I thought maybe you and I could talk for a while. Since it's obvious you don't want to talk to me, I'll respect your wishes and let you go. I guess I should say goodbye for good in case I don't ever talk to you again," Linda didn't know how to handle Mark when he was this forceful. She loved him and didn't want to lose him. Mark was right. She had only thought about herself once again.

"Don't go getting all dramatic on me. I didn't say anything about goodbye forever. But, I would really like to get off the phone before I say something I'll wish I hadn't said. Take care. Bye." Mark hung up the phone without allowing Linda a chance to say goodbye. He had already begun to hear the hurt and pain in her voice and didn't want to hear it swell up even more when she said "bye". It was hard for him to take a stand for himself. He had pined for Linda so long he didn't want to do anything that might chase her away. He wanted her in his life, which was why he proposed. Regardless of his love for her, he had to remember to love himself as well.

Chapter 59

"What is wrong with you Mitch? You've been acting funny since we left Fellowship City." Marsha was highly upset with Mitch because he was acting like a madman this afternoon. She understood her husband sometimes got overly upset about things and reacted passionately.

"Just because I'm not bouncing around on my tail like some cartoon character doesn't mean something's wrong with me! Sometimes I don't feel like smiling and acting happy. You should certainly understand that Marsha! You're not always a joy to be around yourself, let me tell you!"

"Alright Mitch. I see you aren't ready to tell me what happened. When you're ready, your majesty, maybe you'll honor me with an explanation for why you're treating me like this right now. In the meantime, would you like some dessert? I prepared some strawberry shortcake before we went to church this morning. How about I fix you up a big bowl and cover it with a huge mound of whipped cream? Go get comfortable and I'll have it ready for you."

"Marsha, don't tell me what to do. I'm not going to change and have some strawberry anything. I want you to leave me alone. I'll be in my study and I'm not taking visitors or phone calls." Mitch then stomped up the stairs and to the back of the house so he could go into the study and do whatever he felt he needed to do. He always kept a few sets of clothing in the study in case he needed to change and didn't want to disturb Marsha. He went into the study, changed his clothes and retrieved some bottled water he kept in a small refrigerator and his Bible.

Opening the bottle and turning on some music, he tried to figure out why he was acting this way. When he saw Elder Howard, it set him off. Probably because he was upset about what was happening between him and his wife. That also left him with a question in his mind about Marsha and Eric. Was he just innocently keeping Marsha company so she wouldn't be so lonely? Admittedly, he had been an absentee husband and he was jealous of the fact Eric had the time to spend with Marsha. Mitch simply didn't make the time. He had to bear the bulk of the blame.

He needed to cut some of the church business out and make more time for Marsha. However, he still needed to deal with Cassandra and her lies, which would take up a lot of time. Mitch was in a position where he felt he needed to be very visible and involved in order to show he was willing and able to pastor Believer's Church. The balancing act between the church and Marsha would be somewhat challenging. The problem was he couldn't possibly do both well. He didn't want to stop doing any of the things he was doing at the church. After all, he was the pastor. Mitch also didn't want to neglect his relationship with Marsha either. This was definitely a huge predicament.

Then Mitch realized regardless of Eric, he could be relatively certain Marsha would remain in his corner. Since the investigation and all that went along with resolving the "Cassandra" problem would only take a few more weeks at most, perhaps he could do both. He could potentially take care of the church business and keep his marriage going by spending whatever time he could with Marsha. He would be content in being able to hold the church together. Marsha would be happy with the small amount of additional time he would eek out of his schedule. Everything will work out okay, he thought. Won't it? Suddenly, Mitch had a thought. It wasn't clear where the thought had come from but he somehow knew it wasn't his own thought. *Think about your motives, son. Seek me. You'll find the answers you are looking for.*

Chapter 60

Marsha sat in the chair in their family room watching her favorite television preacher on their wide flat-screen TV. It was a gift from Mitch's parents for one of their wedding anniversaries. Her in-laws always thought anniversaries were very special occasions, right up there next to the actual weddings in importance. When she and Mitch reached their tenth wedding anniversary, Mitch's parents gave them the television.

How could Mitch have come from a family who truly valued marriage yet handle his marriage the way he did? It seemed he valued his ministry, the church and his image more than he did the state of his marriage. It was funny how they had come a long way in their marriage but still had some hills to climb. This particular hill, the one they were facing now, was probably one of the most difficult to climb. The time when his ex-girlfriend wanted him back after they were married didn't compare to what Mitch and Marsha were going through now. Moving to a different state, leaving all of Marsha's friends and some family, in order to be closer to Mitch's parents and grandmother was no big deal compared to this. This particular problem was somewhat of a Marsha versus God thing. Mitch honestly thought he was doing this whole thing for God. Apparently, Mitch didn't understand that God would never put us in a situation He knew would tear up our marriage. Did Mitch really think everything else was more important than their union? There had been times since he became a pastor when she would have responded with a resounding "no". More recently, the answer was an even more resounding "yes"!

Marsha's thoughts went to Eric Howard. She remembered how well he treated her and how much fun they had at Fellowship City. She couldn't remember the last time Mitch had shown her a good time. They hadn't even gone out for a night on the town lately. The focus was all on the church. She briefly considered going over to Fellowship City now and perhaps seeing Eric there. Mitch would be in his office for most of the evening since he was upset. She could probably make it there and back before he even knew she was missing. What are you thinking Marsha? You can't go looking for Eric! She was so lonely she'd begun to let her thoughts wander. Her mind was desperately searching for a balm to ease the hurt and loneliness she was experiencing.

Marsha felt an overwhelming desire to pray. She needed to give all of this to God once again. Hopefully, she would leave it with him this time. Marsha had prayed for a few minutes when she felt a presence in the room. Her husband Mitch had joined her on her knees in prayer. It was like they both knew what they needed to pray about and went about doing it as though they planned it. When Marsha stopped, Mitch picked up the prayers and continued. When he stopped, Marsha returned to leading the prayer. She began to pray for Cassandra because she had continued having disturbing dreams about her. Marsha noticed Mitch didn't participate very much where that prayer was concerned but he didn't stop her. When they were finished a lot of time had passed but they each felt a new level of closeness to each other and God that wasn't present before.

"Marsha, I'm so sorry. I have neglected you and not made you a priority. God is not pleased with that. I promise I'll do better. I don't know how to do it yet but I'm going to ask God daily for direction. Don't lose patience with me because I love you Marsha." Mitch was still on his knees speaking to his wife. He hadn't planned to express himself that way but it seemed to have poured out of him.

"I have waited so long for you to change your way of thinking about us. I know you have a charge to pastor this church and I respect that. The question is do you understand your responsibility for this marriage. I forgive you Mitch. I love you!"

"Thank you baby. You won't regret not giving up on us. By the way, I heard you praying for Cassandra. What's that about? She's a big part of the problem, you know. That woman is a liar and a manipulator. I can't continue as her pastor after this. She's going to have to find another church." Mitch waited patiently for a response from Marsha. He was angry about the inconvenience of the "Cassandra and Eric" issues.

"Mitch, you can't put her out of the church. You have to pastor the people God sends to you. I've been having dreams about Cassandra that haven't been pleasant. I really don't know why she did this to you and Believer's Church. But I do have a feeling there's much, much more to this story than meets the eye."

"Cassandra knows exactly what she's doing. She has plotted and planned against me ever since I told her she was not called to be a minister."

"Whatever is happening with Cassandra may be a secret to her as well instead of a deliberate plan she cooked up. I've been praying intensely for her lately. Right now, she's still a member of Believer's church and we have a duty to meet her needs where we can. I know you're angry but if you're going to continue to pastor, you can't react like this. The bottom line is you can't expect people to be anything but people. There will probably be many more situations like this in the coming years and your response can't always be to kick people out of the church."

"You're right Marsha. That's something I'll have to work on. I'm going to trust you on this and keep an open mind. Why didn't you tell me about these dreams anyway? I am Cassandra's pastor you know."

"I felt I needed to be the one to pray for Cassandra. I think it's a woman thing if you know what I mean."

"Alright, I'll let it go. Let's go have some of that dessert you fixed."

Chapter 61

"Hi baby!"

This was Steve's acknowledgement of Maxine's presence in the room. Steve had always spoken to her that way because he'd always seen her as his baby. Steve cherished and cared for her. He wanted her to know she could always depend on and trust him. Yes, Maxine would be his baby again. He would see to it.

"Hi Steve, " Maxine responded elatedly. She was sincerely ecstatic Steve still desired to pursue her. Actually, his persistence tickled her heart and awakened it to the love Steve was showing. She wasn't sure, but she felt like she might be falling in love with Steve again.

Maxine looked at Steve standing before her looking good, smelling good and being good to her in his own way. When he was out there involved with drugs and who knew what else, she was extremely worried about him. That concern covered the anger and embarrassment she experienced. Once she knew he was alive, the anger then revealed itself. This was the emotion Maxine felt when she saw Steve that Sunday at church. After they talked through things, her emotions shifted to those of tolerance, love and a desire to potentially reconcile with this man. She couldn't be obvious about her feelings yet. Soon he would know she wanted him in her life if he continued to pursue her as he had been.

"What are you doing here?"

"I came to see you. Is this a bad time? I know I didn't call first."

"No, you're okay this time but don't make a habit of showing up unannounced!"

They both chuckled and fell into the love seat. There was an awkward silence as they gazed at each other. Finally, Steve reached up and gently stroked Maxine's face. She closed her eyes in appreciation of his attention.

Though she had promised herself she wouldn't respond to him, she kissed Steve lightly on his cheek. Steve then coaxed her face toward him and kissed her more passionately. She acquiesced and Steve realized something had definitely changed between Maxine and himself. She didn't seem to hate him anymore and he wanted to know why.

" Max we need to stop." He didn't want to stop, but he knew it was necessary so he could get some clarity.

"Why?" Maxine had finally released herself to show her vulnerability and now he waned to stop? What's going on she wondered?

"I want to know why you're treating me like this. Not too long ago you almost hated me! Now you're kissing me like you love me!"

"I've been thinking about you and our relationship. I've also been praying about my attitude toward you. The next thing I knew God had truly changed my heart." Maxine was actually giddy about the transformation in her spirit. She was thankful God intervened and changed her outlook. She noticed Steve still didn't seem quite as happy. She wondered aloud, "Why? You don't want my affection? I'm not mad at you anymore, and you're questioning me? What's that about?" Maxine then scooted her body away from Steve in order to be able to observe him when he answered.

"Come on baby. You know I've loved you from the moment we met. I need to make sure you aren't going to flip on me again. You have to admit it's a whole lot different from the way you have been reacting with me. But make no mistake, I absolutely want to be with you for the rest of my life if I can!"

Maxine then scooted back toward Steve and allowed herself to exhale. She had been unsure of what Steve was going to say. She actually felt her emotional wall go back up for a second. When he explained himself, she felt the tension ease. She hadn't revealed herself to him too soon. After all, she didn't want to get hurt again if she could help it.

"So, what does all this mean for us Maxine?"

"Stevie, I would love to spend time with you but I think we should take it really slow. I do need to know, though, that you are completely free from the drugs and we can't tell Linda."

"Yes, I'm completely off of the drugs. Why can't Linda know?"

"I'll tell her in my own time but not now. I don't want her to get too excited thinking we're getting back together. We don't know what's going to happen and I don't want to let her down again."

"That won't be a problem but I think she might already know. She answered the door when I got here today. What's the big secret?"

"I want us to be able to see where this is going without someone else being inquisitive about what we're doing. I know that's how Linda is so I just want some time. Okay?"

Steve agreed and didn't have to wonder what her motives were. It didn't matter anymore. He actually had a second chance with Max.

Chapter 62

Eric moved through his house with the beat of the music he was playing in his home. He even sang along with the choir on the CD. He needed to hear uplifting music after the day he'd had today.

Eric reflected on the happenings of the day. First, he bombed at his first sermon. Then he'd been put on notice that he would be punished for acting the way he had. To top it all off, Mitch was upset with him. Why did Mitch think he had something going on with Marsha? They had only run into each other a time or two at Fellowship City and eaten their meals together. That's all.

Eric felt the stirring in his spirit and knew exactly what it meant. God was revealing to him what was really happening. He acknowledged he enjoyed Marsha's company a little too much. What was wrong with that? After all, she was a wonderful and very attractive woman. Then it became clear to him why time with Marsha was so important. It was a way to fill the void left by Eunice. But Marsha is Mitch's wife. It would be inappropriate for her to fill the spot in his heart left vacant by Eunice's death. Eric began to ask God for what he needed.

"Lord, I love my wife Eunice. I'm thankful You gave her to me for a time but I don't understand why You took her from me! I miss her so much. Lord, I need a companion. I don't need anyone to replace Eunice because no one could ever do that. I'm asking you to bring someone into my life I can go out to dinner with. I want someone who'll go to church with me and pray for me."

"It's about time you talked to me about this. I've been waiting."

Eric heard the still small voice but thought it was his imagination. Who else could have said that? God?

Chapter 63

"Momma? How are you today?" Cassandra had made it out of the church without too much notice because of everything that was going on. The response of those around her shook her and she needed to talk with her mother. The simple act of knowing her mother was listening to her always had a way of calming Cassandra no matter what the problem.

"Baby, I'm doing fine. God had me praying for you last night. That usually means something is going on with you."

"Well Momma, church today was real different. One of the elders took over the pulpit today. The people got upset and a lot of them left. They were yelling at him about what he was trying to do. The church mothers left and went to a different church. I think some people were so displeased they might decide to join other churches. I really felt uncomfortable with all of that going on while we were supposed to be worshipping God. I might leave too!"

"Cassandra, what's the real problem? I'm glad to know you're concerned about others but that's not how you usually operate. Tell Momma what's going on."

"I already told you what's going on. I don't like being around a lot of drama and I know I'm not alone. Church is supposed to be peaceful and not full of trouble."

"Now you know I love you but I have to be honest. Where there's a lot of drama we typically find you somewhere around. So, tell me the truth. Why are you so out of sorts?"

"I don't like drama! I'm shocked you think that about me?"

"Are you going to make me say it Cassandra? I was hoping you were mature enough to be honest with yourself. You thrive on a lot of attention. That's why you dress the way you do and why you act the way you do sometimes. Your father and I built our whole life around you because we wanted you so badly. We catered to your every whim and focused on you the way we thought we should. We raised a child who will not give up until she is right in the center of the limelight. You like getting things going where you can be the center of attention. I love you and I've been praying for you. When are you going to take some responsibility for your own actions?"

"Momma! What happened today didn't have anything to do with me. All I did was go to church like you always taught me to!"

"Okay Cassandra. What did you wear today? Before you even say it, I know you like to look nice and that's okay. But, how long did you stay in the mirror? Did you take extra time to insure everything was perfect? Did you get to church early or were you fashionably late? You don't even have to answer me chile because I already know. You made a grand entrance today and it didn't get you what you wanted. There wasn't enough attention to go around today with all the other stuff going on. Now you're upset because it didn't work"

"She's right you know."

Cassandra didn't have a response for her mother's statements. She began to feel the tingle in the pit of her stomach that said everything her mother said was true. She really was a bad person and couldn't stand it when she couldn't get the attention she craved.

"Are you there, Cassandra? I'm talking to you girl! Did you hang up?"

"I don't know what to say. I can't believe this."

"Don't play with me Cassandra. I'm saying this because it has gone on long enough. God laid you and this issue on my heart very heavily. I can hardly pray for anything or anybody else. Let's be honest. This is not about you dressing up for church or running a little late from time to time.What is your motive honey?"

"That's what I've been showing you. This is her voice but My words for you."

"This hurts Momma. I think I need to hang up."

"Sandra, come out of your denial. I know you understand exactly what I'm saying. God has a reason why He wants to heal you. He needs you whole because He has something for you to do. There is a God-given purpose for your life. The world can't experience it until you get yourself together. I'll let you go. I love you Cassandra." Cassandra laid her phone receiver back on the cradle, stretched out on her floor, and had a good old-fashioned temper tantrum.

"Okay God! What can I do about all of this now? I don't know any other way!"

" *My strength is made perfect in your weakness.*"

Chapter 64

Mother Thomas moved through her house cleaning and humming spiritual songs as she did most of the time. Those songs gave her comfort as she remembered her mother and her grandmother doing the same thing. She suddenly realized the songs they sang weren't very comforting or joyous at all. The melodies always ended up sounding sad and mournful. Mother Thomas' mind explored why her grandmother was so unhappy. Instantly she remembered Grandma Rose only sang sad tunes when Grandpa Howard was somewhere philandering. Otherwise, she was as happy as an ant on a picnic table. Actually, that was the case with her own mother and now she was following suit. Mother Thomas tried so hard to ignore the fact she missed Buddy. He wasn't solely her handyman. That man had given her some other benefits she hadn't realized.

"My Lord that man could sure make a woman feel good!" She reminisced over the good things in their relationship as she fanned herself. Like, how he would take care of her when she was ill. He even kissed her face when she looked like an alien because of an allergic reaction to some flowers he'd surprised her with. Then there were the times when they went out for a night on the town and he introduced her as his jewel, his baby, his everything. Buddy deeply loved her so she didn't understand where everything had gone so wrong. He was gay now. That showed how much he really loved her. It was good no one knew Buddy had moved in with his "man". That would surely be an embarrassment.

Mother Thomas jumped as the doorbell rang followed by a few knocks at the door. She was expecting the Mother's Board so they could have their monthly meeting and fellowship. Though she gave these women a difficult time, she enjoyed it when they were together. They were her only friends and she would do anything for them. The church mothers didn't need to know that little tidbit though. They might see her as weak and that would not be good.

"Hi ladies. Come on in here. Don't forget to take your shoes off y'all know I have white carpeting. Mother Brown it's good to see you today. How are you feeling Mother Goodwin? Praise the Lord Mother Moore."

As the women filed in Mother Thomas began to take their coats, hats and whatever else they had worn to cover themselves on the way to her house. Mother Young arrived with her fox stole complete with its head and paws.

"Aaaagh! Oh, I'm sorry. I didn't expect to see this thing. Did it get its shots Mother Young? Why'd you wear this thing over to my house anyway? You act like President Obama is coming to our meeting today." Mother Thomas bent over with laughter as the other ladies chuckled quietly with their hands over their mouths.

"There you go being so mean again. I'm tired of you always picking on me Mother Thomas and it's time someone puts you in your place! By the way, where's Buddy? You still have him locked up in the basement?" It was now Mother Young's turn to poke fun at her good friend. The other ladies, now seated, looked on at the exchange with surprise. Was Buddy really locked up somewhere in this house? Mother Thomas didn't find the comment funny and she dared her guests to think it was humorous.

"Mother Young I shared that with you in confidence. Now I see I can't tell you anything I want to keep a secret. No, I don't have Buddy imprisoned anywhere. He's out because we're having this meeting. He'll be right back after you all leave."

"That's not what I heard. I heard he moved out a long time ago. As a matter of fact, I think I've been seeing his car parked down the street in that man's driveway." Mother Young had a smug look on her face. She knew she'd hit her target because of the look of surprise on Mother Thomas' face.

The Mother's Board all leaned forward in their seats to hear what their leader's response would be. They missed hearing this rumor. They also didn't want to miss Mother Young get slapped for stepping out of line with Mother Thomas. Everyone knew better than to step out of line with her.

Mother Thomas could not believe her ears. How did Mother Young find out about Buddy leaving? She began to look around at the other women she considered her friends. How was she supposed to react? Did anyone else know about this? What else did Mother Young see or hear? Mother Thomas quickly regained her composure and prepared herself for what she was going to say though she didn't know what that would be yet.

"Mother Young, who would say such things about my beloved Buddy? We've been happily married for over twenty-five wonderful years. He visits his friend up the street sometimes. Why would people gossip about that? Actually, women of God, none of us should be involved in gossiping. What kind of church mothers are you if you talk about others without knowing whether your information is true or not? It sounds like we need to spend some time repenting instead of talking about the problems in our church today. That's what we really need to do. I'm going to get the snacks. Can a couple of you help me?" Whew, that was a narrow escape! Mother Thomas hoped this tongue-lashing would stop all discussion. She turned toward her kitchen and began walking. She suddenly realized no one was following her. Looking around the room, Mother Thomas noticed right away Mother Young still had that confident look on her face. It was painfully obvious she knew more.

"Alright, spill it. What else did they say?"

"Actually, Buddy ran into my husband at the hardware store and told him he moved out. Apparently, the man you say is Buddy's friend is much more than a friend. From what I hear, Buddy is in love with your neighbor. You couldn't even keep your own husband. Now who needs to repent?"

"This meeting is cancelled since Mother Young is obviously out of her mind today. Mother Young we'll start with you. Take this rabid fox you call a fur and get out of my house. The rest of you come get your shoes, coats and hats so you can leave too. I'm not even going to reply to that it's so stupid. I'll see you soon if the Lord is willing."

The Mother's Board reluctantly left their perches on the various couches and chairs in Mother Thomas' living room and prepared to leave. Everyone, including Mother Thomas, knew as soon as the group reached the street they would all share their ideas about the revelation they heard. Mother Thomas had headed up a number of similar curbside conferences herself. By the time today's street meeting occurred, Mother Thomas had collapsed in her favorite chair in tears. Mother Thomas felt a familiar urging and got up from the chair almost as quickly as she had landed there. She took her time, eased her way slowly to her knees and began to ask God for guidance. She missed Buddy tremendously. She treated him so badly and expected him to continue to stay with her. It wasn't her intention to run him right into the arms of another person especially a man. Should she let Buddy live his life out with that man or should she fight for him? Mother Thomas looked to God for the answer.

Chapter 65

Three long days had passed since Linda last conversed with Mark. Her goal was to leave him alone to allow him time to cool down. She planned to be gracious when he called to apologize and beg her forgiveness but that hadn't occurred yet. Linda left the house today for a long walk to clear her head and exercise her body. The next thing she knew, she was standing outside of Mark's door. Though unannounced, she needed to see him and find out where they stood. Linda was ready to fully forgive Mark and be his wife if he still wanted her. She had dreams about him the last few nights. Mark was standing at the altar in a white tuxedo and when he went to kiss the bride, it wasn't Linda. The thought of him marrying someone else disturbed her so much she woke up from her sleep.

Linda raised her hand and allowed it to land on Mark's doorbell. She heard the audible evidence of her action then Mark's footsteps heading toward the door. But it didn't open. Linda knew he was looking out of the peephole because she saw it go dark. Still there was no turn of the locks or pulling on the knob to indicate he intended to allow her to come in.

"Mark," she called, "I know you're in there. I need to talk to you!" There was silence after Linda's request. Undaunted she decided to continue trying to reach him.

"Honey, I'm sorry for the way I acted. Please don't hold it against me. I need to make things right with you no matter what you decide about us. I know I hurt you but let's try to work this out."

"Woman, I told you to give me some time," Mark replied. "Why couldn't you at least give me that much? You always have to have things your way."

"Look! I'm out here pouring my heart out to you in front of your neighbors and you think this is what I want to do? I care about you so much Mark I'm prepared to camp out on your doorstep all night if that's what it takes. I'll sing love songs and beg to get your attention. Don't try me Mark. I already see people peeping at me through their curtains and blinds. This could get ugly!" Once again, Mark responded with silence.

"Okay! Here's the first song of my medley!" Linda began by singing their song. It was romantic at the time they'd first heard it and she thought he might remember.

Mark listened to Linda singing. For the first time it was obvious she was extremely tone deaf. Yet, there she was, standing on his doorstep singing their song as if she was live and in concert. Peeping through the hole in his door, he saw her singing with her eyes closed and her hands moving demonstrating the sentiments of the song. What was he going to do? Mark was very aware of his deep and abiding feelings for Linda. Feelings, that no matter how angry he became with her, he couldn't deny. He was experiencing unfamiliar emotions. As Linda continued singing the song, he remembered the day they met. She looked so cute in her cut-off denim shorts and red t-shirt. She appeared so wholesome and carefree. They were both standing in long lines at the ice cream shop when a new window opened. Linda and Mark moved toward the open window but ended up bumping into each other. Linda apologized but Mark saw no reason to. He had intentionally moved into her path. When their eyes met there was electricity running between the two. When they talked about it weeks later, they each discovered the other had in fact felt it too. They knew from then on they were in love.

Linda went into the second song of her medley. Mark sat on the floor near the door to listen to the woman he loved sing of her love for him. He chuckled as she personalized the song with his name as well as hers. He moved toward the door but stopped short of grabbing the doorknob. Mark remembered the ache in his heart and sat down again. Linda deeply hurt him not once but twice. How much did she really love him? How could she do these things to him and yet really care about him? He wasn't sure if he wanted to put himself in a position to get hurt again.

"Mark, there's a crowd gathering. I might have to sell tickets. There's a front row seat available for you. Are you coming out or am I performing another selection?" Linda truly hoped Mark would come out because she was indeed making a spectacle of herself. She was surprised he allowed this to continue for so long.

All of a sudden, Mark opened his front door to the cheers and applause of his neighbors. He was amazed at the number of people gathered there. Linda ran toward him with tears in her eyes and the completion of a song on her lips. She kissed Mark lightly on his lips and then stood back to look at him. He looked perplexed and a bit worried. The reception was not what Linda had anticipated but she decided to shake off the unease his facial expression caused her and do what she knew in her heart she came there to do.

"Mark, I know I missed an opportunity to show you my love and devotion. When you proposed to me before, it caught me off guard. I was still in pain because of what we had been through and couldn't give you the answer you wanted at the time. Please forgive me for my immaturity and unwillingness to forgive. I've loved you since the day my eyes met yours and it would be an honor to be your wife. Mark, will you marry me?"

The crowd looked on with amazement in their eyes. The anticipation was thick enough to cut. It was really quite intense. With Linda standing in front of him looking even more gorgeous than she ever had before and the throng of well wishers positioned around them, he felt put on the spot. Mark realized this is how it felt when he'd asked Linda to marry him at Fellowship City. He loved this woman so much.

Mark embraced Linda tightly enjoying the feel of her body against his. He whispered his one-word answer in her ear, smiled at her and kissed her tenderly. After several minutes of holding each other, Mark returned to his abode leaving the crowd and Linda on his front porch.

Chapter 66

The Believer's Church board began gathering in the meeting room as the time for the meeting to begin approached. Pastor Mitch arrived while the men were still fellowshipping with each other over a light lunch. Marsha felt it was necessary to provide food because this meeting could last quite a while. Mitch agreed because he wanted to get all of this over with and didn't want to hold other meetings to resolve all of the issues at hand. They were responsible for determining the consequences for Eric, the allegations against Linda and Maxine, as well as Mitch and Cassandra. After everyone arrived, they sat down at the large table. Today was important because the conclusions drawn today would affect the direction of Believer's Church for years to come. There was a brief devotion and a heart-felt prayer asking God for the guidance in making the crucial decisions before them.

Deacon Mays began the meeting by reviewing the agenda.

"Let's talk about Elder Howard first. Brothers, I think we have to come down hard on Eric. He knows better than to do what he did. Our church will never be the same after that stunt he pulled. I've been getting calls since Sunday from confused and angry members. I believe I've been able to convince some of them we don't take their concern lightly. I informed them we would be meeting today to figure out what to do about Elder Howard."

The deacons all nodded and began several mini-conferences with each other about what they thought should happen.

Mitch began to speak, "I agree Deacon Mays but we have to remember that we must show mercy also. I want to do whatever God's will is. Did anyone ask God for His wisdom for handling this situation?"

Mitch began to look around the table and noticed not one of the men would look him in the eye. He realized they all wanted to hurry up and punish the man the way they saw fit. They really didn't care about what God had to say. Then, they heard an unexpected giggle that caught the attention of everyone in the room.

Out of thin air, Sister Cassandra appeared and stood, unnoticed by the group of men in attendance, at the head of the table.

"I know you didn't want me here but I had to come. I have to speak to you before I, before I, well before I leave this earth," Cassandra slurred, "Mitch didn't do anything to me. I set the whole thing up to get my way. In fact, I did some other stuff I need to confess. I don't want to meet God with all of this on my conscience."

The men began to look at each other and Cassandra with both confusion and concern on their faces. No on knew what to think or expect from Cassandra's attendance at the meeting. Everyone wondered about her obvious garbled speech and the fact she looked unkempt. Cassandra always looked exceptionally pulled together and neat, but that was not the case on this day. There wasn't a speck of makeup where there was usually an abundance of lipstick, blush, foundation and eye shadow. Her attire looked as though she'd been in it for a couple of days. It was also obvious that no water had touched her body in quite some time.

"Are you drunk Sister Cassandra?" Deacon Mays asked. "You're talking crazy like you're going to die or something."

"I knew it! She's on that stuff!" Brother Owen said.

"But she's not skinny like those other people on crack." Brother Wilkins observed.

"No, I think she's drunk." Deacon Crutchfield suggested.

"She needs Jesus!" another random voice responded.

Cassandra began to laugh as if she heard the best joke in the world. "I'm going to die real soon, brothers. You won't have to worry about me being a thorn in your flesh any longer. I took a bunch of pills before I left home. I don't want to cause any more pain. God knows I'm hurting so bad on the inside that I can't live with it anymore."

Cassandra began to sway from left to right and front to back as though she couldn't decide which way to fall. Deacon Mays reached out to catch her but missed as Cassandra swayed in the opposite direction. She swayed for the final time and fell face first across the meeting room table.

Several of the church leaders in attendance began to applaud as if this was just a tremendous performance. Pastor Mitch viewed the men and wondered why they were clapping. Obviously, Cassandra was having a breakdown of sorts as evidenced by her lying flat before them.

"What in heaven's name are you celebrating, brothers? This is clearly a cry for help and you all are clapping?" Pastor Mitch stood immediately and moved toward Cassandra to attempt to wake her. If she really swallowed some pills, she would need medical attention.

Pray for her, son! I can deliver her right now.

Mitch heard the words and knew it was God but, caught up in the moment, he didn't stop to consider the message.

Deacon Wilkins explained the board's outburst, "Pastor Mitch this woman is putting on a show. It's a cry for help all right. She wants our attention. This is how she's done it since she pressed her way onto this church board. If she can't get what she wants by asking, she'll make it happen by any means necessary. Get up Cassandra! The gig is up. We know you don't want to talk about what you accused the pastor of doing but we are determined to deal with it. So you might as well cut this little charade of yours short."

By this time, Mitch had already checked Cassandra's pulse and knew she was alive. He called out to the men who were present for their assistance "Someone call 911! I believe she really did take something!"

This announcement caused every one of the deacons, elders and other church leaders to stand and flee the room. It was a wonder that Pastor Mitch didn't fall victim to the stampede.

"Wait! Where's everyone going?"

"We knew Cassandra was trouble from the start and we don't want any parts of this!" said an unknown voice.

"I have warrants and can't be around when the police get here! I might end up back in jail behind all of this!" another voice said.

"If you know what's best for you Pastor Mitch you'll get out of here while you can! Save yourself!"

"What is going on around here?" Pastor Mitch yelled at the men as they ran out of the room.

Pastor Mitch pulled his cell phone out of his pocket and dialed 911 for emergency assistance. He informed the dispatcher that Cassandra appeared to be intoxicated but mentioned taking some pills. He didn't know what type of pills were taken if any. The woman continued to give directions to Pastor Mitch as to what he should do until help arrived. Pastor Mitch, knowing that help was on the way, hung up on the operator's instructions and went back to Cassandra. He decided to do what he'd always seen done on television when someone took pills. He pulled the woman from her position on the table and stood her up. He allowed her weight to fall onto his shoulder and began to call her name in an attempt to bring her back to consciousness.

"Sister Cassandra, " Mitch yelled shaking her at the same time, "Sister Cassandra wake up!"

Cassandra eventually began to cry and Pastor Mitch knew he was successful.

"What's wrong Cassandra?"

"I'm so messed up I don't deserve to live anymore. I'm a bad person."

"What makes you believe you're such a bad person?" Pastor Mitch continued walking Cassandra around the room as the two conversed.

"You don't have to ask me that question. You know what I did to you!"

"I forgave you right after you accused me. We can't hold onto grudges."

"Oh that's so Christian of you to say that you forgave me though I know you couldn't have. No one could overlook someone who does what I do. Not even God."

"If you ask God to forgive you He'll forgive you and forget it even happened. Why don't you confess it all to him right now?"

"You don't know who I really am. I'm so terrible if you look in the dictionary for the word wretch, you'd see my picture! I don't think God even wants to hear from me."

"Sister, you're His child aren't you? What parent doesn't want to hear from their child? He wants you to talk to Him. Don't you pray Cassandra?"

"Yeah I pray. I tell God what I want Him to do. I let Him know how to punish others when they don't do what I want."

Pastor Mitch decided that the best course of action in this situation was to ignore Cassandra's answer to his last question.

Tell her that I love her with an everlasting love.

"God loves you with an everlasting love."

Cassandra began to cry even more profusely. "No!"

"One of the most often quoted scriptures in the bible tells us just how much God loves us. In the book of John, it says that He loved us so much He sent His only Son to die for our sins. I know it's hard to fathom that kind of love."

"But that was before I started acting the way I do. God didn't know me way back then when He sent Jesus."

"That's not true either. God knew us before He formed us in our mother's womb. Read the first chapter of Jeremiah. Like Jeremiah, God brought you here for a purpose. Isn't that something Cassandra? Even though God knew you, He still allowed you to show up on this earth. He knew you were going to make some mistakes Cassandra. You are no surprise to God."

Cassandra attempted to sit in a nearby chair as the two walked past it. Pastor Mitch pulled her closer to him in order to insure that she would keep moving.

"Look at Paul in the New Testament. Talk about someone who did some bad things! Paul used to seek out God's people in order to persecute them."

"Sounds like some stuff I would do."

"You know what? God stopped Paul in his tracks while he was on his way to harass some Christians. God changed Paul. After that, Paul was a major part of Christianity. He wrote a lot of the New Testament. See, God can forgive people who make mistakes and use them to do His will. You are not that far away Cassandra. I don't think anyone can get so far away from God that He can't reach them."

"I hurt Pastor Edwards too."

"What did you do to Pastor Edwards?"

"He didn't deserve it like that other man did!"

"What happened Cassandra? Who hurt you?"

The emergency personnel entered at that very moment. They pushed Pastor Mitch out of the way just as he was making progress with Sister Cassandra. Who was "that other man"? He realized how disturbed Cassandra really was as they were wheeling her out of the church.

Chapter 67

Mother Thomas was in a rush to get down the street to where Buddy lived. She needed to get there and do what she'd planned to do so many times before. Mother Thomas had some serious questions for her husband and she had to ask them before she lost her nerve.

She loved Buddy. Resolving the issues surrounding his departure was necessary for her understanding and closure. The answers may not be what Ilene wanted to hear, but she would listen anyway.

Mother Thomas walked up to the gate that separated the house's property from the city's and opened it. She noticed there was mail peeking out of the mailbox. There was a letter addressed to her husband and his "friend". That one observation broke Ilene's heart even more. She had completely lost him. He was gone. Mother Thomas began to think that since she was too late there was no need to be on this doorstep. Mother Thomas hesitantly knocked on the front door anyway. Within a few seconds, the man who stole her husband answered the door.

"Is Buddy here? I'd like to speak to him." Ilene's words felt as though they'd never left her mouth but someone else had spoken them.

"What do you want," the man yelled at her, "You know that man don't want you anymore! Don't ever come here bothering us again! You've already messed up one relationship and I'm not going to let you destroy ours!" As the door began to close, a hand appeared stopping the door from slamming shut. It was Buddy.

"Man, don't you ever treat Ilene like that! She doesn't deserve your disrespect! I don't treat your loved ones that way and you're not going to treat mine like that! Now you owe the lady an apology and make it a good one."

Ilene heard all the words Buddy said but her ears held on to the words he used to describe her. She was one of Buddy's "loved ones". That meant he might still love her. While "old yeller" apologized to her, she pondered those words and what that could mean for her and Buddy. After Mr. Attitude was gone, Mother Thomas stood and looked deeply into Buddy's eyes. What she saw there was both suspicion and concern.

"Ilene, you've never come here before. Is everything okay? You know whatever I have is yours if you need it. Say the word and it's done." Buddy stood with both hands outstretched in front of him with his palms up. Ilene knew he always did this when he sincerely wanted to help her.

"Since you're being so generous I'm going to ask for what I really want. Why did you leave me? I know you mentioned some things the day you left but I think there's more to it. Actually, I know there is more you haven't shared with me. Please tell me the truth. Was there something I did?"

"Woman, you know I love you and always will. The problem is I don't know for sure that you ever really loved me. You said the words very rarely. It felt like you only needed me to help you around the house and to pay the bills. I wanted more from our relationship. So, did you love me? Do you love me?"

"I love you, Buddy! I always have and always will. I'm hurt it wasn't obvious to you."

"Ilene, what was very obvious was you had another love."

"I can see you're going to make me knock you out! I was totally committed to you!" Mother Thomas began doing arm stretches so she wouldn't pull a muscle when she hit Buddy.

"No, Ilene I don't see things that way. It was obvious to me that you loved and were committed to church and those church folk. I couldn't ever get your time or attention. I was always sitting around waiting for you to remember us. Our relationship was so important to you before. Over the last few years, you didn't even have the time to see the problems. When you did have time, it was only to get what you wanted or needed. It was never about feeding our marriage. You never made the investment our marriage required to survive. You did make sure the church and all of those people saw your commitment to them."

Mother Thomas didn't have a response for Buddy. He was right. She hadn't shown him the love he needed and deserved from her as his wife. However, now wasn't the time to swallow her pride.

"You were always trying to keep up a front for people. You wanted people to think that everything was perfect. Ilene, we weren't perfect! So what? You ignored the opportunities we had to actually improve our marriage. You chose to put the effort into convincing people that everything was great instead. You know, the funny thing is all those people you were trying to trick, were tricking you. They all knew exactly what was going on. Those folks who you cared so much about were all laughing at you behind your back. "

"They knew what was going on because you were telling our business to people in hardware stores."

"What I said in the hardware store that day was the truth. You still don't get it do you? It's past time to tell the truth. Ilene, is there something else you want? If not I'm going back inside now because you're not taking this seriously."

"Okay Buddy, you're right. I did do all of those things. I thought I needed to be deeply involved in church to show God that I loved Him. I did take you for granted. I thought you'd always be there regardless of how I treated you."

"Be honest Ilene. You weren't trying to show God anything. The God you always told me about knows you love Him regardless of what you do."

"Okay, I'm sorry but God has been working on me so much. It's taking me a long time to accept what I did. I was trying to show everyone else how perfect I was. I think it was my way of controlling people around me. In the process, I ignored you and our marriage. Buddy, I never meant to do any of this. I love you and I want to fix everything. Buddy, will you come home? I want you back."

"Baby, I need to think about coming home but I do accept your apology. Right now, we don't have very much trust in each other. We need to rebuild it and it's possible with a lot of work. I don't know if I feel like putting in all of the effort. Ilene, are you sure this is what you want? I mean you still need to get yourself together."

"I know with all of my heart I want my marriage back. More than our marriage, I want you back Buddy. I need you honey. I know I still have a lot of changing to do but it won't mean a thing if you're not with me."

"I'll think about it. I promise I will. You know you're not the only one who God is dealing with. God's been working on me too. I know I'm not gay. I never was. I haven't figured out how to tell him yet but I will. Ilene, to tell you the truth, I didn't want to leave. I wanted to get away from the pain of knowing you didn't love me."

"I never really believed you were gay. Again, Buddy, I'm sorry for hurting you so deeply. You need to pray and ask God what you should do. I want to be sure whatever we decide is God's will. I love you and I'm sorry. Please remember that." Mother Thomas slowly moved back down the walkway, through the gate and out to the sidewalk. She turned to look at Buddy once more. He was still standing in the same spot looking at Ilene with a look she recognized. This man still loved her deeply.

Chapter 68

Maxine and Steve walked hand in hand through the park they chose for their date. Spending time with each other had become both a ritual and a priority for the couple as they explored the possibility of a rekindled engagement. Maxine removed her hand from Steve's and placed it around his body instead. Steve, noticing Maxine's actions, followed suit and pulled her closer to him.

"Max?" Steve said as to get Maxine's attention.

"Yes." Maxine responded.

"This feels so right. Don't you think so?"

Maxine needed to be extremely careful about how she answered Steve's question. She was truly enjoying the time they spent together but she wasn't sure about letting him in completely yet. She still felt a deep-seated need to keep him at a distance. Glancing at her former fiancé, Maxine knew she wanted him to be a part of her life forever. Losing him to the streets was hurtful. Watching him walk out of her life the man he was at that moment, would be a disaster. What was her reason for pushing him away now? Maxine decided to throw caution to the wind and answer from her heart and not from her fear.

"It does feels good Steve. I don't ever want to lose what I'm experiencing right now."

Steve led Maxine over to a bench positioned near a fountain. The ducks floating in the pond, the dance of the water from the fountain, the gentle breeze and the quietness of the park created a very romantic ambience. Steve leaned over and kissed Maxine gently on her lips. The two fell into an embrace that allowed the other to feel their heartbeats.

"I'm ecstatic you feel that way. I'm surprised you actually opened up and told me."

"Why are you so surprised?"

"Max you usually guard your feelings like it's gold in Fort Knox. When you do it with me, it says our relationship isn't special. It says I'm like everyone else in your book. Not worthy of being trusted."

"I wasn't going to bring it up Steve but you did move down a notch or two in that category when we were engaged."

"That's understandable. Things are different now. I just wonder if the conversation is always going to go back to what I did back then. If it is, I'm not sure what we're doing together."

"I'm working on letting it all go with God's help. I promise that when I get through it, I'll make another promise to never bring it up again."

"That's fair and I'll definitely wait. I promise to never lie to you again. I'm committed to always being there for you and protecting you. I'll do whatever I have to do to get you to trust me with your heart again. I vow to make you second only to God in my life. I pledge my undying love to you forever. Maxine you are my life."

"Steve," Maxine said with tears streaming down her face, "it means so much to hear you say those things. I've needed to hear those words for so long."

"I want you to be my wife. I want to propose but I don't think you're ready right now. One of these days I'm going to ask you to marry me again."

"Why do you have to wait?"

"Today's not the day because I don't think you'll say yes. A brother wouldn't be able to take the heartbreak if you said no!" Steve and Maxine both let out a hearty laugh. "I'm waiting until I think we're both ready. I want to guarantee you say yes to that question."

"What about Momma Doris? I know what she did was wrong. But, she is your mother and the two of you need to resolve your issues."

"I can't stay mad at my mother for long. I don't know when or how but I'll talk to her. Don't worry, we'll all get through this."

They sealed the deal with a kiss, and another, and another until Steve and Maxine remembered they were on a park bench.

Chapter 69

Once Pastor Mitch insured that Cassandra was safe and resting in the hospital with her mother by her side, he pulled out his cell phone and began calling those whose attendance at the emergency church meeting was necessary. He contacted Marsha, Eric, Linda, Maxine, Mother Thomas, and the members of the Church Board. Pastor Mitch arrived at the church first and began to pray for Believer's Church. He didn't understand how things had gotten to this point. Things were in disarray and he didn't know what to do. However, he knew exactly who to go to for answers. Why did Sister Cassandra find the need to lie on him? What was going on with the normally supportive and cooperative Eric Howard? Was Marsha somehow romantically involved with the church elder? What about what Mother Thomas alleged? What was the truth? He noticed Marsha had arrived as she knelt beside him. Other church members, who he didn't summon, appeared around him on the altar. They all prayed for Cassandra's healing. They asked God to help her to overcome the issues that caused her to attempt to take her own life. They requested God strengthen Cassandra and show her His love because they knew she would need both in the days ahead. The people showed their love for another as the group talked to God on Cassandra's behalf and for each other. After a time, Pastor Mitch gathered the people he had requested to come to the impromptu meeting and left the sanctuary.

Mitch could feel the tension as the group wondered what was going on. It was apparent some of them didn't know what had happened earlier in this very room. After everyone was settled, Pastor Mitch began to speak.

"Some of you may be wondering why you were asked to be here. I'll explain but first I need to inform you of something that transpired this afternoon. Some of you were present and ran out of here. I'll speak to you about your behavior later. While the board was meeting earlier, Sister Cassandra came though we asked her not to attend. It was obvious she was intoxicated. She required medical attention and she's getting it right now. I think it's inappropriate to reveal what was behind her being in that state of mind. I will say she is a very sick woman and in need of our prayers and support. Obviously, the congregation knows something or they wouldn't be here right now. As leaders of this church, I'm reminding you it is of the utmost importance we don't spread information we really don't know is true and we keep everyone focused on praying for Cassandra. If she decides to give her testimony, that's up to her. It's not my place to tell her story." Mitch took a break from speaking to allow the information to sink in. He also took the opportunity to look at Marsha to gauge her response to this news. She smiled and placed her hand on his in a show of support.

"The doctors say Cassandra will completely recover. She may need intensive counseling. In any case, when she returns to Believer's Church, I expect for all of you to treat her with the utmost respect despite what you personally feel about her. I require you to be examples to the rest of the congregation. We have to show her love and concern but not pity. Does anyone have any questions?" Pastor Mitch once again looked around the room at those who were there. No one said a word. Everyone nodded their heads letting Mitch know they understood.

"You're all here because of issues involving you. Let's start with you Mother Thomas. Do you know why you were asked to attend?"

"Yes, Pastor Mitch, I do." Mother Thomas responded though she didn't like that Pastor Mitch put her on the spot as he had.

"Would you mind sharing your thoughts?"

"I admit I was the person who accused Maxine and Linda of being involved with each other. Most of you probably knew that and I'm sure there's a good reason why I had to admit it in front of all these people."

"Mother, you had no problem saying it to all of these people before. You're in charge of the Mother's Board and as such you're supposed to be a model of Christian behavior. Honestly, your actions have been anything but Christian. You spread ugly rumors about these two young women with no proof whatsoever. Mother Thomas what you did was very damaging not only to Maxine and Linda but also to the fabric of our congregation as well."

"I want to apologize to everyone here especially Maxine and Linda for causing this problem. I witnessed some things that caused me to think of them that way. They are very affectionate with one another. They're very touchy feely all the time. You never see one without the other. I thought they should've been spending time with young men instead of each other all the time. The icing on the cake was they'd both broken up with wonderful young men who loved them in order to move in with each other. I wondered why Maxine ended her engagement to Steve, my friend Doris' son. He was heartbroken over you, Maxine. I know because Doris told me all about it. That's why I thought but…." A voice interrupted Mother Thomas keeping her from completing her thought.

"First of all, what you said about Linda and I is a blatant lie. We do not have nor will we ever have a romantic relationship with each other. I don't want it and neither does Linda. As far as what we do during Praise and Worship, we are free in our praise. While we're showing God how much we love Him, it's only natural we'd begin to show each other love as well." Maxine spoke gently to Mother Thomas out of respect for her age though she was extremely angry with the woman.

"I shouldn't have to explain what happened between Steve and I but I will because you apparently received some bad information. Besides, it's time I stop hiding this secret anyway. Did Momma Doris tell you that Steve had a drug problem at that time?"

This revelation stunned everyone in the room. It was clear now why the nuptials didn't take place. Mother Thomas was blindsided.

"No she didn't tell me that but…"

"Well he did. I was in love with Steve. Not long before we were to be married, he went on a drug binge and spent all the money we had saved for the wedding. He also sold a truck that was in my name so he could get more drugs. I didn't even know Steve's whereabouts. Once I found out about his problem I didn't think it would be wise to marry him. I still love him even to this very day. So, to answer your question, Steve's drug problem was the reason we didn't get married."

"I really don't want to discuss the reasons behind Mark and I breaking up. But, in order to close down the devil's workshop in my life, I will. Mark and I got into a sexual relationship with each other. That went against my beliefs about premarital sex but it happened because I put too much trust in my own strength. I found myself in situations I thought I could handle because I thought I was so strong in the Lord. Well, to make a long story short, I became pregnant. Mark disappeared and I didn't know what to do. I was ashamed and didn't want to walk in here pregnant and unmarried. The church tends to frown upon women like that. I can only imagine the reaction had that occurred. It's hard to admit but I got an abortion. I lost my ability to trust men because of what happened with Mark. I started clinging to Maxine as my friend and protector. It may have looked strange to some people but it felt very natural for us because we were already extremely close anyway. Maxine and I may have an inappropriate relationship but not in the way you think Mother Thomas. We've clung to each other instead of allowing our circumstances to draw us closer to God. We trusted each other more than we trusted God. That was our mistake." Linda finally exhaled the breath she had been holding the entire time she'd been talking. It was clear to her that holding all of that in had likely been the cause of the turmoil she'd been experiencing.

"What I've been trying to say to you is I used to think those things about the two of you because of something that was happening in my own life. My husband left me and moved in with a man down the street. Buddy told me he was gay and he couldn't live with me anymore. Apparently, that wasn't the only reason Buddy left. Anyway, before Buddy left, I caught him in a compromising position with a different man. I noticed him becoming very friendly with men. That's why I'm very suspicious of people being so close to folks of the same sex. That's why I reacted that way with you. I've repented to God about what I did and I'm asking you two to forgive me. I was wrong. I'm sorry I've caused all this disruption in the church and I'll do whatever I can to help repair it. The talk Buddy and I had recently helped me to see myself more clearly. I don't really like what I see and I'm going to clean it up with the help of the good Lord."

Everyone in the room was silent. Mother Thomas losing her husband was the last thing any of them expected to happen. They'd always appeared happy though they did notice Buddy didn't come to church with his wife very often. Pastor Mitch decided to break the silence and continue moving the meeting along.

"Mother, why didn't you tell me about this. I would've prayed for you and counseled you if you wanted.

"What about Elder Howard? We have to address that dilemma as well don't we." Deacon Mayes asked.

"I talked to God about this and I believe I know the direction we should take. Elder Howard, explain yourself first." Pastor Mitch wanted Elder Howard to speak on his own behalf so everyone could understand his position. He was still acutely aware of the feelings of the other board members. They wanted to hang the man by his toenails and keep things moving. Hopefully, hearing from the man himself would soften their stance.

Through tears, Eric Howard began to speak. "I have been coming to this place we call church for most of my life. I have supported every leader God sent to Believer's Church. I've smiled and given my time and service. Everybody thought my life was great. That's what a good church member does. We keep our heads up and a smile on our face regardless of how we feel on the inside. The truth is my life was awesome until Eunice passed away. That woman prayed for me, cared for me and loved me like no one else. I miss her so much." Elder Howard allowed his tears to flow freely. He felt he was shedding the load he'd been carrying for years. Several members of the church board shook their heads as though they didn't believe him. Others understood his pain and worked hard to push back their own tears.

"What does that have to do with what you did to this church? I feel bad you lost your wife and everything but I don't believe that's what caused you to act that way." Deacon Crutchfield spoke for the skeptics in the group who readily agreed and reiterated his sentiments.

"We are going to be respectful here. That's unnecessary. You'd want someone to show you compassion if you lost someone special." Pastor Mitch interrupted the attack that was gaining steam. "Go ahead Eric. Finish what you were saying."

"I'm so lonely and I sometimes fight depression. I'm an old man who lost his wife. I don't have anything else but this church. For a long time I thought I should be the pastor but it didn't happen. I needed to feel useful and needed. I really did think I was within the rules of this church to step into those shoes at least temporarily. Once I stood behind that pulpit and watched the church members walk out the door, I felt rejected. No one even wanted to hear what I had to say. Now you're turning against me because I made a mistake. I don't know why this is all happening. Lord, I don't understand what's going on!"

"First of all, Eric, you are more than a widower. You are a man of God." Marsha began, "Those times I had conversations with you I knew you wanted to please God. I think you stepped ahead of him a little bit. You do have something to give to the world. Just because you don't see the plan God has for your life doesn't mean He doesn't have one."

"Elder Howard what my wife said is true. God does have a work for you to do. You were born for a reason. It's not too late." Pastor Mitch began to realize he understood the undercurrent he felt in Believer's Church. Tears began to come to his eyes as it became clear that he'd been as out of touch with the church body as everyone else. All of a sudden, he felt forgiveness for Elder Howard though he still believed he got too close to Marsha. The two men would definitely clear the air as soon as possible but this was not the time.

"That's all fine and good. We all have a work God called us to do. All of us here are leaders and we should operate at a higher level. Are we just supposed to let everything slide? I mean, I didn't expect for any of these people to admit wrongdoing. How can we just take everyone's word for it and ignore the accusations?" Deacon Crutchfield questioned.

"Deacon, do you have any proof that any of this is true?" Pastor Mitch responded.

"No, but I don't have any proof it's untrue either. We never did discuss you and Cassandra. How do we know you didn't come on to her? Her coming in here under some kind of influence and saying she set you up isn't enough. She was out of her mind and didn't know what she was saying."

"Crutchfield, you are out of line! No one was here except the two of us. How are any of us supposed to prove anything? What would satisfy you? Huh?" Pastor Mitch was losing his patience. It appeared some people just wanted to keep drama going so they had a reason to argue.

"Pastor, I respect you as the person God put in place to lead this church. I don't think we should treat you any different from anyone else. Mother Thomas may have cleared up the issue with Linda and Maxine. But, this other stuff is still hanging out there and I don't think we should let it go because you say so."

"I didn't get a chance to say how I think we should approach what Eric did. However, I do believe Cassandra cleared everything up."

Deacon Crutchfield and Pastor Mitch stared at each other as if daring the other to make any type of move. The other attendees were still and silent as well as the tension rose. Deacon Crutchfield looked around the room in an effort to gauge support for his position. One by one five of the board members slightly nodded their heads to indicate they agreed with the deacon's position. The actions weren't lost on Pastor Mitch who decided to wait for their next move. He could end this all but felt God was teaching him and those in attendance a much-needed lesson. Believer's Church needed to learn how to operate in forgiveness, compassion and love for one another. This situation highlighted that fact.

"It's not appropriate for you to decide your problem should be swept under the rug. We will not sit by and let you do that. Brothers?" Deacon Crutchfield and his supporters stood and prepared to leave the room.

"I saw what happened that night," confessed Elder Howard. "No one knew I was still in the building. I went past Pastor Mitch's office and saw Sister Cassandra trying to seduce him. He asked her to leave and she did. Nothing happened."

The group that was planning to leave returned to their seats. Elder Howard once again had the attention of everyone in the room.

"You knew nothing happened but allowed all of us to go through this anyway? I ought to come across this table and…." Pastor Mitch stood up and began to proceed across the table in Elder Howard's direction.

The loud responses of the group snapped Pastor Mitch back to reality. It was ridiculous to handle this in this manner. He just concluded this church needed to show forgiveness and here he was ready to hurt Eric Howard. He had to be an example. Though he was angry, he sat down at Marsha's insistence.

"Marsha, why are you always protecting this man? You spend an awful lot of time with him, you're always comforting him, and now you're protecting him. What is going on between the two of you?" Mitch yelled.

"Nothing is going on Mitch. I can't believe you brought this up in front of the church."

Mitch lowered his head as he recognized he was out of line in speaking about his marital problems in front of the church. He apologized to Marsha silently and expected the normal softness in her eyes. Instead he saw the fire.

"You weren't there... You and I have discussed this before and I won't do it here. So there's no confusion, it just so happened I ran into Elder Howard at Fellowship City a few times. We've forged a friendship and I don't see anything wrong with that. We don't go out on dates. We don't talk on the phone. It's nothing like that. I refuse to live in a bubble. None of you has to live like that and that includes you Mitch. Eric was wrong to withhold this information but I think we're getting off the subject."

"I'm sorry I didn't mention what I witnessed before. We were all being so honest and I thought I should come clean as well. I'm so sorry." Elder Howard begged.

"Eric, I forgive you. You're going to confess what you've done to this congregation. You are going to explain why you hijacked that pulpit. I'll allow you time very soon to do that. We are done with all the rest of this. Everyone bow your heads. We need to pray that God restores our church and that He heals every wound we've discussed today." Pastor Mitch led the prayer then stood by the door to the room. As people began to leave, he hugged each one of them and told them he loved them. Everyone followed his lead and began to hug one another in the hall. The praying in the sanctuary had ceased and the people had left. The others left the building happy with the resolutions that had come out of the meeting and ready to get on with their lives.

Chapter 70

"Momma, are you here?" Steve called to his mother as he walked into the quiet house. He knew she was here because her car was in the driveway. He walked further into the house through the various rooms and areas filled with memories of his childhood. He wandered into the master bedroom and saw his mother, curled into the fetal position, sleeping peacefully. Immediately, he felt remorse over the time he spent away from her because of his anger. If something had happened to one of them while they were upset with each other, it would've been a terrible disaster. He silently vowed not to allow this to happen again. After observing her for what seemed like hours, he turned to leave the room deciding to return later.

"Where are you going? I haven't seen you in I don't know when and you're going to leave without talking to me? Boy you'd better get yourself over here!" Momma Doris slowly sat up in bed and leaned on the headboard. She patted the bed to indicate where she wanted her son to sit. "I've been praying you would come by here and see me."

Steve moved to the bed and sat on the edge of the mattress as directed. Once in place, he reached for his mother and embraced her tightly.

"Baby, where have you been?" Momma Doris wondered aloud.

"I've been around. I got a place and I've been getting it together the way I like it."

"Maxine? Have you been seeing Maxine?"

"Yes, we've been spending time together. But Momma I don't think we should be discussing that."

"Why can't we talk about you and Maxine's relationship?"

"Because I don't want you getting involved this time. You really hurt me and Maxine before."

"What did I do?"

"You helped spread those rumors about Maxine and Linda. That is so far from the truth."

"I didn't accuse them of anything. Mother Thomas told me they were that way."

"Momma, I'm going to settle this once and for all. They are close friends who live together. There is nothing more to it than that."

"Okay son. I'm sorry and I won't do anything like that again. Now, tell me about you and Maxine."

"You're going to have to let me be a man. I can look out for myself. If I mess up it's on me. Do you understand Momma? You're going to have to loosen the reigns a little."

"I understand now. After all this time I get it. I've raised you the best I knew how. Now it's time for you to live your life as you see fit. My job now is to keep praying and trusting that you remember your upbringing. Now what's been going on?"

"We've been spending time together and that's all there is to say about it right now."

"I'm praying that God's will be done in your life. I love you, Stevie. Don't ever forget that."

"Never stop praying for me. I need your prayers. I love you too Momma."

"Go on in there and get something to eat. There's lots of food in the refrigerator. Take some home with you if you want. I can't eat all that food."

"Why'd you cook so much food if you couldn't eat it all?"

"Because I knew you'd be here soon."

The two walked into the kitchen. Momma Doris opened the refrigerator door and began to pull out food containers. Each chose what they wanted to eat, warmed it, and sat down to their first dinner together in quite some time. There was laughter and joy where an hour ago there'd been sadness. God had repaired the relationship of Momma Doris and Steve once again.

Chapter 71

Marsha walked through the corridors of the hospital looking for Cassandra's room number. Though her husband didn't reveal her condition to everyone else, he shared more details with his wife. She decided to visit Cassandra and determine if she could be of help to the woman. She' was very angry with Cassandra because of all she'd put everyone through seemingly for no reason. However, regardless of Cassandra's actions, she was still one of God's children and Marsha felt she should visit with her for a bit. Besides, the dreams she'd had about Cassandra and the man were occurring almost every time she closed her eyes. Marsha had worn through the knees in her clothing praying for Cassandra because of the nightly movies. Reaching Cassandra's door, Marsha stopped long enough to gather her self and knock on the door. The door opened revealing a slightly older version of Cassandra. She looked at Marsha with an obvious question in her eyes.

"May I help you?" the woman asked.

"You must be Cassandra's mother. I'm Marsha, Pastor Mitch's wife." She extended her hand toward the woman.

"I'm Cassandra's mother. It's very nice to meet you Marsha. I met Pastor Mitch when he brought Cassandra into the hospital. You all are good people I can feel it. Oh, I'm sorry for rambling on. I'm sure you came to see my daughter. I've been sitting here around the clock but I'd like to go get some refreshments and make some phone calls. You can go right on in. She's awake."

Marsha entered the room quietly. Cassandra kept her gaze towards the window on the other side of the room.

"Cassandra? It's me, Sister Marsha." There was no response.

Marsha stood for a few minutes trying to figure out what to do next. Should she leave and come back later or should she stay and hope to converse with Cassandra? She decided to stay even though the interactive visit she planned might not occur. Once Marsha got to the other side of the room, her breath caught in her throat once she saw Cassandra's appearance. The figure with no makeup, whose hair flowed freely with the wardrobe of hospital gown and socks, was not the normally glamorous Cassandra Marsha knew. Marsha sat in the chair and waited for whatever was to happen next. After several minutes void of conversation, a whimper escaped Cassandra's mouth followed by a deluge of tears. Marsha placed her arms around the woman and embraced her until she felt she should release her.

"I'm sorry for what I did to Pastor Mitch. " Cassandra sobbed.

"You need to focus on getting well now."

There were a few awkward moments before Cassandra pulled away from her visitor.

"I want to get some things off my chest. I'd like to talk to you about it but I need to know you'll keep it confidential though."

"You can trust me." Marsha pulled the chair up next to the bed so she could hear clearly. She waited patiently for the words to flow.

"Laying here thinking about my life I realize a lot of what I'm going through now is because of something that happened to me years ago. Please don't judge me because of what I'm about to tell you. We all have secrets."

"Go ahead Cassandra. I'm listening."

"I've been having these uncontrollable urges to get back at men for a real long time. That's what drove me to say those things about Pastor Mitch. Just so you know, he really didn't try anything with me that day."

"I know my husband Cassandra. From the beginning, I knew you were lying. I didn't understand why you would do that to him. He cares about you and all the other members of Believer's so much."

"I didn't care how he felt about me as long as he did what I wanted him to do. All the other men I've tried to manipulate have always appeased me to get me to go away. I've held affairs, sexual encounters, dirty business deals over men's heads all to get my way."

"What do you mean?"

"Well, I don't know if you knew Pastor Edwards. He was our pastor before you and Pastor Mitch came. I flirted with him and led him to believe we could have a more intimate relationship. I really wasn't interested in him like that. I used it to get on the church board and some other things I don't remember. I think he left because he thought I was going to tell the congregation about us. He actually asked me if we could get together sometimes. I knew I had him right where I wanted him."

"I hear your reason for why you did that to Pastor Edwards. Now I'm seeing the connection to what you tried to do to Mitch. Both situations were extremely unfair and wrong mind you. But, why do you think you have to plot and scheme your way to get your desires?"

"I think that's where DeWayne McAllister comes in. He was the pastor at a church I went to when I was in college."

"Cassandra, every man you've mentioned so far is a pastor. Do you have a problem with men of God?"

"No, I've influenced my boss, police officers and even the cable man before." The chuckling woman sat up in bed. She rested her back and looked off as if reminiscing. "I admired Pastor DeWayne so much. He was so handsome and charismatic. He was attractive to me because he was so powerful. At first, he acted as though he didn't notice me. Every chance I had to be in his immediate presence I took advantage of until he acknowledged me. I became his right-hand woman." Cassandra's expression darkened. "He asked me to come into his office one day to tell me about a special assignment from God. I was exhilarated and frightened all at the same time. That was probably a sign that I shouldn't involve myself with whatever was going on. I mean, what would God Himself want with me? Anyway, since I was so attracted to him, I overrode my first mind and did it anyway. It turned out to be a big mistake."

"What was God's assignment?"

"It wasn't really God who had the assignment for me. When I look back on it, DeWayne was the one who had a mission for me. He took advantage of my admiration of him."

"I don't understand what you're trying to tell me Cassandra."

"He said God ordained that I be a special help and support to him. I was very excited when I found out I would be closer to Pastor DeWayne than I had been. I was probably falling in love with the man but didn't know it. My parents sheltered me when I was growing up. When I went away to college, I was very naïve and a virgin. I didn't leave college that way thanks to DeWayne. I found myself satisfying his sexual desires. I did whatever he asked. Nothing was off limits even when I knew I shouldn't be doing it. I lived for his approval."

"I had no idea something like that had happened to you!"

"I vowed no one would ever hurt me like that again. I started doing things the same way he did. I attracted men who had something I wanted by flirting and implying we could have more until I got what I wanted. I simply dropped them once I was successful."

"Wow! I guess I know why I had those dreams about you. I've been praying for you. I'm glad you have some understanding about why you do what you do. Now you can start to get past it. The thing is, Cassandra, you still don't know why you were so desperate for DeWayne's approval. You have to dig a little deeper to really get to the root of all of this."

"Do you still care about me Marsha? Did my story change how you see me?"

"No, none of that has changed. You should know I believe you're dealing with a sense of shame. Shame causes a person to feel they're defective. Like something's wrong with them. Unfortunately, sexual abuse, which is what you encountered, causes a lot of shame. You're not alone and there is help and healing available. Don't forget to ask God to help you and He will."

"Thank you Sister Marsha. Somehow, I knew I could talk to you."

"I'm going to leave now so you can get some rest. Call us if you need anything and we'll see you real soon."

Chapter 72

"Last week we had a meeting to discuss some rumors that have been spreading through our congregation." The congregation was silent. "Don't act like you haven't heard them. I know most of you have. That's why many of you showed up at a time when I expected less than ten people to an impromptu meeting." The congregation laughed because they all knew what Pastor Mitch was referring to.

"After the meeting, my wife and I went home and continued to pray. We really do love this church and all of you that make up this body. Once we completed our prayer time together, I went to my home office and began to ponder what I would minister to you today. God began to lead me to talk to you from the topic Secrets: The devil's workshop. Now I know the saying goes that an idle mind is the devil's workshop but how many of you can agree that the devil has more than one workshop. If he only had one way to attack us, he would be an easy foe to defeat. Amen?"

Those in attendance lifted their hands, some yelled, some stood but they all let their agreement with their pastor's statement be known.

"You see our enemy will fight you on any and every front. Someone mentioned the other day that she was going to shut down the devil's workshop. This person had a secret they'd been keeping for quite some time. Our secrets provide a dark place where the enemy can set up shop. He uses that secret to torment you by threatening to reveal it to others. He uses that information to convince you that people won't look at you the same if they knew what you did or what happened to you. You think people won't like the real you. Sometimes, his game plan is to make you feel bad about yourself because of the thing you are hiding. The devil's workshop I'm talking about this morning is your secret. Can you say amen?" The crowd replied with a loud voice, "Amen Pastor Mitch!

Preach! Tell it like it is!" "Sometimes we see people and think they're acting strangely. To us, their behavior is questionable. We make up stories to explain why they act the way they do. We don't really know what's going on in their lives. That person may be acting out because of the impact of their secrets. Believer's Church, we aren't supposed to judge one another and we shouldn't gossip either. We're supposed to pray for each other. Instead of talking about him or her, try praying for that person. You may be the one God wants to use to help that person through their problem. People of God, let's help each other tear down the devil's workshop in our lives! Let's get free from our secrets together! We can do it!" The crowd was on their feet responding to their pastor's words and praising God. "Tell your neighbor you're tearing those dark places down. Tell them there are no more secrets. Let your sister or your brother know you'll help them demolish the devil's workshop!"

The people responded by speaking words of encouragement and support to their fellow believers. People were leaving their seats to speak to others and show their willingness to help. Several people came to the front of the church prompting Pastor Mitch to make an unusual altar call.

"I'm going to give each of you an opportunity to free yourselves. I need the greeters to pass around some prayer request cards. Write your secret anonymously on the card. You can identify yourself if you like. The Believer's Church leadership will be praying over these so you can find the freedom you are seeking. You can also find someone you trust and reveal your secret to them. Tell them what you feel comfortable talking about. Remember, regardless of the route you choose, the moment your issue isn't a secret anymore it loses its power."

For the next thirty minutes, people rushed around the church ministering to one another. They revealed everything big and small. All were obviously weighing heavily on those who carried them. Folks who always kept a stern face were openly weeping as they disclosed why they'd acted so mean. It was a day they would celebrate year after year. Pastor Mitch would see to that. Today was the birthday of Believer's Church without the masks.

Chapter 73

One year later…

The harpist began to play the love song softly as the lights in the church dimmed. The many candles lit in the key areas about the church sanctuary illuminated the otherwise dim space. The groom, best man, Elder Howard and Pastor Mitch stepped out of the office and the spotlight immediately followed them. Elder Howard was now the Assistant Pastor of Believer's Church. He followed through with the confession of his faults before the congregation. After much counseling and prayer, Eric recovered from the loss of Eunice. Shortly afterward, he became Assistant Pastor and worked by Pastor Mitch's side as his helper. Once the men were in place, the harpist stopped the song and several couples began to proceed down the aisle. Each couple had different facets of love to characterize in their own way. As the various scenes of love played out, the groom took a deep breath as he realized he was going to meet his bride at the altar in a matter of moments. They had been through a lot on their journey together but this moment and those to follow made the tough times worthwhile. Everyone was now in place. The soloist began to sing the couple's favorite song along with the harp. The heavy wooden doors to the sanctuary closed as the bride made her move to the entrance. When the doors opened, a sheer lace curtain hung over the open space. A spotlight positioned behind the woman of the hour came on and revealed only her outline. As if on cue, caged doves began to make their own melodies adding to the ambiance of the moment. The bridal coordinator took down the drape and the groom caught a glimpse of her. His breath caught in his throat once he took all of her beauty in. She was normally a gorgeous woman and he never thought she could look any better. Today, she had proven the assumption incorrect. There was obviously no end to her splendor.

The woman began moving up the aisle holding tightly to the arm of the man who had raised her and loved her first. She wanted to walk alone but her father refused to allow his daughter to walk down the aisle without the benefit of his arm to steady her. She was his "baby girl" as she always would be. The groom's face showed both the love he felt for this woman as well as the assurance that came from knowing she'd always be his to love.

"Baby girl?" the man called out to his daughter, " are you sure you still want to do this? You know, even now, you don't have to. We can go right back through those doors and out to my car. So, tell me what you want to do."

"Dad, why would you wait until we're moving toward the altar to ask me this? I love him and I'm going through with this."

"Even with all he's taken you through you still want to be with him?"

"Yes, in spite of all that's happened we belong together. There is no other man for me."

"Well daughter, I'm okay with that."

The groom watched as the conversation took place wondering what the topic of discussion was. It looked serious until they ended it, smiled at each other and then turned their happy faces toward him. The two joined hands as they met in front of Pastor Mitch. Her dad moved to his seat and sat down. The ceremony didn't call for him to give her away.

"Everyone can be seated. This is a joyous occasion and I feel privileged to have been asked to participate."

The ceremony proceeded with words of expression and love. There was laughter and tears. Elder Howard spoke a heartfelt prayer over the couple. Once all was completed, the couple, facing each other while holding hands, looked at Pastor Mitch, as he stood ready to make the expected announcement.

"Ladies and gentleman, I'm ecstatic to present to you once again, Mr. and Mrs. Buddy Thomas! Brother Buddy, you can salute Mother Thomas!"

The two sealed their reunion with a kiss and began to leave the sanctuary followed by their support team seated in the first couple of rows of the church. A very pregnant Maxine waddled down the aisle as one of this elite group. She and Steve were married and now expecting their first child. Steve and Maxine purchased a home large enough to provide room for Momma Doris to move in which she didn't hesitate to do. Maxine would need her help once she had the baby. Seated next to Maxine in this special section was Linda. Though Mark had rejected her wedding proposal, the pair had continued seeing each other. They were currently in a non-monogamous relationship and Mark was seeing someone else in addition to Linda. Linda didn't like it but she'd have to wait and see what happened. In the meantime, she filled her time heading up the singles ministry along with Cassandra and spending time with God. Cassandra was a completely different person after she completed her prescribed course of treatment following her suicide attempt. Gone were the sexy clothes and attention-getting ways. It was no longer important for Cassandra to control her relationships because she'd learned pain was an inevitable part of life. She found out from her experience, God could heal her from every hurt she would ever encounter.

Pastor Mitch reached for his wife's hand as he made his way out of the sanctuary. Their marriage had faced every possible challenge since Mitch had become pastor of Believer's Church. Mitch and Marsha had established boundaries around their relationship in order to keep their relationship strong. There was a weekly date night and it was mandatory except in the case of a true emergency. They also went on a get-away at least once every other month providing extra special time for them. Mitch realized how necessary it was to nurture his relationship with Marsha during the whole Cassandra debacle. He didn't know it then but he had been missing the intimacy of their marriage. By protecting their time, the two developed a level of closeness they never imagined. Once Elder Howard came on board as his assistant, someone was capable of carrying on if Mitch was away without concern for the church's welfare. Marsha had formed "Heart to Heart" which was very successful in helping women with their needs. Desiring to be more effective, she entered into a psychology program at the local university in an effort to gain her degree.

Believer's Church had grown consistently over the past year even more so than expected. Known as a ministry free from pretense and judgmental attitudes, people came from all over to experience the love of God in a refreshing way.